The Body in
the Back
Garden

The Body in the Back Garden

A CRESCENT COVE MYSTERY

Mark Waddell

CROOKED LANE

NEW YORK

Published in the United States by Crooked Lane Books, an imprint of The Quick Brown Fox & Company LLC.

Crooked Lane Books and its logo are trademarks of The Quick Brown Fox & Company LLC.

Library of Congress Catalog-in-Publication data available upon request.

ISBN (hardcover): 978-1-63910-440-6
ISBN (ebook): 978-1-63910-441-3

Cover illustration by Brandon Dorman

Printed in the United States.

www.crookedlanebooks.com

Crooked Lane Books
34 West 27th St., 10th Floor
New York, NY 10001

First Edition: August 2023

10 9 8 7 6 5 4 3 2 1

For Matt

Chapter One

"Look, I'm only going to be there for a couple of days, so can we meet today?"

"Of course," Daisy Simpson assured me, the Realtor's low voice coming clearly through the speakers of my rental car. "My afternoon is flexible. What time were you thinking?"

I glanced at the dashboard clock. "I'm on my way up-island right now. How about two PM?"

"I'll be there." There was a small pause before she added, "And once again, Mr. Tremblay, I'm so sorry about your aunt. She was a very special person."

"Thanks," I replied, a little tersely. "See you soon." I disconnected the call.

Settling back in my seat, I exhaled slowly and loosened my grip on the steering wheel. The road ahead of me curved and wound its way through the lush greenery of Vancouver Island, situated off Canada's west coast. Dense stands of Douglas fir, broken occasionally by jagged outcroppings of rock, lined the highway on both sides. I'd just left Nanaimo and had about an hour and a half before I reached Crescent Cove.

I didn't want to be here—not on the island, and definitely not headed for Crescent Cove. I hadn't been back in more than twenty years. Once upon a time, it had been my favorite place in the whole world . . . but a lot had changed since then.

My phone's ringtone played through the car's speakers, and I glanced over at the screen. Bryce was calling. Again. Teeth clenched, I stabbed the *ignore* button with a little more force than necessary and told myself for the hundredth time that I would block him for good as soon as I had the chance.

In an effort to distract myself, I fiddled with the radio until I found a local station playing bland pop hits. I didn't want to think about Bryce back in Toronto and his halfhearted attempts at contrition. I didn't want to think about my aunt, who'd been struck by a car and killed just over a week ago. I didn't want to think about those magical summers I'd spent here on the island back when I still had a family. I didn't want to think, period. So I rolled down the windows and turned up the radio and sang along to Taylor Swift as I sped toward the last place in the world I wanted to be.

Crescent Cove was a village of maybe two thousand people situated on the eastern shore of Vancouver Island. Sitting as it did between the larger towns of Courtenay and Campbell River, it attracted a fair number of summer tourists who were drawn by its quaint Main Street and gorgeous views across the Strait of Georgia. I'd spent my own summers there too, arriving in early July and reluctantly returning to my parents in Edmonton just before school started again at the end of August. I'd loved staying with my aunt Marguerite, and under her warm, benevolent supervision I'd run through the hushed forests behind her cottage, explored the tide pools that dotted the local beaches, and eaten an ice cream cone every single day.

It was idyllic while it lasted.

Numbed by an unceasing stream of today's greatest hits, I found myself passing the exit for Courtenay sooner than expected. Not long after that I turned off the Island Highway and followed the gently curving road eastward as it burrowed through dense forest before emerging at the top of a small rise. Around me appeared the small, well-tended houses and expertly manicured lawns of Crescent Cove's westernmost border, with the rest of the town sloping gently down toward the ocean in front of me. I felt my breath catch a little as I drove through the familiar streets and then past the grounds of the Collingwood estate, the big house rising in solitary splendor behind wrought-iron gates. The neighborhood was postcard perfect, bungalows and quaintly historical homes sitting behind lush lawns and colorful profusions of flowers, with glimpses down to the water almost everywhere you looked.

Turning north after the Collingwood estate, I bypassed Main Street and the inevitable snarl of tourist traffic, choosing another route that took me past the incongruously imposing facade of the local library and the redbrick fire station before turning, with some trepidation, onto Ravenwood Lane. The street was named for the rain forest that crowded close to this end of town, its cool air filled with the croaks and calls of half-seen ravens. Trees towered overhead as I drove slowly to the very end of the winding road. There, down a curving gravel track,

I came at last to my aunt's cottage, a one-story bungalow built in the craftsman style. It sat on a small rocky rise, its sprawling garden enclosed by a white picket fence that held back the encroaching forest. This side of the cottage was cloaked in perennial gloom by the trees, and my aunt had filled the garden here with ferns and hostas and shade-loving flowers, artfully arranged around a big stone-lined pond at the garden's center.

I parked the car next to a sleek, dark red sedan that had been pulled up close to the fence and slowly got out, taking in big lungfuls of cool air as I did so. There was another car parked at the far end of the gravel patch, an old blue Volvo that I guessed had belonged to my aunt. Stepping into the garden for the first time in more than twenty years, I paused, one hand still on the gate, and closed my eyes.

It was so peaceful here, so beautiful. I could almost imagine my aunt's voice calling to me from inside, telling me that dinner was ready or asking if I wanted to walk down to the beach.

But my aunt was gone, and with her any real connection I had to this place. My eyes opened, the tranquil atmosphere suddenly oppressive somehow. Troubled, I latched the gate behind me and set off down the winding paths of crushed stone that looped through the garden.

The cottage looked unchanged, its shingled siding painted a bright yellow that glowed even in the shadows of the forest. It took up a comfortable amount of space, its tall lattice windows surrounded by cheerful white trim that also decorated the overhanging eaves of the steeply gabled roof. Heading left along the side of the building, I passed beneath the crooked limbs of an enormous oak tree, the picket fence rather whimsically running up and over the gnarled hump of its roots, and patted its trunk fondly as I wandered past. Then I came to the front of the cottage, and before me opened a vista so lovely and familiar that I felt my heart catch in my chest.

There was the ocean, deep blue under the brighter cerulean of the sky, stretching toward the dim shadows that were all I could see of the mainland nearly twenty miles away. The view was spectacular, and the cottage had been built to take full advantage of it. The front garden ran another fifty or sixty feet to the edge of the bluff, which then dropped off precipitously to a rocky beach below, accessed by an ancient, rickety staircase. The front garden was mainly lawn, bordered on three sides by wide flower beds filled with a riot of color. All along the edge of the bluff, spindly sea grasses bent and fluttered in the wind, forming a nice contrast with the expertly tended grass my aunt had cut every week, rain or shine, with her decrepit push mower.

I paused and drank it all in, but before I could do more than that, someone fluted, "Yoo-hoo!" at me. I turned to see a smiling middle-aged woman waving from the small front porch. Daisy Simpson, I presumed. Plastering on a smile of my own, I went to meet her.

Dressed in a rather chic striped blouse and pencil skirt, Daisy extended a hand to me as I joined her on the porch. "Mr. Tremblay? Daisy Simpson, Shoreline Realty." Her grip was firm as she shook my hand. "Lovely to meet you, though obviously I wish it were under better circumstances."

"Thanks for meeting with me," I responded, working to keep my polite smile in place. "I appreciate it."

"Of course! Anything for Marguerite's family. She was an amazing woman." She sighed. "Knocked down by a car not half a kilometer from here. So tragic."

I nodded noncommittally and turned toward the front door, which was standing open. "I'd like to put this place on the market as soon as possible. Today, if we can."

Beneath her sensible bob, Daisy's dark eyes watched me appraisingly. "We can do that, certainly. Given the state of the market, you should walk away with a fairly significant amount of money." She paused for a moment before adding delicately, "There are some people in town who were disappointed to hear that this place would be sold."

"I live in Toronto. I can't afford the upkeep on another home." I knew I was being brusque, but I already resented having to make the trip out here and wasn't interested in the disappointment of people I'd never met. "I'd also appreciate any suggestions you might have for getting rid of my aunt's things," I added after a small pause.

She nodded once. "Sure. Let's just take a quick spin through the cottage, shall we? Then we can discuss pricing."

I nodded again and followed her into the tiny foyer. The air inside smelled a little stale, but with hints of the sandalwood incense my aunt had loved. As we headed left into the living room, I was struck once more by a powerful sense of déjà vu—everything looked the same, though I knew she must have made changes over the years. The floors were the same honey-colored wood, the wide boards scarred by decades of use but still gleaming with polish, covered here and there by an assortment of colorful rugs. The room's focal point was the big fireplace made from rounded river stones, its wooden mantel lined with knick-knacks, and various pieces of mismatched furniture had been arranged around it. And of course, there were plants, maybe a dozen or more, ranging from a single dark-blue orchid in the center of the mantelpiece to potted ficus trees flanking the wide entranceway bridging the foyer and the living room.

I looked to my left, out through the tall bay windows with their lovely view of the sea. Behind me, Daisy was saying, "As you can see, everything is in terrific shape. Marguerite really took good care of this place." Her voice receded as she walked toward the back of the house. "And she updated the kitchen a few years ago."

Turning, I followed her through into the little space that my aunt had used as a dining room and then into the open kitchen beyond. Sure enough, it looked significantly different from the small, homely space I remembered—now it had dark granite countertops, stainless-steel appliances, and glass-fronted cabinets, all tastefully done so that none of it looked at odds with the rest of the cottage. Here, too, there were plants sitting on top of the double-wide fridge, trailing down the sides of the cabinets, and lining the windowsill over the sink.

Daisy smiled at me as I took it all in. "Your aunt had excellent taste," she said, and I couldn't disagree.

The cottage was laid out in a square, and from the kitchen we continued around the back of the building—passing the French doors that opened onto the garden—to the bedrooms and small library on the north side. My aunt's bedroom was at the far end, with views over the water, and next to that was the book-lined room where I'd spent countless hours as a kid, whiling away rainy days by absorbing information like a sponge. The library had always been my favorite room in the house, and I couldn't help smiling as I paused in the doorway. For a moment I could almost see my younger self, pale and pudgy with thick glasses, sprawled on the old Persian rug with half a dozen books scattered nearby.

Back in the foyer, Daisy's continual stream of chatter—most of which I'd tuned out—paused as she took a moment to study me. Then, linking her arm companionably with mine, she pulled me gently out onto the porch once more. "As I said, the property is in excellent shape," she said. "Given that, and these views"—she paused again to admire the sweep of ocean that unfurled itself in front of us—"you'll have no trouble selling this place quickly. And for a pretty penny, I should add." She gave my arm a little squeeze before releasing me.

"I'm glad." I took a deep breath of sea air and tried to shake off the layers of nostalgia that had settled over me. The smile I gave her was more genuine this time. She was trying to be helpful, I knew that. The complicated history I had with my family wasn't her fault.

"Okay," Daisy said with a small nod. "Then I'll head back to the office and get the paperwork started. I'll email you with the details, and once I get your approval, we'll get this place listed. How does that sound?"

"Great," I replied. "Thanks." I glanced down at my watch. "I guess I should head into town and try to find a hotel room."

"Good luck," she said drily. "This time of year, you'll be lucky to find a room at the old Seahorse Motel out on Barton Road, and I wouldn't stay there for a million dollars."

I was a little surprised. "I didn't realize the tourist trade had picked up so much in the summers."

"Oh yes," Daisy said, as she descended the creaking wooden steps to the front yard. "It's a madhouse around here. Which is great for local businesses, of course, but a tad inconvenient for the rest of us." Her smile was rueful as she turned back to me. "In any case, you don't need a hotel. Stay here! There are clean linens in the spare bedroom, and the local grocery store delivers. You could have them send over whatever you need."

I hesitated. The thought of staying in the cottage was suddenly powerfully appealing . . . but painful, too. In the end, though, my tiredness won out and I nodded. "Sure. That's a good idea."

"Wonderful." She beamed a dazzling smile at me as she drew her phone out from the purse looped over her arm. "I'll text you the number for the greengrocers." Once she'd done so, she said brightly, "I'll be in touch!" before bustling away, her shoes crunching quietly on the stone path as she headed around the side of the cottage and back to her car.

I stayed where I was, hands in pockets and staring out over the ocean, for a long time. The breeze was cool and occasionally carried the sounds of shrieking children from somewhere along the beach that ran below the cottage. *It really is beautiful here*, I thought to myself. But the sense of refuge I'd felt when I was younger had long since evaporated. Now it was just a place that needed to be sold.

I still didn't understand why my aunt had left the cottage to me, along with the small antiques shop on Main Street that she had run for close to forty years. I'd loved both places when

I was younger, but I hadn't spoken to my aunt since I was a teenager. In fact, I'd learned of her death only when I received a tersely worded email from a law firm in Crescent Cove, notifying me that I was the primary beneficiary of my aunt's will. Even more surprising was the fact that she'd added my name to the deeds for both properties, meaning that they passed directly to me without having to go through probate. That was lucky, since it meant I could sell them both and return to my life back east as soon as possible.

Retracing Daisy's steps, I headed around to my rental car and grabbed my suitcase from the trunk before walking through the back garden and across the small patio to the French doors that led into the rear of the cottage. It didn't take long to unpack what I needed in the guest bedroom next to the library, and then I took another tour of the building, pausing this time to linger over remembered pieces of art on the walls or to examine the dozens of curios and other little objects my aunt had scattered throughout the place. Most of them were items she'd borrowed from her shop, a habit of hers that had made her cottage seem, to my youthful imagination, like a homey sort of pirate's den full of treasures.

I replaced the old windup fire engine I'd been admiring on the mantelpiece and, on a whim, decided to go for a walk on the beach. I needed to stretch my legs a little after the long drive up from the Victoria airport. First, though, I called the number Daisy had sent me and ordered a few staples—bread, coffee, milk—along with some prepared meals before heading out the front door. Leaving it unlocked behind me, as I'd always done, I crossed the front lawn and then carefully descended the rickety old stairs that plunged down the steep hillside to the beach some thirty feet below. I spent the better part of an hour walking up and down the sandy shore, watching the small waves as they rolled in.

Eventually, though, the constant breeze off the water started to feel chilly, so I hauled myself back up the stairs and onto the wild, untamed edge of the hillside. Before me sat my aunt's cottage, the Ravenwood towering behind it . . . and someone standing on the front porch, peering avidly through the living room windows.

Chapter Two

I paused, a little taken aback, before advancing across the front garden. "Can I help you?" I called out as I approached.

The stranger whipped around, and I saw that he was a middle-aged man dressed in a red-and-black tracksuit. He was a little shorter than me, his pale hair combed back from narrow features and a pair of slightly protuberant eyes. "Who are you?" he demanded.

"Funny," I said as I reached the porch and slowly ascended its three steps, "that's just what I was going to ask you." He stared at me with a blank expression, so after a brief pause I added, "I'm Luke Tremblay. Marguerite was my aunt."

The man crossed his arms across his chest and squinted at me. "Yeah, I heard you might be coming. Well, I'm Joel Mackenzie. I'm here to pick up something that Marguerite sold to me."

I studied him from several feet away, noting his defensive body language and the lack of condolences. "You bought something from her before she died?" I inquired politely.

"That's right." He shuffled his cheap white sneakers across the weather-beaten wood of the porch. "I traveled a long way to this flyspeck town to collect a particular piece that your aunt had in her store."

"Her store is on Main Street," I pointed out.

Joel grimaced and glanced back toward the window next to him. "It's not there. My guess is that she brought it home."

I felt my eyebrows drawing downward as I listened. "Why would she take home an item that she had sold to you?"

The other man grew agitated, uncrossing his arms and flinging them out to either side. "Look, I just want the thing I paid for, okay? It's not in her shop, so it's probably here. If I could just get inside . . ."

I cut him off with a raised hand. "Nope, sorry," I said, trying to keep my tone polite but firm. "I'm not giving anything away unless you have a receipt to show me."

"I, uh, lost the receipt," Joel said, looking away for a moment. Then he stepped closer until his bulging blue eyes were staring up at me. "But if you just let me inside right now, I'll—"

"Whoa. Back up, please."

His face screwed up into a furious glare, and then before I could react, he shoved me aside with an elbow to the ribs. I staggered a couple of steps with a muffled *ooof* as he reached for the front door, but I managed to regain enough equilibrium to put a hand on his polyester tracksuit and push him away.

"What the . . . ?" I wheezed, outraged. "Okay, you need to leave, right now." Massaging my side with one hand, I set myself squarely in his path and pointed to the front garden with my other hand. "Get out of here before I call the police."

Joel's lip curled. "Move, before you regret it," he snapped at me.

Heart pounding, I started to fumble my phone out of my pocket just as he bulled forward once more, trying to reach the front door. We ended up in a bizarre tussle, me holding him back with a hand in the middle of his chest, him grabbing hold of my shoulders. His eyes looked deranged, and this close I could smell stale cigarettes and liquor on his breath.

"Your aunt was a thief," he spat up at me, "and she got what she deserved."

Propelled by a surge of unexpected anger, I set my feet and hurled him back with a single convulsive shove. I saw his expression turn from rage to surprise as he let go of me, arms windmilling and sneakers sliding, before he fell backward off the porch, landing with an audible *whump* of expelled air on the crushed stone path below.

"Get out of here!" I yelled down at his spread-eagled form. "And if I see you back here again, I'll make sure *you* get what you deserve!" I was shaking, both hands clenched at my sides, watching the shorter man struggle to catch his breath as he rolled feebly from side to side.

Abruptly, I realized that we weren't alone: a teenage Black girl was watching us both from a dozen feet away, eyes wide and mouth hanging open. She was carrying two bulging cloth bags with *Crescent Cove Greengrocers* printed on them. My anger collapsed along with the adrenaline rush, leaving me sick to my stomach.

Joel, meanwhile, had managed to get to his hands and knees before stumbling to his feet. He brushed furiously at the dust on his tracksuit as he scowled up at me, but then he followed my gaze and saw the girl as well. "This isn't over," he snarled, before scurrying away. The girl barely avoided being knocked over as he rushed past.

"Sorry about that," I said to her, feeling suddenly abashed.

Turning her gaze back to me, she shook her head slowly, her hair waving in the breeze as she did so. "That seemed pretty intense," she noted uncertainly.

I ran a shaking hand through my own hair, unsurprised to find it damp with sweat. I felt like I'd run a half-marathon. "He was trying to break into the house," I mumbled. Then, looking again at the bags she was holding, I said, "You must be here with the groceries I ordered."

We both turned at the sound of an engine revving behind the cottage, then the loud crunch of wheels spinning on gravel. I darted off the porch and past the teenager in time to see an old, rusted-out pickup fishtail slightly before correcting itself and charging back up the driveway. Part of me had expected him to drive straight into the back of the house and try to get in that way, as crazy as that sounded. Given his behavior, though, I wasn't prepared to put anything past Joel Mackenzie.

"Here you go," the young woman muttered as she set down the bags next to me.

"Thanks," I told her sincerely. "And sorry again. That wasn't . . ."

"No worries," she said, giving me a quick wave even as she turned and hurried away. I couldn't blame her. That probably hadn't been a fun scene to witness.

15

Feeling disoriented, I grabbed the bags and let myself back into the cottage, taking a moment to lock the door behind me. Then, moving mechanically, I headed back to the kitchen and unpacked everything. There was plenty of food to tide me over for a couple of days, and after I put everything away, I found myself standing at the kitchen sink, staring out at the back garden and the dense rows of trees rising beyond. The afternoon had gotten away from me, and everything was cloaked in gloom as the sun sank out of sight behind the forest. Suppressing a shiver, I locked the French doors leading onto the patio before turning on the oven, grabbing a foil pan of lasagna from the fridge, and getting some dinner going.

It was with mixed feelings that I finally sat down to eat at the round table situated between the kitchen and living room. There was little to see out of the large picture window in front of me—just my reflection, set against the dark backdrop of the forest outside. I felt very lonely as I ate the excellent lasagna. The cottage around me was warm and familiar and comfortable, but it also felt empty without my aunt's larger-than-life presence. In my memories she was always telling elaborate stories or laughing at something, her green, expressive eyes crinkling at their corners. She'd had a way of filling a space just by being herself. I'd loved her so much as a kid, finding in her the warmth I'd never received from my parents. When she stopped talking to me along with the rest of my family, I'd been crushed. And now here I was, in the home she'd made for herself, the little cottage by the sea that had once been my favorite place in the world . . . and she was gone.

I sat there for a long time, watching my blurred reflection grieve against the impenetrable blackness of the Ravenwood.

Given my maudlin state of mind over dinner, I was a little surprised at how well I slept that night. I opened the window in the guest room just enough that I could hear the waves sighing and whispering in the distance, and I felt immensely comforted as I curled up beneath the down comforter and drifted off to sleep.

I came awake at one point, a bleary glance at the digital clock next to the bed telling me it was almost one in the morning. Something had woken me, I thought, a sound . . . but after lying there for a few minutes, listening, I decided I had been mistaken. Taking the opportunity to shuffle my way into the adjoining bathroom, I fell asleep again almost as soon as I returned to bed. The next time I awoke, my eyes opened to deep golden sunlight streaming through the window and a cacophony of birds trilling and singing in the trees outside.

Dragging myself out of bed with some reluctance, I wandered into the kitchen and fired up the coffee machine. Glorious sunshine was spilling through the bay windows in the living room and coloring the old wood floors a deep shade of amber as I leaned against the countertop and waited for the lifesaving elixir to brew. Steaming mug finally in hand, I decided to greet the morning out on the back patio.

I went to unlock the French doors, then stopped when I found them already unlocked. That was strange. I was certain I'd locked them last night, after Joel Mackenzie's belligerent visit. Bemused, I pushed one door open and stepped outside, my bare feet stepping gingerly across the cold stones of the patio. In front of me, the Ravenwood had been transformed from the brooding darkness of last evening to a splendid wash of greens and browns and grays illuminated by the rising sun.

I paused to soak it in, coffee mug cradled between my hands, and then noticed I wasn't alone in the garden. There was someone sprawled across the crushed stone surrounding the ornamental pond, clad in a familiar tracksuit.

It was Joel Mackenzie, and he was lying facedown in the water.

Chapter Three

Fifteen very tense minutes later, I was still standing on the patio, though I'd had time to shove shoes onto my feet and chug the rapidly cooling coffee while waiting for the authorities to arrive. I'd called 911 as soon as I realized that Joel wasn't moving and, in fact, would never move again, something I'd ascertained after one look at the blood matting his pale hair and the grayish pallor of the hands flung limply to either side. Not to mention that he apparently no longer needed to breathe.

There was a dead body in my aunt's garden. Noting with distant relief the arrival of two vehicles on the other side of the picket fence, I returned my attention to Joel's pathetic, crumpled form. I couldn't stop staring at the ominous stain that discolored the back of his head. My morbid fascination was so profound, in fact, that it took me a while to realize that someone was speaking to me. Giving my head a brisk shake, I turned and found a tall, imposing figure standing at my side, wearing a blue tactical vest with POLICE emblazoned in white letters across the front. His uniform consisted of a pale-gray short-sleeved shirt and navy trousers with a wide gold stripe down the side, and the rugged, handsome face watching me below the peaked cap was utterly expressionless.

"There's a dead body," I blurted, pointing to the pond.

"Yes, we're aware," the officer said in a dry tone. He was what my aunt might have described as a strapping specimen of a man: several inches taller than me, with broad shoulders under his tactical vest and a pair of flinty hazel eyes that watched me with seeming dispassion. From his uniform, I figured he was a Mountie, which made sense, as Crescent Cove was too small to have its own dedicated force. The Royal Canadian Mounted Police often stepped in to police smaller or rural communities. "I'm Sergeant Munro," he went on, after a slight pause. "And you're Luke Tremblay."

"Right, yeah."

"You called this in."

Nodding, I let my gaze slide back to Joel's body. Two people were crouched to either side now, a young Black woman in a Mountie uniform like Munro's and an older white woman dressed more casually in jeans, sweater, and fleece vest. "I found him right before I called 911."

There was another pause. I tore my attention away from the corpse in my aunt's garden and saw that the burly sergeant had extracted a small notepad and pen from a pocket in his tactical vest. "Had you ever seen the deceased before?" he asked as he flipped open the notepad, his cool gaze fixed on me. He really was good-looking, I noticed distractedly. Or maybe it was just the uniform. No, I decided a moment later, it definitely wasn't just the uniform. His square jaw had a dusting of dark stubble, and his voice was deep and warm and actually a little thrilling . . .

"Sir?"

Clearing my throat, I tried to stop mooning over the nice policeman and gather my thoughts. "Uh. Had I seen him before? Yes. He came to the cottage yesterday. He said his name was Joel Mackenzie."

The sergeant nodded as he jotted that down. "He came here yesterday? What did he want?"

"He claimed that my aunt had sold him something—a piece from her shop, I guess. She owned Forget-Me-Not Antiques on Main Street," I added by way of explanation. "He came here looking for it, though, which was strange. I caught him peering through the windows, and then he tried to push his way inside." I wrapped my arms around myself and shivered as I remembered the man's desperate rage. "He was very upset."

Munro looked at me, unblinking. "He tried to get inside? What happened then?"

The sergeant's blank stare and taciturn demeanor were making me nervous. "Nothing happened. I stopped him and he left."

Munro made a note in his pad. "How did you stop him exactly?"

I shrugged and looked away, unable to meet his gaze. "I stepped in front of him and told him to leave. That's all."

There was a slight pause. "Okay," he said in a neutral tone. "Did you hear or see anything during the night?"

I started to shake my head and then hesitated. "I'm not sure," I said, after a moment's thought. "I did wake up around . . .

one, I think? I thought I'd heard something through the open window. But I listened for a while and didn't hear anything else, so . . ." I trailed off with another shrug.

Next to the pond, the two women had now straightened to their feet and were talking quietly to one another, casting the occasional glance in my direction. Their expressions were thoughtful, and I shuffled my feet uncomfortably as they watched me.

"Was there anyone else in the house last night, Mr. Tremblay?"

I turned back to the sergeant. "Nope. Just me," I replied with a weak smile. He didn't smile back.

With the crunch of boots on gravel, the other Mountie approached and held up a clear plastic bag containing a wallet. "This is all he had on him, Sarge," she told Munro. She looked young—younger than me, anyway—and her face wore an expression of open curiosity as she studied me for a moment before turning her attention back to Munro. "Driver's license IDs him as Joel Arthur Mackenzie, from Hamilton."

I listened with interest. He had said he'd traveled a long way to be here, I recalled, and Hamilton was way back east, just south of Toronto. It would take several days to drive that distance.

"Okay. Head back to the detachment office and see if you can find any family or next of kin." Munro turned the full force of his unsettling gaze on me. "I'm going to need you to head there as well sometime today to make a formal statement."

Nodding jerkily, I said, "Of course, sure. I'll, uh, shower and get dressed and then stop by."

He flipped shut his notepad and returned it to its pocket. "In the meantime, don't make any plans to leave Crescent Cove, Mr. Tremblay."

"But . . ." I stopped as his lips curved into a frown, then rallied and continued. "I'm only supposed to be here for a couple of days. Just long enough to put the cottage and the antiques shop on the market and find someone to dispose of my aunt's assets. Then I need to get back to Toronto." He watched me impassively. "My whole life is back there," I added, a little desperately.

"You're not going anywhere," the sergeant informed me bluntly, "until we solve this murder. You have a dead body on your property, and we require your cooperation. Is that clear?"

I looked up at his implacable features and saw a spark of genuine dislike in his eyes. That was almost as unsettling as finding a dead body in the ornamental pond. Swallowing, I nodded again and kept my mouth shut.

"Good." He turned away from me without another word, leaving me standing there in my ratty old T-shirt and sweatpants. "Cassie, get going. I'll follow once I've spoken to the doc." The young woman nodded and made a beeline for one of the police vehicles parked on the other side of the fence. Munro, meanwhile, strolled across the patio toward the other woman and spoke with her for a few minutes while I stood there, uncertain what to do. Finally, I went back inside and washed my coffee mug, my movements mechanical. From the sink, I could see one of Joel's feet splayed awkwardly from behind the sergeant's polished boots. Then Munro clomped off, leaving the older woman gazing down at the body.

Hesitantly, I went back outside. "Excuse me," I called to her, unwilling to come any closer to the pond. "Is there something I'm supposed to do now? I mean . . ." I gestured helplessly at the body.

With a quick grin, she moved closer to me and extended a hand to shake mine. "Juliana Kestenbaum. Local doctor." She was a sinewy woman who moved with a barely repressed energy somewhat at odds with her mane of graying curls. I placed her at around sixty, but she exuded the vitality of a much younger person. I decided I liked her immediately. "No need for you to do anything right now. I'm going to finish up my preliminary inspection of the body while I wait for the medical examiner to arrive from Campbell River. She'll perform a full autopsy."

I nodded. Once again, I couldn't take my eyes off Joel's corpse, but Juliana shifted deliberately so I found myself staring at her sympathetic expression instead. "How did he die?" I asked, after a moment's pause.

"Blow to the head, it looks like," she replied briskly. "Though that might have stunned him long enough that he drowned instead. Won't know until they open him up." I must have looked unaccountably queasy at the thought, because she started gently pushing me back toward the house. "Just head back inside, okay?"

I complied, stumbling a little over my own feet, and then treated myself to a long, hot shower in the remodeled bathroom attached to the guest room. Once I was shaved and dressed, I found the back garden blessedly empty of doctors and corpses. Everything looked rather spookily unchanged, in fact, apart from an ominous gap in the water lilies dotting the pond's surface and a few flowers crushed either by Joel himself or the careless boots of the police.

I glanced at my watch and saw that most of the morning was gone. I was supposed to meet Daisy Simpson at my aunt's antiques shop in less than an hour to discuss putting it on the market as well, but I really wanted to get my standing appointment at the RCMP detachment out of the way first, so I texted her and asked if we could meet after lunch, to which she speedily agreed. Then I hurried through the back garden to my rental car and headed for the center of town.

The heart of Crescent Cove was laid out in a simple grid that sloped eastward toward the water. I had to use my phone to find the RCMP detachment, and then I had to find a place to park nearby, which proved more challenging than I'd expected. Daisy hadn't been kidding when she said business was booming in the summer—there seemed to be people and cars everywhere. Fortunately, it was a beautiful sunny day and I didn't mind hiking an extra two blocks back to the detachment from the parking spot I'd nabbed. I weaved my way around throngs of tourists as they meandered along the town's picturesque little streets, each lined with an impressive collection of buildings dating back to the nineteenth century, until I reached a rather unassuming structure sandwiched between a quaint café and a local purveyor of fancy candles. With considerable trepidation, I pushed my way inside.

I was greeted at the front desk by a young man who couldn't have been more than fourteen but was nonetheless wearing a uniform. Were the Mounties hiring high school students? Maybe I was just getting old. Introducing myself, I told him that Sergeant Munro had asked me to stop by and provide a statement.

"Oh, right, the murder!" he said, his boyish features beaming with unbecoming enthusiasm. "I'll just see if he's free." A quick phone call later, he escorted me through a collection of desks toward a glass-walled office at the back of the central area. With a jaunty knock on the door, he pushed it open and ushered me inside with a grin before closing it again behind me.

I found myself staring at Sergeant Munro once more, but this time he was seated behind a desk that looked to be organized with ruthless efficiency. He'd removed his hat and tactical vest and sat stiffly in his short-sleeved uniform shirt, big hands folded together atop his desk. "Mr. Tremblay," he greeted me. "Have a seat."

Giving him a weak smile, I sank into one of the two chairs positioned opposite him while taking a surreptitious glance around. The office was small and as well organized as his desk, with numerous filing cabinets along one wall and an enormous whiteboard stretching across another. Apart from a couple of houseplants in glazed ceramic pots, there didn't seem to be many personal touches.

"I'll try to keep this brief," Munro went on after a moment. "But we do need a formal statement about your interaction with Joel Mackenzie and your movements yesterday evening and this morning."

Wiping damp palms on my jeans, I nodded. "Sure, of course."

The sergeant took a slim file folder from the top of a pile on his desk and opened it. "You live in Toronto, is that right?"

"Yes. I've lived there for . . . about fifteen years, I guess."

"And before that?"

"I went to Dalhousie for university, out east in Halifax. I'm from Edmonton originally."

His hazel eyes studied me from beneath a pair of thick eyebrows. Now that his hat was off, I could see that his hair was styled in a crisp side part, and for some reason that jogged something in my memory. Was it possible I'd met Munro before? It seemed unlikely, considering I hadn't been back to Crescent Cove in more than twenty years. But there was something about that boyish haircut, the square lines of his face, his pale-bronze skin . . . all of it suddenly seemed so familiar.

He cleared his throat, and I realized I had been staring. I felt my face warm as I quickly became absorbed in studying a convenient filing cabinet instead.

"When did you arrive in town, Mr. Tremblay?" he asked, after another small pause.

"Yesterday afternoon. Around two, I think. I met with Daisy Simpson at the cottage and discussed putting it on the market."

"Right," Munro said. "So you can go back to Toronto." Was I imagining the sardonic edge to his voice?

Blinking at him, I said, "Yes. So I can go back home to my life." I put a bit of an edge on my reply as well, though a mutinous part of my brain pointed out that since I'd kicked Bryce out of our townhouse, there wasn't much of a life to go back to. I told that part of my brain to shut up as I added, "I found out I'm the beneficiary of my aunt's will less than a week ago, at which point I decided to get this trip over with—sell the cottage and my aunt's shop, tie up any last details, and then head back east."

Munro's mouth curved into a wry smile as he made a note in the file in front of him. "You don't seem to want to be here," he observed.

"Where? Sitting in this office? Or in Crescent Cove?" I replied sharply. "Well, you're right on both counts, Sergeant. I *don't* want to be here."

He gave me an impassive stare. "What do you do in Toronto?"

I tried to wrestle down my indignation and respond in a civil tone. "I'm a freelance writer. I worked as an investigative journalist at the *Toronto Star* for a long time before deciding to strike off on my own."

Nodding, he made another note. "Okay. So let's return to yesterday afternoon. You met with Daisy Simpson. What then?"

"I went for a long walk on the beach. When I came back to the cottage, I found Joel peering through the front windows. I asked if I could help, and he told me he was looking for something—an object or piece that my aunt had sold him but never delivered."

"What was this object exactly?"

I shook my head. "I don't know. He never said. He seemed desperate to get it, though. He claimed that it wasn't in her shop. Then he insisted that it must be inside the cottage. I explained that I wasn't going to hand over anything until I saw a receipt, and he became really angry. He shoved me aside and went for the front door."

Munro's eyebrows lifted at that. "He physically pushed you?"

"Yeah, he did," I agreed with some vehemence. "I managed to stop him from getting inside, and then . . . then he left."

I cursed my small hesitation and hoped that the sergeant wouldn't dig any deeper. Once again I was reluctant to admit to shoving Joel Mackenzie off the porch and threatening him if he ever returned, even though I knew it would look very bad indeed if Munro ever learned that fact and I hadn't mentioned it. But I couldn't shake this feeling of animosity radiating from him, and I really didn't want to give him any more reason to dislike me.

Thankfully, however, he didn't appear to have noticed my brief pause. "You didn't see or hear from him again?"

"No. I stayed in for the rest of the night. With the doors locked, I should add. I made myself some dinner and went to bed early. I'm still on Toronto time."

"But you mentioned hearing something last night?"

"I'm not sure about that," I said carefully. "I did wake up around one in the morning. The window was open and I thought I'd heard something outside, but I listened for a while and didn't hear anything else." Watching Munro write this all down, I asked, "What time did he . . . you know, die?"

The look he gave me was scrupulously neutral. "We won't know that until the medical examiner performs an autopsy. At the moment, we know it was sometime between you running him off your property yesterday afternoon and you finding him dead on your property this morning."

I really didn't like the way he said that.

"Is there anything else you want to tell me?" Munro asked, after we'd stared at each other for a few moments.

"Nope." I hesitated before asking the question that had been on my mind for a while now. "Can you tell me anything about my aunt's death?"

He closed the file folder and carefully put it to one side as he considered his response. "We don't know much," he finally admitted. "She was struck on Ravenwood Lane sometime between nine PM and midnight, and the vehicle that hit her was going at least fifty kilometers an hour. No one heard or saw anything—not surprising, since the houses around there all sit well back from the road. And the dry conditions meant that there were no tire tracks that might help us." He let out a small sigh. "As best we can tell, Marguerite was walking toward her cottage when it happened. The car came up from behind her, and since the road ends at her driveway, the perpetrator must have turned around before fleeing the scene."

I swallowed and gave him a jerky nod. "Still no suspects, then?"

Munro slowly shook his head. "No. We've asked people to come forward if they hear anything or if they see a vehicle with damage consistent with an impact, but so far we have nothing."

I nodded again as an uncomfortable silence fell between us. The sergeant watched me steadily, his gaze cool, before folding his hands together and asking abruptly, "Do you really not remember me?"

I gaped at him, momentarily lost for words. "I . . . I'm afraid not," I finally stammered. "Should I?"

A muscle twitched on one side of his square jaw. "We used to hang out as kids. Those summers when you visited your aunt."

The Body in the Back Garden

"That was a long time ago," I said, a little defensively.

He acknowledged the point with a stiff nod.

"I don't think I knew anyone named Munro," I went on, casting my mind back more than twenty years.

Shifting slightly in his swivel chair, the sergeant said, "My first name is Jack."

"Jack." I stared across the desk at him. "Wait a minute. *Jack*? No way. I don't believe it." Unbidden, I felt a smile creep across my face. "You were the skinniest little kid I knew. And you had braces, didn't you? Like, for *years*." He grimaced faintly, and I let out a soft laugh. "Man, you've changed. Who would've thought that you'd go from scrawny to . . ." I gestured rather helplessly, trying to encompass his strapping frame.

Munro's dark eyebrows drew downward. "I was a little small for my age, yes," he allowed. "But I'm not the only one who changed." That edge was back in his voice, and my smile slowly faded under his glower.

"What does that mean?"

"We were friends," he said crisply. "Or I thought we were. I remember looking forward to Canada Day every year because I knew you'd arrive in town not long afterward. You were . . ." He frowned and shook his head sharply. "You were fun, and you didn't care that I liked reading fantasy novels or that I had braces or that I was the smallest kid in my grade. We spent every single day running around the beaches or the Ravenwood or exploring your aunt's shop. You don't remember that?"

"I do remember," I started to say, but he kept going.

"And then you just disappeared. The summer after I graduated from high school, I waited for you to show up, or phone, or write. But you never did. I was stuck in this town with people my age—kids I'd grown up with—calling me *half-breed*, *nerd*, *loser*. Worse things too. They made my life miserable. Why do you think I was always so happy to see you? Hanging out with you was a break from dealing with . . . everyone else."

I listened in growing dismay, watching as Munro clenched his big hands into fists on top of his desk. "Jack," I said, when he paused. "I'm sorry. I really am. I didn't mean to do that to you."

"Then why did you?" he demanded quietly, his gaze hard.

"I . . ." I stopped and closed my eyes. When I opened them again, he was still staring at me. "That's a long story," I said, a little huskily. Then, clearing my throat, I added, "It's also not something I want to talk about right now."

I watched as his expression shuttered and his eyes cooled to subzero. There was a twinge in my chest, a little twist of hurt, but I fought to keep my gaze steady on his.

When he spoke at last, his words were clipped and precise, with chilly formality. "I see. Well, thank you for coming in, Mr. Tremblay. I'll let you know if I have any further questions for you." He turned his chair toward the computer sitting on the corner of his desk and started clacking away at the keyboard without another word.

I'd never been so thoroughly dismissed in my life. Awkwardly, I got to my feet and headed for the door, but before I could exit, I heard him say from behind me, "Don't even think about leaving town." A glance over my shoulder showed him still frowning at his computer monitor, but I didn't need his full attention to appreciate the threat in those words.

Chapter Four

I was still shaken a couple of minutes later when I stepped onto the sun-drenched sidewalk outside the detachment building.

Well, that hadn't gone well, I thought sardonically. *Of course* the person in charge of investigating a murder on my aunt's property also had an ax to grind. I mean, why not? With my luck, any number of ancient grudges would resurface over the next day or two and I'd be the next person left for dead in someone's backyard.

Shoving my hands in my pockets, I turned right and started to amble down the sidewalk, past the little café I'd noticed before. The Bluebird, it was called. A couple of old ladies sitting in the front window watched me go by with keen interest while talking animatedly to one another, and I gave them a toothy smile that made them blink at me from behind their bifocals. As I turned away, however, my thoughts veered straight back to Sergeant Jack Munro.

I'd loved my visits to Crescent Cove as a child and then as a teenager, but they'd been a little lonely as well. As an outsider and a very shy person, I'd found it difficult to make friends. Until, that is, I met Jack. I'd come across him crouched next to one of my favorite tide pools on a little beach that I usually had all to myself, staring down at a bright-purple sea star that I'd named Henry. I was eleven at the time and desperate for friends, so I'd clambered up the slippery rocks to join him. He'd given me an uncertain look when I settled myself nearby, but then he smiled when I introduced him to Henry. We spent the next hour inventing increasingly implausible events in the sea star's checkered past, and from then on we were fast friends. I remembered him as all knees and elbows and crooked teeth, that last soon corrected by the biggest pair of braces I'd ever seen. We spent endless hours in the Ravenwood, making up stories and games or just wandering between the massive trees, and I still had fond memories of rainy afternoons reading comic books in his mother's tiny house on the edge of town. She was a member of the K'ómoks First Nation and legitimately the nicest person I'd ever known as well as the town's only librarian.

I hadn't thought about Jack in a long time. He'd been consigned to the deepest recesses of my mind along with all my other memories of Crescent Cove, firmly locked away after my aunt stopped talking to me. With the typical self-absorption of youth, I'd been too caught up in my own pain to consider that he might have missed me. How strange that he should reappear now, at the center of this horrible business. It wasn't the reunion I would have predicted.

Rising from the depths of memory, I found myself at Main Street. Gazing left, down toward the water, I couldn't help but smile. The street was unchanged since the last time I'd seen it, lined on both sides with two- and three-story buildings made of brick or pale stone and accented by colorful awnings, shutters, and painted trim. Old-fashioned streetlamps supported enormous hanging baskets overflowing with flowers that trailed toward the ground, and the sidewalks were thronged with people wandering slowly from one shop window to the next or enjoying their lunch outside small eateries that catered to a range of tastes. This was the beating heart of Crescent Cove, and it made me happy to see it thriving.

Sea gulls swooped and cried against the crisp blue sky as I made my way down the street toward my aunt's shop. The muscles in my shoulders and neck began to unclench in the warm sunlight, and for the first time since waking that morning, I started to feel okay. Joel's battered head bobbing gently among the water lilies, Jack's mistrustful gaze—they both faded a little as I soaked in the cheerful ambience of a seaside town at the height of summer. Ahead of me, the ocean rippled and shone as it ran toward the horizon, dotted with the sailboats of people enjoying a day out on the water.

Forget-Me-Not Antiques occupied a prime corner location three blocks up from Shoreside Drive and the ocean beyond. I paused outside and studied the huge window, in which dozens of items had been arranged with obvious care. As a rule, my aunt had tended to acquire smaller objects for her shop; there were often a few big pieces, usually furniture, but the bulk of her inventory had been given over to little treasures. There might be more money in selling the big things, she'd told me once, but most of her business came from tourists in town for the day. They weren't going to buy an antique desk and then pay a small fortune to have it shipped home—they wanted things they could take with them, cameos and watches and exquisite little objets d'art. Accordingly, the window display glittered with everything from brooches and cigar cutters to snuffboxes and cuff links, with three small painted landscapes suspended overhead in three different frames.

Ordinarily, the shop would be filled with people, but today the door was locked, with a CLOSED sign visible. I peered through the beveled glass and saw something moving inside, so I knocked briskly, assuming it was Daisy. I waited, then knocked again, more insistently, when no one answered. Nothing. I'd just started a third round of knocking when the door was flung open with a peeved rattle of jangling bells and a young man loomed in front of me.

"We're *closed*," he informed me loudly. "Didn't you see the sign?"

I paused, taken aback. He looked to be in his midtwenties but was dressed like someone from a Regency novel: flared jodhpurs, riding boots, tweed waistcoat, and a blousy shirt with its laces undone. His attire made a sharp contrast with the aggressively modern number of piercings decorating his ears, nose, and lower lip, to say nothing of his extravagantly curled and waxed mustache. Behind a pair of small round glasses, his dark eyes watched me with undisguised annoyance.

"Whoa," I finally murmured as I took it all in. "Is there a Jane Austen convention in town?"

"If you stopped by just to insult my clothing," he said frostily as he started to swing the door shut, "feel free to sod right off."

"Wait, wait, sorry," I replied hastily, lifting my hands to stop the door from closing. "I'm Luke Tremblay." His expression of disdain didn't waver. "Marguerite's nephew." Still nothing. "She . . . owned this shop?" I ventured.

"I know who Marguerite was," he snapped. "She was my boss, after all."

"Okay, great," I said slowly. "And who exactly are you?"

Rolling his eyes as if I'd demanded something unspeakably onerous, he finally muttered, "I'm Barnabus Delacruz. I've worked here for more than two years. And we are *closed*." Once again, he attempted to close the door in my face.

"Hang on," I protested, stepping forward so that I could push it open bodily. I had an uncomfortable flash of Joel Mackenzie attempting to do the same thing at the cottage, and with that my good mood of a moment ago evaporated. "I'm in charge of this store now," I said, more sharply than I'd intended, "and I'm meeting a Realtor here. So just back up and let me in."

With a snort, Barnabus retreated so abruptly that I practically fell into the shop. I shot him a furious glare as I caught my balance, but he only smirked in reply before turning and marching farther into the store. His black hair was knotted messily on the back of his head in a man-bun, at odds once again with the genteel character of his clothing. "Thanks," I said loudly to his back. He whipped around the edge of the jewelry case, planted both hands on its glass surface, and gave me a chilly smile by way of response.

Shifting my attention away from him for a moment, I glanced around. The shop, like almost everything else I'd seen in Crescent Cove, looked largely unchanged. Its floorboards still squeaked underfoot as I stepped forward, and the air smelled of dust and beeswax and violets, all of it creating a familiar, comforting blend of scents that took me right back to being a kid again. In front of the right wall ran the long jewelry case behind which Barnabus had sequestered himself; against the back wall was the numismatics section, with dozens of old coins neatly arrayed on dark-green velvet. Scattered across the battered old floors were antique tables, dressers, and other pieces of furniture on which rested hundreds and hundreds of items. Normally, the space would be filled with warm, golden light from the dozen or so lamps stationed around the store, but today the only illumination came from sunlight streaming through the two enormous windows in the front and left-hand walls.

Taking a deep breath of warm air, I steeled myself and approached the jewelry case. "I'm sorry we got off on the wrong foot," I said to Barnabus with deliberate politesse. "I think your outfit is very interesting." I paused for a beat before adding a little uncertainly, "Did my aunt make you wear stuff like that?"

"No. I like to wear *interesting* things," he informed me loftily, with a scornful little emphasis on *interesting*.

"Oh. Okay. Great." I searched for more polite chitchat and came up empty, so decided to cut straight to the chase. "What are you doing here? I thought the store's been closed since my aunt died."

"It has," Barnabus said, "but I got a call from Marguerite's lawyers. They want a full inventory. So . . ." He gestured sardonically. "Here I am. *Inventorying.*"

"Ah." I nodded. "That's very helpful. Thanks."

He watched me silently as I turned away and started to wander the shop, occasionally stopping to pick up something and look at it more closely. Then, abruptly: "You said you're meeting a Realtor here."

"Yup. My aunt left me this place as well as her cottage. I'm selling both of them."

"You're getting *rid* of it?" He sounded scandalized.

I shrugged. "I'm certainly not going to run it. And a location like this, on Main Street, will go for a lot, I'm guessing."

A profound silence met this response. Glancing over my shoulder, I saw Barnabus glaring at me with his arms folded across his chest. "What did you think would happen after she died?" I asked, genuinely curious.

"I thought that whoever inherited this store would recognize its value to the community and keep it open," he said with some vehemence. "It's a local institution!"

I felt a momentary pang of guilt before firmly quashing it. "The town will survive without this store," I said, trying not to sound defensive. "And you may not like hearing this, but the money I can get from selling this place will change my life." At the very least, it would allow me to buy Bryce's half of our townhouse back in Toronto, once I convinced him to sell. I'd finally have a home that belonged just to me.

Barnabus clearly *didn't* like hearing that. He gave me a deeply unfriendly stare before turning away, his back stiff with outrage. It didn't look like we were going to become buddies anytime soon.

I spent another few minutes wandering around the store, steeping in pleasant memories as I did so. Then, abruptly, something occurred to me. Joel Mackenzie had claimed that my aunt had sold him something but then kept it for herself. Would there be a record of that purchase? Steeling myself once more, I headed toward Barnabus, who was still behind the jewelry case. He was dusting the contents with singular care, pausing occasionally to rearrange a particular piece. Clearing my throat, I said, "I wonder if I could ask a favor."

No response.

I tried again. "Um. Barnabus? Could you help me with something?"

Silence.

Annoyed, I rapped sharply on the glass top of the case, at which point he straightened from his dusting and fixed me with a gimlet stare. "Oh, sorry," he said sharply. "I was just doing my job. You know, while I still have one."

I plastered on a fake smile. "No, sure, I understand. I'd like to take a look at the last few transactions my aunt made before she died. Would you mind grabbing those records for me?"

Muttering something under his breath in Spanish, Barnabus stalked to the small office at the back of the store and emerged a minute later with a slim ledger. He placed this in front of me on the jewelry case with more force than necessary. Thanking him with a nod, I opened the ledger and paged to its final entries.

There were two different styles of handwriting evident— I recognized my aunt's messy scrawl and assumed the other belonged to Barnabus. Every sale was carefully noted, including the date, a brief description of the objects sold, to whom, and the price. But a quick scan revealed no sign of Joel Mackenzie. In fact, I realized as I stared at the final page that there had been no sales at all for well over two weeks. My aunt had died just over a week ago, so these dates didn't make sense. There was no way she would have closed the store for that long in the middle of summer.

"It looks like nothing was sold for a while before my aunt died," I observed aloud, then looked at Barnabus, who shrugged.

"The store was closed," he said shortly.

"What do you mean? Why would she close the store?"

He shrugged again. "She didn't tell me. Marguerite just gave me a week off—with pay—and locked the place up. So I went to see my parents in Saskatoon. When I got back, I heard she'd passed." I looked up from the ledger to see him blinking furiously behind his glasses, and realized after a moment that he was trying not to cry.

"That's . . . unusual," I said, feeling a little uncomfortable at this display of emotion. "Closing the store during the most profitable time of year, I mean. I remember when she broke her arm, and even then she only closed for a single afternoon."

Barnabus looked away from me, out one of the store's windows. "Like I said, I don't know why she did it. But I'll tell you this." He returned his attention to me, his dark features suddenly serious. "She was acting strange beforehand. Like, cagey. She kept looking out the windows, wouldn't answer the phone. I asked her what the problem was, but she insisted everything was fine. You know how she was." I did. My aunt would have said everything was fine if the store was on fire and all her limbs were broken. "When she gave me that week off, I didn't even question it. I just left. And then she . . ." He broke off and took a deep, shuddering breath.

41

"Hey," I said quietly. "There wasn't anything else you could have done." I didn't particularly like Barnabus, but clearly he had taken my aunt's death hard. I felt bad for him.

He removed his glasses and wiped at his eyes with the back of his hand, but before he could reply, the door opened with a melodious tinkling of bells and a voice fluted, "Yoo-hoo!" It was Daisy Simpson, issuing her traditional greeting. She came bustling in, chunky heels thumping against the wood floors and her round face alight with sympathy as she hurried over to me. "Oh, I've just heard," she said breathlessly, reaching out to put a hand on my arm.

"Heard?" I replied blankly.

"About the body you found this morning!"

I stared down at her. "Wow," I finally said, "news travels fast around here."

"Jules told me. Sorry, Dr. Kestenbaum." Daisy shook her head. "What is this world coming to?" she asked no one in particular. "A dead body!"

"Wait a minute," Barnabus piped up, "you found a *body*?"

"Yes," I replied testily. "I found a dead body in my aunt's garden." I focused my attention on Daisy once more. "Is this going to affect the cottage being listed?"

She removed her hand from my arm. "Well," she said hesitantly, "at the moment the property is a crime scene. I can't list it for sale while that's the case. And then . . ." She trailed off and gave me an uncertain look.

"And then?" I prompted.

Daisy clasped her hands together tightly. "Well. Someone was murdered there. Now," she added, as I opened my mouth,

"I'm not required to disclose that fact, and neither are you. It's not a material defect of the kind that would need to be acknowledged to a potential buyer. But this is a small town. People talk. And I can't promise that this information won't become available to a buyer."

I felt my stomach sink as I considered the implications. Thanks to Joel Mackenzie meeting his end on the property, the cottage might become a very costly albatross around my neck. I'd been counting on a sale to supplement my meager savings, now that Bryce wasn't around.

"There are plenty of people who wouldn't care that someone died there," Barnabus volunteered. "Might even be a selling point for some."

I shot him a glare that bounced right off his many piercings and left him unfazed.

"That's true," Daisy said thoughtfully. "But in any case, there's nothing we can do about that now. I'll put the listing on hold until the police tell me differently. As for *this* place . . ." She paused and turned in place, surveying the shop. "I assume you want it sold as well?"

"Yes." I wanted to cut ties with Crescent Cove and get back to my life as soon as I could, though it seemed uncharitable to admit that. "As soon as the inventory is finished. Barney here is already working on it." I favored him with a flinty smile.

"Don't call me that," he said sharply, and I felt my smile widen. It was petty, but it also felt good to focus my feelings on a convenient target.

Daisy seemed oblivious to the tension between us. She was gazing around with a wistful expression. "Main Street won't be the same without Forget-Me-Not. It's been here for almost forty years, did you know that?" I made a noncommittal noise, and she added, "Plenty of businesses in town would love to snap up this spot, though." She gave me a faint smile and patted my arm again. "I'll draw up a listing and send it to you."

"Thanks, Daisy. I appreciate it." I looked over at Barnabus. "And I would also appreciate it if you could get me that inventory as soon as possible."

"Oh, sure," he drawled, "I'll get right on that for you." His insincerity put my teeth on edge, but I could do nothing but nod. Unless I wanted to wade through the shop's records myself—which would take weeks—I had no choice but to rely on his help.

I probably should've been nicer to him, some part of me reflected. Then I looked at that man-bun and thought to myself, *Nope*.

Chapter Five

Saying good-bye to Daisy and giving Barney a tight nod of farewell, I left the shop and stepped, squinting, into the bright sunlight. A family of tourists almost bowled me over, veering aside only at the very last second, and the smell of the hot dogs their kids were eating made my stomach growl with surprising vehemence. I'd skipped breakfast after finding Joel's corpse, but now I was ravenous, so without really thinking about it I turned and ambled across the street to the Sand Dollar Café, a local favorite.

I'd clearly missed the lunch rush, as only half of the tables in the place were occupied, and I was heading for a quiet spot next to one of the windows when I realized that people were watching me. A lot of people, actually. They were locals, I guessed, and they'd heard about the body in the pond from the one-woman gossip column that was Dr. Juliana Kestenbaum. An older woman clutched her purse tightly to her chest, as if my mere proximity to a crime meant that I was likely to be a criminal myself, and her companion tutted and shook her head, presumably at my daring to be seen in public after such a disgrace. Others eyed me sidelong and murmured to one another. The atmosphere in the quaint little café went from friendly to suspicious in the space of five heartbeats.

Coming to a halt, I looked around at the other diners and abruptly decided to have my lunch on the go. I reversed direction and approached the counter, doing my best to ignore the people seated on swivel stools to either side as I leaned in and ordered a sandwich from the young woman working there. She nodded and smiled at me as she wrote it down, clearly oblivious to the events of the morning, and I swiftly retreated to an unobtrusive spot against the wall where I could stare at my phone and pretend no one else was there.

Alas, my self-imposed exile lasted all of thirty seconds before someone said, "That can't be Luke Tremblay, can it?" I looked up into a pair of smiling turquoise eyes that belonged to a statuesque older woman who had to be in her sixties, her silver hair knotted into a fashionable chignon at the base of her neck. She was wearing a long silk blouse striped vertically in blue and green over a pair of white capris. Before I could do more than register her presence, she enfolded me in a strong hug. She smelled of a heavy, old-fashioned perfume that tickled some long-forgotten part of my brain.

"Oh, okay, and we're hugging," I observed as she squeezed me tightly. Then, hands on my upper arms, she pushed me away so she could study my face.

"You don't have the slightest idea who I am, do you?" she murmured with a soft laugh. "And why should you? I'm Evelyn Collingwood. Your aunt and I were great friends."

It took me a moment to process this, but once I did, I could see in her features the younger woman I'd known as a child. "Mrs. Collingwood! I'm sorry. I was just a little distracted . . ."

"Of course you were, Luke dear. And please, you must call me Evelyn now that you're all grown up." She lifted a hand and gently pushed a stray piece of auburn hair off my forehead. I smiled uncertainly. "So handsome. You look so much like Marguerite, it's . . ." She trailed off, and I was unnerved to see tears well up in her eyes.

"Thank you," I said quietly. It was true that I favored my aunt strongly, from the unruly curls of my reddish hair to my dark-green eyes and pale, freckled skin. "And you look lovely, Mrs. Collingwood. I mean Evelyn."

"I look old," she insisted with a self-deprecating smile. Her hands dropped away from my arms as she went on. "I had hoped to see you at Marguerite's funeral."

"I didn't know she'd died until her lawyers contacted me a few days ago."

Evelyn shook her head and sighed. "Of course. But I'm very glad you're here now. Your aunt would be thrilled that you've come back to Crescent Cove."

I looked away, feeling suddenly awkward. My memories of Evelyn Collingwood were vague, but I'd always liked her. She had sometimes stopped by the cottage to visit my aunt, and once or twice we'd been invited to the vast Collingwood estate that sprawled on the ridge behind the town. The Collingwoods were old money going back at least two hundred years, and they weren't just a local institution—their family was one of the wealthiest on the island. Renowned philanthropists and patrons of the arts, they were the reason Crescent Cove was more than an unknown pinprick on the map. The Collingwood fortune had built the library, the performing arts center, and other local institutions, and their family's prosperity had paved the way for the town to prosper in turn. To say they were beloved was an understatement.

"I'm actually selling the cottage," I finally admitted. "And my aunt's shop." I looked back at her and found her watching me with a sad expression. "My life is in Toronto, and has been for a long time."

She reached out and gave me another hug. "I'm sorry to hear that," she said quietly. "Crescent Cove won't be the same without a Tremblay to make things interesting."

I felt my eyes prickle with unwanted tears and looked away again, blinking furiously.

"Now," she said more briskly, "we're having our usual summer soiree tomorrow, and I absolutely insist that you be there." I turned back to her, protests already forming, but she gave me a steely gaze that brooked no refusal. "I can't imagine you'll be running back to Toronto until the police sort out this dreadful murder, so you have no excuse, Luke. We can raise a glass to Marguerite's memory, and I'm sure Kieran will be thrilled to see you." Her only child had been about my age, I recalled, though we'd rarely interacted during my visits. I had no idea why he would be thrilled to see someone he barely knew.

Seeing that arguing would do no good, I nodded and tried to smile. "That sounds great."

"Wonderful." Her own smile was considerably more genuine than mine. "In the meantime, how are you holding up?" There was no need for her to clarify what she meant.

I shrugged. "I'm doing okay. Still a little surprised at how quickly news travels here, though." I cast a glare across those seated in the café as I spoke and noted that most of them were watching my interaction with Evelyn with open interest.

"Small towns," she agreed ruefully. "I'll drop by with a little something later this afternoon." Before I could tell her that wasn't necessary, she leaned forward and pressed a kiss to my cheek. "It really is lovely to see you again, Luke. I just wish it had taken something other than your aunt's death to bring you back to us."

It was said without accusation or rancor, and I was mortified to realize I was on the brink of tears once again. "I'll see you this afternoon," I murmured, giving her a tremulous smile before heading back to the counter to retrieve and pay for my order. By the time I was done, she'd left, and I hurried out of the café before I could break down completely.

It took a couple of blocks before I regained my equilibrium. I wasn't sure why Evelyn's gentle demeanor had unsettled my emotions so thoroughly. Maybe because it had been a long time since someone had just *hugged* me like that. Or maybe it was remembering better times. Maybe Crescent Cove was starting to get to me.

Lunch in hand, I started to make my way back toward my rental car and then stopped in the small but lovely park that surrounded the town library. Finding an unoccupied bench beneath a craggy oak tree, I ate my sandwich while studying the library's imposing sandstone facade. I wondered if Jack's mom was still the librarian. She'd turned the library into a haven for anyone who needed a quiet place to sit, much to the dismay of the town's more conservative residents who would rather not have ne'er-do-wells cluttering up their cultural institutions.

Having finished my lunch, I sat there for a while longer listening to the birds call and sing to one another in the trees around me. Then, with a sigh, I got to my feet and headed back to the rental car. The drive back to the cottage took no more than five minutes, and when I got there, I found a Jeep Wrangler with RCMP markings waiting for me.

My heart sank. I really didn't want a third encounter with the police today.

With some reluctance, I trudged around the side of the cottage and found Jack Munro waiting for me, brawny arms folded across his tactical vest as he gazed out at the sea. My heart sank even further, but also fluttered a little as well. I had no idea how to behave around him now that I knew he was my old friend.

As I approached, shoes crunching on the stone path, he turned to face me. I paused. Jack looked *mad*. His square jaw was clenched and his eyebrows were drawn downward in a fierce glower.

Uh-oh.

"We need to talk," he informed me, and I nodded jerkily after a moment's hesitation.

"Sure. Okay. Do you want to come inside?"

With a shake of his head, Jack advanced toward me until he was close enough that I had to look up into his face. "I want to know why you lied to me."

I had to work moisture back into my mouth before I could reply. "What do you mean?"

"I spoke with Aleesha Perkins." At my blank stare, he added, "Her mom runs the greengrocers in town. She delivered some groceries here yesterday."

Oh, yeah. I nodded again, mute.

"Aleesha claims that she witnessed you assault Joel Mackenzie and then threaten him." Jack's resonant baritone was tight with anger. "Is that true?"

"I wouldn't say *assault* exactly," I hedged. "I did push him, that's true."

"She says you pushed him off the front porch and that he landed on his back on the ground."

"Uh. Yes." Jack's eyes narrowed, and I added hurriedly, "But he provoked me. He called my aunt a thief and said she got what was coming to her. I . . . I got upset and pushed him harder than I intended."

"And then threatened him."

"No!" I protested. "No, I just told him that if he came back here he'd regret it." I paused. "Okay. That sounds bad, I admit. But I didn't mean anything by it. It wasn't a *threat*."

Jack said nothing. His features, familiar and yet not, were completely blank.

On a rising tide of panic, I reached out involuntarily and grasped his forearm. "Jack, please. Please believe me. I did not kill Joel Mackenzie. I didn't see him again until I found his body this morning. I know how this looks, but . . ."

Jack stepped back from me, breaking my hold on his arm. "You assaulted and threatened a man who later turned up dead on your property, Luke." His voice was cool now, dispassionate. "And you have no alibi for last night. *How this looks* is extremely bad for you."

My feeling of panic increased as I stared up at him. "But you know me. You know I would never . . ."

He cut me off with brutal finality. "I used to know you. I'm not sure I do anymore."

I had no response to that. There was nothing left to say. My panic slowly subsided, leaving hurt and fear in its wake.

A deep silence fell between us. Waves crashed in the distance, and gulls screeched overhead. "Is there anything else you want to tell me?" he finally asked. "Because if there is *anything*, you need to tell me now."

I shook my head once. "There isn't," I said, barely able to speak through the tightness in my throat.

He nodded without taking his eyes off me. "I strongly advise you to stay put here at the cottage while we continue our investigation."

I said nothing, and after a long pause Jack brushed past me as he headed back to his Jeep. I watched him go with something close to despair.

I was now the only suspect in a murder, and the person in charge of investigating that murder clearly disliked me. I wanted to trust that Jack would figure out who the killer was rather than pin this on me, but given our recent interactions, that seemed far from certain. If I didn't want to end up in prison, there was only one option left.

I needed to solve this myself.

Chapter Six

I wasn't a genius, but I'd watched every episode of *Murder, She Wrote* as a kid, so I figured that had to count for something. More to the point, my whole career at the *Toronto Star* had been about digging up facts and piecing them together. The best investigative journalists had an uncanny instinct for the truth that helped them see past the lies and the false leads, and I'd been a pretty good investigator in my time.

The first thing I needed to do was figure out what I knew and what I didn't know. Finding a pad of lined paper in my aunt's desk in her library, I grabbed a pen and started scribbling.

- *Joel Mackenzie. From Hamilton. How long in town? Staying where?*
- *Apparently hit over head. (With what?)*
- *Bought (?) something from Aunt M. No record of sale. Must be antique.*
- *Aunt M acted strangely before death. Why?*
- *Joel found with wallet but nothing else.*

I looked at that last note for a while, then added two more items to the list.

- *PHONE???*
- *Truck??*

The fact that Joel had been found without his phone struck me as important. Maybe his murderer had taken it. And what about the battered old truck I'd seen him driving yesterday? Where was it? Was it still parked wherever he was staying in town? If so, it might contain clues.

I sat there for a while, pen tapping against the paper in front of me. Barnabus had said my aunt was acting "cagey" before she died. It sounded like she was on the lookout for someone. Had she been avoiding Joel? Maybe she'd sold him something off the books and then regretted it, though that didn't sound like her at all. Had he threatened her?

I stared at my messy notes for a while, my mind jumping from one question to the next. Finally, I wrote *WHY?* and circled it several times. What had Joel been doing in Crescent Cove that had resulted in his death? What was he chasing that someone else was so desperate to keep away from him? On the face of it, it seemed absurd that something sitting in my aunt's poky little shop had been the catalyst for murder . . . and yet here I was, the prime suspect in a brutal death.

Suddenly exhausted, I pushed the pad away from me and slumped in the old wooden swivel chair, staring blankly out the window at the enormous oak tree that dominated this side of the cottage. I have no idea how long I sat there, lost in an endless spiral of bleak thoughts, but what brought me back to life was the sight of someone hurrying past the window, little more than a human-shaped blur that whisked past before my eyes could focus properly. I sat up, heart pounding with sudden anxiety, before heading straight to the front door. I had another nasty moment when I saw a silhouette on the other side of the beveled glass set into the door, clearly that of someone bent down and trying to peer into the house. Images of Joel Mackenzie pressed against the bay window flashed through my brain and I felt a queasy spike of adrenaline as I flung open the door, prepared to confront whoever was skulking outside.

"Oh!" Evelyn Collingwood breathed in surprise, straightening from her half-crouch. She'd added a white sweater knotted loosely around her neck and had a large casserole dish cradled in both hands. Her turquoise eyes were very wide as she gazed up at me.

I stared at her in surprise before remembering that she had promised to stop by. "Hi, Mrs. Collingwood. I mean Evelyn. Sorry for . . ." I gestured mutely to the door. "I'm a little on edge, I guess."

Letting out a shaky little laugh, Evelyn said, "No, no, it's my fault for sneaking around. I didn't want to disturb you and was going to just leave this on the doorstep." She hefted the dish as she spoke. "But since you're here, I'll just bring it inside, why don't I?" And before I could stop her, she suited action to words and squeezed past me into the little foyer. "This really should be in the fridge," she called back as she made her way through the living room and toward the kitchen.

I stood there for a few moments, lost for words, before slowly closing the door and then trailing along behind her. She was just closing one side of the double-wide fridge as I entered the kitchen, and then she turned and gave me a rueful smile. "I thought I'd find you entirely without food, but I see you're well stocked."

"Uh, yes. Daisy Simpson gave me the number of the local grocery store."

"How thoughtful." Evelyn studied me and then added, "I can go if you'd rather be by yourself, Luke."

I opened my mouth to agree that yes, actually, I did want to be alone, but then heard myself saying, "No, you don't have to go. I'd . . . like to talk. About my aunt. If that's okay."

Her expression softened. "Of course it is. Why don't you go into the living room and I'll make us some tea? Don't worry, I know where everything is."

Nodding, I turned and shuffled away as she busied herself with the electric kettle. I found myself next to the fireplace, staring at a framed photo on the mantel. It showed my aunt standing in front of Forget-Me-Not Antiques with a big smile on her face, one arm around the waist of someone I belatedly recognized as Barnabus Delacruz. He was wearing a smoking jacket and what looked like an actual monocle, and he was smiling as well, with an arm resting across my aunt's shoulders. Reaching out, I picked up the photo and studied it more closely. My aunt's red hair was liberally streaked with white and her face carried more lines than I remembered, but aside from that, she'd changed relatively little over the years. I felt a twinge of . . . something . . . as I looked at the two of them. Envy? Regret? They'd been close, obviously.

I was still studying the photo when Evelyn returned, bearing two ceramic mugs along with milk and sugar on a small tray. "There we are," she murmured as she placed the tray on the low table in front of the fireplace. "Help yourself, dear." I did so before sinking onto the old sofa while Evelyn made herself comfortable in an overstuffed chair.

Cradling my mug between my hands, I said quietly, "Was my aunt happy before she died?"

The older woman looked thoughtful as she considered my question. "I think so, yes," she finally said. "Marguerite was a naturally happy person."

"You didn't notice anything . . . unusual in the days and weeks leading up to her death?"

Evelyn shook her head slowly. "Unusual? No. But then, I didn't see your aunt in the last week or so."

I absorbed this in silence as I sipped my tea. Around us, the room had started to darken almost imperceptibly as the sun sank behind the Ravenwood and the cottage fell into shadow.

"You know, Marguerite loved you very much," Evelyn volunteered after a little while.

"Maybe she did, once," I said, unable to meet her gaze. "But not for a long time."

Evelyn shook her perfectly coiffed head. "That's not true. She was incredibly proud of you, Luke. And I know she regretted that things had gotten so difficult between you."

I laughed bitterly. "Difficult? That's one way of putting it, I suppose." Lifting my eyes to her, I said, "She cut me out of her life. Told me I couldn't visit here again. *Difficult* doesn't quite capture what that felt like."

"Oh, Luke," she said with genuine distress, "it wasn't like that at all. After the . . . the argument you had with your parents, she received a call from her brother. Your father. He warned her not to meddle, to just leave you alone. The family were united in their decision to . . . let you go your own way, and if Marguerite didn't toe the line, your grandfather would disinherit her." She shook her head. "Your aunt was in serious financial trouble at the time. Her shop wasn't doing well and the cottage had become something of a money pit. When you wrote to her and asked to visit, she felt she had no choice but to refuse." Leaning forward in her chair, she held my gaze with her own. "That was the single greatest regret of her life, Luke. By the time she realized what a mistake she'd made, she thought it was too late. She was afraid you would reject her as she'd done to you, so she just . . . let you be." Her eyes were warm and sad as she watched me.

I listened, face blank. "I wouldn't have done that," I started to say, but my throat closed around the words.

Evelyn placed her mug on the table and rose to her feet. "I'm going to show you something. Wait here." And then she headed through the foyer and over to the other side of the cottage.

She was gone for a long time. Dusk had truly fallen outside now, and I finally got up and switched on several lamps so that the room was flooded with golden light. Through the windows I could see that the sky had gone a deep blue and the sea was like slate, smooth and dark. Finally, Evelyn returned with what looked like a photo album in her hands. She settled herself on the sofa and beckoned for me to sit next to her.

"Marguerite kept track of you," she told me quietly as she opened the album. At first it was filled with old photos taken during my many visits to Crescent Cove—smiling, youthful versions of me standing on various beaches, or sprawled next to the picnic lunches my aunt loved to make for us, or exploring the towns we visited on our many road trips around the island. My heart twisted painfully as I spotted a photo of me and Jack with our arms around each other's shoulders, both of us grinning like fools. But then Evelyn turned more pages and the photos disappeared, replaced by newspaper clippings and, later, printouts from the internet. I craned my neck to read one of them and saw that it was the first article I'd written for the *Dalhousie Gazette* when I was a student there. All of my *Gazette* articles were there, I realized, followed by everything I'd published during my time as a journalist and then my work as a freelance writer. My entire career, all of it carefully documented and preserved by my aunt, who'd thought she could only ever know me from afar.

My vision blurred, and I felt Evelyn's thin hand come to rest on my shoulder. "She never stopped loving you," she murmured. "Right up to the day she died. I know that for a fact."

I couldn't reply. As if against my will, I slowly leaned into her and let the tears fall while she patted my shoulder and said quiet, sympathetic things.

It took a while for my grief to recede enough that I could regain a little control. When I finally blinked away the last of my tears, I levered myself upright again and sniffled once or twice. "Sorry about that," I mumbled, mortified to my core. "I cried all over your sweater."

"Nonsense," she responded briskly. "You needed a good cry. You've had a difficult time of things."

I couldn't argue with that. As she got to her feet and gathered up the tea things, I slumped on the sofa, utterly exhausted. I felt wrung out, emptied. It took all the strength I had left to pull myself up and say good-bye to Evelyn before she left, giving me another hug on her way out. Then I stumbled to my bedroom and, pausing only to kick off my shoes, collapsed onto the bed and fell instantly into a deep and dreamless sleep.

Chapter Seven

The next morning brought an unwelcome surprise only slightly less traumatizing than finding a corpse in the garden—namely, Bryce. He appeared not on my doorstep, thank God, but on my phone. It was midmorning in Toronto but extremely early in Crescent Cove, so I was minimally conscious when I answered with a mumbled, "'Lo?"

"So you've finally stopped ignoring my calls," Bryce observed in his deep, urbane voice.

"Ugh," I replied with feeling.

"You sound like you're barely awake."

"I *am* barely awake," I said as I struggled to sit up in bed. I was still wearing my clothes from yesterday, and my eyes felt like they were filled with sand.

"Luke," he said, with that note of disapproval that always put my teeth on edge, "it's past nine in the morning."

"For you it is. I'm out west."

"What? Why on earth would you do that?" For Bryce, the civilized world ended at the Toronto city limits.

"It doesn't matter. What do you want?" I heaved myself to my feet and started to shuffle toward the kitchen.

"Sounds like someone woke up on the wrong side of the bed this morning."

I let out a frustrated sigh as I put the phone on speaker and placed it on a granite countertop, then grabbed the ground coffee from a cupboard and started measuring it out. "What do you want, Bryce?"

Silence followed, then stretched long enough that I checked to see if we were still connected. Finally, Bryce said quietly, "I was thinking about you. Wondering how you were."

I rolled my eyes. "Making sure your mess won't inconvenience you, you mean."

"Luke, that's not fair." I could picture Bryce shaking his head in disappointment, eyes regretful behind steel-rimmed glasses. He'd always been a consummate actor, able to convey a wide range of emotions with little more than a tilt of his head or the lift of an eyebrow. It was one of the things that made him such an effective litigator. People found themselves saying far more than they intended after he batted his baby blues at them a few times.

I could feel the old irritation starting to grow and tried to tamp it down as I filled the coffee machine with water and then switched it on. "*You* cheated on *me*, remember? So let's not talk about fairness."

His sigh reverberated through my phone's speakers. "You asked for space and I gave it to you. I even handed over my keys to the house when you asked for them."

"Because I didn't want to see your lying, cheating face again!" I shouted. Okay, so maybe I wasn't doing a great job of stifling my irritation.

His voice turned steely. "I'm not going to hash this out with you again."

"Then why did you call? *What do you want?*"

More silence, followed this time by, "I need to pick up a few things from the house. And as you know, I no longer have my keys."

"Well, you can't get your things, Bryce, because I'm not *at* the house." I opened and closed a few cupboards with considerable force to punctuate this statement.

"Then tell me where I can find a key, and I'll . . ."

"Nope," I interrupted. "No. You're not taking a single thing until I'm back in Toronto."

Another sigh. "Luke, you're being unreasonable."

"I don't care!" I yelled, my voice echoing through the kitchen. "You made this mess when you decided to fool around with your intern."

"He's a law clerk, not an intern," Bryce interjected.

I was momentarily tempted to smash my phone to dust with the ceramic mug I now clutched in one hand. Instead, I did a slow count to twenty in my head while trying to breathe through my rage.

"Luke? Luke? Are you still there?"

"You're not getting into the house until I'm back in Toronto," I said at last, my voice close to normal. "I'll text you a time when you can stop by. Don't call me again." Then I stabbed my finger at the little red circle on my phone and hung up.

The coffee machine burbled and chattered to itself as I struggled to regain my composure. Undoubtedly, Bryce would spin our conversation as yet another example of my hysterical irrationality. I'd been so impressed by his calm strength, his demeanor of effortless expertise at everything he did, that it had taken me years to realize how thoroughly he manipulated people. Particularly me.

I gave my whole body a shake and reminded myself that I had more pressing problems than Bryce—namely, my being a suspect in a brutal murder. So, once the coffee had finished brewing, I poured myself a mugful and set about waking up my frazzled little neurons with a healthy dose of caffeine.

The silver lining in Bryce's calling so early was that I could watch the sunrise, so I decamped to the front garden and settled myself in one of the Adirondack chairs that sat on the very edge of the bluff, affording me a stellar view of the beach below and, of course, the waters of the Georgia Strait as the sun climbed slowly up from behind the vague, mist-shrouded contours of the mainland off in the distance. The breeze off the water was chilly, but the coffee warmed me along with the soft old hoodie I'd thought to bring from Toronto, and it was with a sense of much-needed clarity and peace that I cast my gaze across the brightening expanse of the skies overhead.

Evelyn's revelations of the evening before had come as an unexpected balm for my bruised and battered heart. I knew now that the distance that had grown between my aunt and me had been the result of fear and misunderstanding rather than contempt or indifference. It couldn't restore all the lost and wasted years we'd spent apart, but I found the knowledge comforting nonetheless. The cottage behind me, and even the town itself, were no longer sources of pain. Even with my life upended by murder, I felt relief.

I closed my eyes and basked in the light of the rising sun for a while, and when I felt sufficiently prepared for whatever the day might bring, I returned to the cottage to shower and eat some breakfast. I grabbed the notes I'd scrawled the day before and studied them as I ate.

How long in town? Staying where? I read those first questions over and over again. Jack and his colleagues were probably investigating them already—might have answered them by now, in fact. But I couldn't sit here and wait for them to tell me what they'd found. Our last conversation the day before had convinced me that Jack was all too willing to throw the book at me for Joel's murder. If I wanted to exonerate myself, I'd need to do some sleuthing of my own.

Okay then. Rather than canvassing every hotel and motel in the area, I considered where Joel was likely to have stayed. As a journalist, I'd cultivated a knack for noticing what people wore, using that to make educated guesses about their behavior and habits. In Joel's case, he'd worn cheap sneakers and an ill-fitting tracksuit that looked a little frayed around the edges. It was possible that he simply didn't care about clothing, but it was also possible that he couldn't afford to care. His truck had looked ancient too, its sides pitted with rust as it bounced down the driveway on crappy shocks.

What if Joel had been strapped for cash?

Grabbing my phone, I did a quick search for local hotels and quickly compiled a list. I mentally crossed off B and Bs and other boutique offerings, then considered the businesses that remained. One of them caught my eye: the Seahorse Motel. Daisy had mentioned it at our first meeting, hadn't she? In fact, she'd implied she wouldn't be caught dead there, which suggested to me that it was a seedy dump. The kind of place where someone on a budget might stay.

I was in my rental car two minutes later, following my phone's directions to the Seahorse. It wasn't too far from the cottage, situated on a quiet stretch of road outside of town. It was the kind of secluded spot that might have been charming once upon a time but now was the ideal location for sordid affairs and other clandestine business. The ancient neon sign next to the road had burned out in several places until it read SEA RSE M TEL, and the word *Vacancy* flickered fitfully below as I turned into the parking lot and stopped the car in an empty spot.

The motel consisted of one long row of rooms facing the parking lot, with an office at one end and a decrepit vending machine at the other. The building had been painted seafoam green and pale pink at one point, but both colors were now dull with grime and age. Even the white clapboard shutters on the windows looked dingy. As I exited my car, I looked around for Joel's truck but didn't see it anywhere. That wasn't a particularly encouraging sign—maybe he hadn't been staying here after all. On the other hand, maybe he'd driven it closer to the cottage on that fateful night and left it somewhere. Either way, its absence was unfortunate. I'd hoped to take a look inside.

I approached the office and entered. Wood-paneled walls and shag carpet of an indeterminate orange color made me feel, rather queasily, as if I'd been whisked back to the seventies, an impression only heightened by the tinny sound of David Bowie's "Rebel Rebel" blaring from a back room obscured by a beaded curtain behind the desk. Cautiously, I approached said desk and then rapped smartly on the service bell, which chimed with startling volume. The music died immediately, just before a man swept aside the beaded curtain and fixed me with an impassive stare. He was tall and gaunt, balding on top but with a long ponytail of graying hair falling past his shoulders. He watched me from behind a pair of glasses perched atop a truly stupendous nose, and I could discern little in the way of welcome in his forbidding expression.

"Can I help you?" he intoned in a gruff monotone.

"Hi there," I greeted him, turning on my brightest smile. "I'm looking for Joel Mackenzie."

His eyes narrowed. Then he consulted the huge ledger lying open on the desk before turning to cast a glance at the row of hooks on the wall behind him. There were three room keys hanging there, each affixed to a blue plastic tag. "He's not here," the man informed me. "His key's hanging up."

I tried to keep my excitement well hidden. I'd guessed correctly: Joel had been a guest at the Seahorse. "Oh, that's too bad. Do you know when he left?"

The tall man shrugged, supremely uninterested.

"Okay." Propping myself up against the desk, I leaned closer. "Here's the thing. I'm a reporter with the *Times Colonist* down in Victoria, and Joel has some information for me. It's in a manila folder and I'd bet anything it's just sitting in his room. I don't suppose you'd let me in there, just for a minute?" I gave him another winsome smile. "I know that's usually a no-no, but I'm up against a tight deadline and my editor will kill me if I don't get this copy to him by this afternoon. So if I could get in there and grab it—"

"Yeah, I'll let you into his room," the man laconically interrupted, "but only if you pay what he owes me."

I stopped and considered this for the space of several moments. "What he owes you?" I repeated cautiously.

"Hasn't paid up since he got here."

"Right. And, uh, when was that?"

He consulted the ledger again. "Two weeks ago."

Now *that* was interesting. Two weeks was a long time to hang around a small place like Crescent Cove. Then I realized that would have put his arrival a few days before my aunt died. A shiver worked its way down my spine. *She got what she deserved*, he'd told me. Had *Joel* been driving the car that killed her? I hadn't considered it before, but now . . . I swallowed and pressed a hand to my stomach, feeling a little sick.

"He's got almost two hundred dollars outstanding," the motel owner said, oblivious to my reaction. "You pay up, and I'll 'accidentally' leave his key on the desk here."

Fumbling my wallet out of my back pocket, I saw with some relief that I had a healthy pile of twenties, which I dutifully counted out onto the desk. Our little transaction cleaned me out, but I walked out of the office with the key to Joel's room clutched in my hand and the gaunt man wearing the closest thing to a smile he was likely to possess.

Hurrying along the row of rooms, I reached number four and found the curtains drawn across the window. I was about to push the key into the lock on the peeling door when I realized there *was* no lock. Instead, there was a splintered hole about a foot above the doorknob. I paused, bemused, before leaning down to take a closer look. The wood around the hole was scorched in places. I wasn't a ballistics expert, but it sure looked to me like someone had shot out the lock.

My skin pebbled with goose bumps as I quickly glanced around. No gun-waving lunatics, which was good. Just the quiet, sun-soaked parking lot and the woods on the other side of the road. Given the decibels that David Bowie had been putting out in the office, I could believe that a gunshot would go unnoticed by the owner. But what about the other guests? I eyed the rooms to either side. Maybe gunshots were a regular occurrence at the Seahorse. Or maybe the people staying here had decided it was better for everyone if the police never heard about them.

Hesitantly, I pushed against the damaged door, and it swung open with a suitably atmospheric squeak of its hinges. Peering into the dim interior, I could make out the shape of an unmade bed covered with a tangle of sheets and pillows. No sign of movement. Grabbing my phone, I turned on the flashlight and played it across the room from where I stood to one side of the open door. Was there someone in there? I strained my ears, trying to catch any hint of noise from within, but all I could hear was a TV blaring from a couple of doors down.

Slowly, my heart thumping in my chest, I stepped across the threshold. The room contained about what you'd expect: a battered old dresser with an ancient TV sitting on top, a pair of cheap-looking nightstands on either side of the bed, appallingly bad art on the walls, and the half-open door to a bathroom on the far wall. Channeling every police procedural I'd ever seen, I quickly spun around to peer behind the door. Nothing there. I tried not to think about gun-toting murderers hiding under beds as I cautiously advanced farther into the room, swinging the bright beam of my phone's flashlight across a chaotic mess of discarded clothes and fast-food containers. I couldn't tell at first if Joel had been a slob or if someone else had torn through the room, but after crouching on the threadbare carpet to check under the bed—no murderers there—I rounded the mattress and found a suitcase lying facedown on the floor, surrounded by what I assumed had been its contents. It seemed highly unlikely that Joel would have ripped through his own suitcase and then tossed it on the floor like that.

Someone had shot out the lock and then torn the room apart. They were clearly looking for something. But what?

Trying to ignore my mounting apprehension, I took a couple of minutes to comb the room myself, careful not to leave any fingerprints. Apart from a lot of dirty laundry and more tracksuits than I thought strictly necessary, Joel didn't appear to have left much behind. A fake-leather jacket had been tossed into the corner next to the dresser, and when I moved it with my foot, I found lurking beneath it a plain white trash can half full of garbage. Eureka! The thought of pawing through whatever Joel might have tossed in there was not a pleasant one, but it appeared to be the only thing that hadn't been turned upside down by the mysterious intruder.

I started to remove the thin plastic trash bag, then froze at a sudden rustle from the bathroom. Silence fell, broken after an agonizing pause by another rustle. My heart pounded in my throat as I let the trash bag slip to the floor and directed my flashlight into what I could see of the tiny bathroom. "Hello?" I said in a quavery voice. Nothing. "Is someone there?"

The only response was another soft sound.

Adrenaline roared through my body as I closed the distance to the bathroom. Then, with one decisive kick, I slammed the door open and peered inside. Toilet, sink. There was another noise, from behind the door this time, and with an inarticulate growl I pivoted into the tiny space and pushed the door shut. A mildew-spotted shower curtain obscured the rest of the room from view until I whisked it aside and found . . . nothing. Just an empty bathtub in desperate need of a good cleaning and, high on the wall, a small window that had been pushed open. From where I stood, I could feel a cool breeze rush through the opening and dance across the shower curtain still clutched in my free hand, rustling the cheap vinyl.

Sagging against the bathroom door in relief, I waited a few moments for my heart rate to slow before turning to examine the sink. Various toiletries had been knocked onto the ground or into the grimy basin. There was nothing else.

I wobbled on shaking legs back into the motel room just in time to hear a car door slam outside. Rushing across the room, I peeked past the cheap curtains drawn over the window and saw the young constable from yesterday's crime scene standing next to one of the Wranglers the RCMP detachment used here in town. After taking a moment to put on her hat, she started across the parking lot toward the office.

There was absolutely no way I could be caught in this room. Even if I wasn't arrested for trespassing, it would look unbelievably suspicious. Frantically looking around, I spotted the trash bag sitting where I'd dropped it and lurched forward to grab it. With Joel Mackenzie's garbage clutched in my hand, I turned off the flashlight, stowed my phone, and crept to the door. I was about to pull it open when I thought about finger-prints and instead used the hand covered by the thin plastic bag to swing the door inward and stick my head outside. The RCMP officer was nowhere to be seen, so I slipped out of the room, pulled the door shut behind me, and raced toward my car. I was certain that I would hear her shouting at me to stop, but thankfully, I was able to wrench open the door and fling myself inside before hastily shutting it behind me. Then, tak-ing in huge gulps of air as if I'd run a marathon rather than sprinted several dozen feet, I slid down in my seat while reach-ing up to angle the rearview mirror so I could see the door to the motel office.

Mere seconds later, the motel owner stalked out, followed closely by the officer. "I don't know what happened to the key!" I could hear him say through the open windows of my car. Oh God. The key. I'd shoved it into a pocket when I found the lock had been shot out. Wriggling around until I could extract it, I used the hem of my T-shirt to wipe off its plastic tag with the number 4 marked in peeling gold paint. Then I watched as the pair approached the door to Joel's room. There was consider-able commotion when they discovered that the lock was gone, with the owner waving his skinny arms around and the officer unholstering her gun before pushing the door open just as I'd done minutes before. As she stepped cautiously into the room, I used the opportunity to open my car door and hurl the key into the long grass that grew at the edges of the parking lot. Then I started the car, backed out, and made a beeline for the exit leading to the road, praying desperately that she wouldn't notice the crunch of my tires on the gravel. One last glance in the rearview mirror showed me that she was still inside before I spun the steering wheel and got the hell out of there as fast as I could.

Chapter Eight

I had no idea where I was going—I just drove until I stopped hyperventilating. Then, my hands shaking on the wheel, I turned onto another quiet road and pulled over onto the weed-choked shoulder. I was sweating freely and actually thought I might throw up, but after a few minutes of deep breathing, I started to feel better. I really wasn't cut out for this adventure nonsense, I reflected, and that had been an absurdly close call.

As I tried to calm down, I wondered if the taciturn motel owner would sell me out to the police. Presumably he knew that I hadn't shot out the lock, since he'd given me the key, and I doubted he was in a hurry to admit to subjecting me to a little light extortion in return for said key. He struck me as the kind of person who wasn't exactly tight with law enforcement.

My gaze drifted to the clear plastic bag filled with trash sitting next to me, and I turned off the car before opening the bag and carefully sorting through its contents. There were candy wrappers and quite a few used Kleenexes, all of which I piled neatly on the passenger seat, but it wasn't until I was almost at the bottom that I found a tightly crumpled piece of paper. I unfolded it slowly and saw that it had been ripped from something larger. Written across it in a surprisingly neat cursive was part of a sentence:

> $50,000
> ~~$20,000~~
> *~~ay me $10,000~~ I'll tell everyone your secret.*

"Blackmail," I murmured to myself as I read it again, filling in the missing pieces. *"If you don't pay me $50,000, I'll tell everyone your secret."* Studying the previous amounts Joel had scratched out, I shook my head. "Looks like he got greedy." Paying out fifty thousand dollars would put a substantial dent in just about anyone's bank account, if they could even afford it. This definitely looked like a motive for murder to me.

I leaned back in my seat and stared blankly out the windshield. Someone in Crescent Cove had a secret so damning that they'd killed to protect it. But how would Joel Mackenzie, a stranger from Ontario, know a local secret? "Maybe he *wasn't* a stranger," I said slowly. It was an interesting idea. Perhaps he'd known someone in town already—someone with a secret that he could exploit.

Checking the rest of the trash revealed nothing further, so I stuffed everything except the note back into the plastic bag. Then I paused. The note was evidence, clearly. Just as clearly, however, I knew I couldn't just hand it over to Jack Munro, not without facing a barrage of potentially incriminating questions. So what was I going to do?

The answer came to me quickly enough: I needed to find a more plausible suspect for Joel's murder than me. If I could find an existing connection to him somewhere in town, someone who already knew him, then I could bring *that* to Jack and get myself off the hook. If I handed him the solution to Joel's death, hopefully he wouldn't care how I'd come across this note. "Okay," I said out loud. "Great. I have a plan."

Starting the car again, I tried to orient myself and, after a few wrong turns, eventually reached the center of town.

As I drove, I thought. Joel had been here for almost two weeks. That was a long time to sit in that dingy motel room, night after night. I was willing to bet he'd ventured out occasionally. And where would someone like Joel Mackenzie go to have a drink? From the picture I was forming of him in my head—a blackmailer who skipped out on his bills and spent as little money as possible—I couldn't quite imagine him ensconced in one of the higher-end restaurants or bistros that catered to tourists and well-heeled locals. On the other hand, Crescent Cove didn't exactly have an abundance of less salubrious locales.

Paused at one of the town's three stoplights, I watched abstractedly as a gaggle of young people crossed in front of me. This wasn't a very exciting place to be a teenager, I thought to myself, at least not a teenager who wanted to do typical teenager-y stuff. The only source of vaguely illicit excitement I could remember from my summers here was . . .

I sat bolt upright in my seat. Of course!

As soon as the light turned green, I took a right and headed for the southern part of town. Less than five minutes later, I was parked outside a boxy building made of dark-red brick with a mostly empty parking lot on one side. Sal's was the closest thing to a dive bar in Crescent Cove, but just about anywhere else it would qualify as a fairly average watering hole. The original owner, Salvatore Domenico, had built this place more than sixty years ago so that the men who worked the commercial docks on this side of town—men like him—had somewhere to go after work. Its blue-collar character and the flamboyantly Italian persona of Salvatore himself meant that the bar had swiftly come to occupy the metaphorical wrong side of the tracks, as far as most people in town were concerned. It was the kind of place where customers occasionally brawled in the parking lot or shouted at hockey games on the TV. It was also the kind of place where Sal and, later, his daughter might turn a blind eye to a little underage drinking. I'd been too straitlaced to visit it myself, but I'd heard plenty of stories from other kids.

Getting out of the car, I strolled up to the front door and stepped inside. It smelled like stale beer and onion rings with just a hint of cigarette smoke from bygone days, and it took a while for my eyes to adjust to the deep gloom. Once I could see properly, I noticed a few people slumped on stools around the U-shaped bar at the center of the space, either starting very early or working off their hangovers from the night before. Huge TVs in every corner played an endless loop of sports, and a few obligatory neon signs advertising Heineken, Corona, and other beers glowed warmly through the murk.

Feeling absurdly self-conscious, I shuffled up to the bar and levered myself onto a creaking stool. The bartender was a woman in her fifties, I estimated, with jet-black hair pulled back into a no-nonsense ponytail and a lot of eyeliner. She slid a square napkin in front of me and offered an inquiring look.

"I'll, uh, have a Coke, please."

"We've got Pepsi."

"Great. Sure."

It took her only a moment to fill a large glass of ice with pop, which she then thumped down in front of me. Before she could turn away, however, I said, "I'm looking for someone, actually, and I wonder if you've seen him." She gave me a weary stare, so I plunged on. "He's a little shorter than me, with fair hair combed back from his face and slightly protruding eyes. He might have come in here a few times over the last couple of weeks."

Her eyes narrowed ever so slightly. "You got a picture?"

I shook my head regretfully.

Tapping her long acrylic nails on the sticky bar, she studied me for a few moments before saying, "I know the guy, sure. Name's Joel something. Tried to leave without paying his tab once or twice."

"That definitely sounds like him."

She snorted and shook her head. "Bothered a couple of my servers too. Typical creep." She said it with the frustrated vehemence of a woman who's seen more than her share of creeps. Grabbing the towel draped over her shoulder, she moved a couple of steps down the bar and started drying highball glasses. "Why are you looking for him?"

I shrugged as casually as I could. "He was snooping around my house."

"Haven't seen him for a few days," the bartender told me. She obviously hadn't connected the dead body in my aunt's pond with Joel Mackenzie, erstwhile creep, though I wondered how long that would last. "If you find him, give 'im a punch for me."

Smiling weakly, I said, "Oh yeah, for sure." Then I hesitated for a moment before adding, "Did he come here with anyone else? Or did he meet anyone here?"

She paused to size me up once more. "He was good at making friends. Always had one or two people hangin' around, laughing at his stories and buyin' the next round."

An old man slouched over the bar a little ways down leaned toward us and said in a creaky voice, "Don't forget about that bust-up he had with Samuel."

The bartender frowned at him as I looked from one to the other. "Who's Samuel?" I asked.

"Samuel Beckinridge," the old guy responded as he turned back to the half-empty pint in front of him. "Runs the library here in town."

I pondered this new piece of information. Jack's mom wasn't the librarian, then. Maybe she'd retired. "What were they fighting about?" I asked, but got two shrugs in response.

Having exhausted any further information I might find here, I quickly drank my Pepsi and then placed a five-dollar bill on the bar before heading back out into the sunlight and fresh air.

Chapter Nine

My memories of the Crescent Cove library were little more than blurry recollections of gleaming wooden shelves lined with books and the hushed, reverent sound of pages turning. After meeting Jack and getting to know his mom, I'd passed a lot of rainy days roaming through the stacks, but I'd spent more time with my nose in a book than I had studying my surroundings, so it was with real surprise that I stepped into the library and saw that it was beautiful.

Pushing through the big wooden doors, I found myself in an enormous open space that rose two stories, surrounded on the upper floor by a mezzanine bounded by wooden railings. The floor on the main level was a checkerboard pattern of black-and-white marble tiles, the walls entirely given over to bookshelves, and at their center stood a circular desk of dark walnut polished to a warm shine. Behind the desk, two grand staircases swept up and around to meet again on the second floor. Massive tables lined with chairs and illuminated by the green glass shades of banker's lamps were scattered across the floor, and I saw a few people quietly reading or flipping through newspapers.

I stopped and stared. It was like the Platonic ideal of the perfect library, possessed of an elegant grandeur complemented by the intimate coziness of a space given over to quiet contemplation. I craned my neck back to gaze up at the panels of blue, green, and yellow stained glass set into the ceiling high above, through which dappled sunlight fell, and I couldn't help smiling. As someone who adored books and libraries in equal measure, this felt like coming home.

Someone coughed off in the distance, and I returned to my senses, though I was still smiling as I approached the central desk. Seated within its circumference were two young people of high school age, one clacking away at a computer while another carefully applied labels to a stack of waiting books. "Excuse me," I said quietly, and the closest teenager lifted their head to give me a friendly smile of their own. Their head was completely shaved and their clothing—cardigan, T-shirt, jeans—had what I interpreted as a deliberately gender-neutral appearance.

"How can I help?" they asked in a quiet voice.

"I'm looking for Samuel Beckinridge."

"Sure. His office is located on the rear wall there." Pointing past the staircases, they waited for my nod of understanding before returning to the computer in front of them.

Walking past the graceful curve of the left staircase, I found myself in a brightly decorated area intended for little kids, complete with small chairs, colorful rugs on the marble floor, and handmade wooden puzzles and other toys for children still learning how to read. This gradually transitioned to the YA section, and shortly after that I reached the back of the library. There were several glass-walled rooms here, all of them dark; I surmised they were meeting rooms of some kind. Next to them, tucked into a corner, was a wooden door with a brass plate attached that read LIBRARIAN. I knocked briskly on the door, and almost immediately a voice called out from the other side, "Come in."

Samuel Beckinridge was a rotund Black man with an open, friendly face. His short hair was speckled with white, and he had deep laugh lines around his eyes. He looked up from behind his desk as I entered, then popped to his feet with a smile. "I can guess who you are," he boomed enthusiastically as he bustled toward me with a hand extended. "You're Marguerite's nephew."

I shook his hand, a little taken aback. "I am," I conceded. "Luke Tremblay."

His smile widened as he noticed my bemusement. "The red hair was a clue," he said, "but actually you look very like her." His grip on my hand tightened. "I was devastated when she died. We all were."

"Thank you," I said automatically.

Releasing me, Samuel shook his head and sighed. He was wearing a red-and-blue-striped bow tie and a bright-green sweater-vest, and while very few people could have pulled off that sartorial combination, he did it with panache. "I was friends with your aunt for years, ever since I moved here. She was a lovely woman. Chaired the library committee, you know, and after Kiara Munro stepped down, Marguerite did her utmost to get me appointed in her place."

Nodding politely, I cast a swift glance around the office. It was small but scrupulously neat, with a large window that looked out across the park that surrounded the building. "I didn't know there was a library committee," I said, for lack of anything else to say.

"Oh yes. Established by the Collingwoods after they built the library in 1898." He gave me a shrewd look. "But I don't think you came here to talk about that."

"Uh, no." He gestured me to a chair before retaking his own seat behind the desk. "Actually, I wanted to ask you about an incident that took place at Sal's." His brow furrowed slightly. "I believe you had an altercation with someone named Joel Mackenzie."

Samuel's expression turned stony, though I couldn't tell if he was displeased with me or with Joel. "I did, yes," he said stiffly.

I waited for more, but when he remained silent, I prodded gently, "Do you go there often? No offense, but Sal's doesn't seem like the kind of place where you find a lot of bow ties."

"They have amazing onion rings. Sometimes I like to treat myself."

"Okay. Can you tell me what you and Joel talked about?"

He sighed and looked away from me. "It was nothing, really. Mr. Mackenzie came here to consult the town archives, which we keep in the basement. He wouldn't tell us what he was looking for, though. Just wanted to . . . rifle through everything." Samuel grimaced at the thought. "I explained that we couldn't allow that, and he got upset. A few days later, he saw me at Sal's and decided to express his indignation in . . . more forceful terms." He paused. "I believe he was drunk."

I thought about this for a moment. "How forceful was he exactly?"

"He threw his beer in my face. Ruined my favorite tie, in fact." His hands curled into fists atop his desk. "He was about to hit me when Dani intervened." At my inquisitive look, he clarified, "Daniella Domenico. She owns Sal's. Not a woman to suffer fools. She threw Mr. Mackenzie out all by herself."

I nodded. "And was that the last you saw of him?"

Samuel shook his head. "No. He came back here once or twice after that. Harassed the kids who work the desk during the summer. And that made me very angry."

Momentary silence fell as I digested this. Drunkenly assaulting people, harassing employees . . . Joel had certainly made himself a nuisance. Was it enough of a motive to kill someone, though?

"On top of that," Samuel added, voice tight, "he managed to break into the archives downstairs and steal some papers."

Aha. There we go.

"Do you know what he stole?" I asked, leaning forward in my chair a little.

He winced. "The archives are a bit of a mess," he admitted. "They were last cataloged more than sixty years ago, and my predecessors did a sloppy job of it. I found two accordion folders lying empty on one of the tables after I chased him out, however, and I know that one of them contained copies of the *Crescent Cove Dispatch* from the first half of the twentieth century."

Nodding, I stared abstractedly out of the window. Joel had wanted something from my aunt—something from her store, more specifically. That meant an antique of some kind. At the same time, he'd been taking things from the archives here, newspapers and possibly more going back decades. Evidence of this secret he'd uncovered? A lot of local families had lived in Crescent Cove for generations, but it was hard to see how something in the distant past could lead to murder in the present.

My gaze slid back to Samuel. The librarian didn't look like the kind of person who would commit murder. But then, who did?

"What's your interest in Joel Mackenzie?" he asked me suddenly.

I cleared my throat. "He was found dead at my aunt's cottage yesterday morning." Samuel stared at me. "That is . . . I found him dead. Murdered."

The other man leaned back in his chair. "And you think that I . . . ?"

"No, no, no," I hurried to assure him. "I don't think you had anything to do with it. I'm just trying to figure out why he was in town."

Samuel didn't look remotely mollified by this. "Yesterday morning, you said? Well, I couldn't have killed him," he insisted. "I was in Victoria until around noon yesterday, attending a meeting of the BC Library Association. I drove down there the day before and stayed overnight."

I raised a hand in a placating gesture. "Mr. Beckinridge, please. I really don't think you killed Joel Mackenzie."

He stood up abruptly and said, "I'm afraid I'm very busy right now." I looked at him with some bemusement and saw perspiration gleaming on his forehead. "You'll have to forgive me," he added with a meaningful look at the door to his office.

"Okay," I said as I got to my feet as well. "I'm sorry, Mr. Beckinridge. I didn't mean to . . ."

"Good-bye," he said firmly, right before he all but pushed me out of his office and closed the door in my face.

Chapter Ten

I was thoughtful as I left the library and slowly wandered through the surrounding park. Samuel Beckinridge, with his bow tie and his friendly face, truly did not strike me as someone who was capable of murder. Everyone has their limits, however, and if anyone could be said to have pushed Samuel past *his* limits, it was Joel Mackenzie. In fact, Joel seemed to have pushed a lot of buttons in Crescent Cove.

Lost in thought, I ambled away from the library until I found myself in front of the Bluebird Café, next to the RCMP detachment. Thinking black thoughts about Jack Munro, I decided to pop into the café for lunch after what had turned into a long morning of investigating. When I stepped inside, however, I almost ran into Juliana Kestenbaum, the local doctor, who was hovering close to the door. "Sorry," I mumbled.

She turned, and her eyes lit up when she recognized me. "Hey there. You look like you could use a sandwich. Care to join me?"

I'd been looking forward to a quiet lunch by myself, in fact, but a good journalist always takes pains to cultivate a reliable source, so, with a smile and a nod, I followed her to a table in a corner of the little café. She collapsed into her chair with a sigh, and I cast her a series of surreptitious glances as I perused the menu.

Almost instantly, a tall young woman materialized next to us, wearing a blue apron over her T-shirt and jeans. "What can I grab you to drink?" she asked, giving us both a smile.

"Just water for me," I replied, while Juliana ordered a Coke. Then we looked at each other as the waitress hurried off.

"So," the doctor drawled, "you've had an exciting couple of days, huh?" Her wry little smile deepened the lines around her eyes and mouth as she watched me.

"You could say that."

Leaning back in her chair, she slowly pushed her hands through the thick tangle of her graying hair. "I heard that Jack Munro gave you a talking-to."

I felt a brief stab of irritation as I stared at her. "How?" I demanded with some asperity. "It was a private conversation."

She shrugged. "People talk."

"They sure do," I grumbled, folding my arms and slouching back in my chair. Casting her a baleful look, I added, "Thanks to you, the whole town knew what happened about an hour after I found the body."

Juliana smiled, unfazed. "It's true, I'm a terrible gossip. Unless it has to do with my patients' confidentiality, of course. But that didn't apply in this case, so . . ." She shrugged again.

I wanted to be annoyed with her, but I couldn't help admiring her cheerfully bluff demeanor and give-no-crap attitude. "Fine, then," I said after a small pause. "If you want to gossip, tell me what you know about Joel Mackenzie."

The waitress returned with our drinks as I said this, and her hand jerked slightly at the mention of Joel's name, spilling some of my water on the wooden table. "Sorry," she whispered as she grabbed a handful of napkins from her apron pocket and started to mop up the spill. I glanced up at her freckled face and saw that she looked miserable.

"Are you okay?" I asked, and she shook her head so that her long brown hair fell across one side of her face.

"I just heard you say that name. He came in here once, and he . . ." Her voice lowered until it was almost inaudible. "He grabbed me."

I exchanged a look with Juliana. "You mean, inappropriately?" I hazarded.

She bit her lip as her face flushed a deep red, then nodded.

"Doesn't surprise me at all," Juliana declared, her expression fierce with dislike. "By all accounts, he was a real bastard."

The young woman gave Juliana a grateful look, then said confidingly, "My dad was so angry. He said he'd kill him if he ever saw him again." Her eyes widened almost as soon as she'd said this, and then she looked panicked. "He didn't, though," she assured us, and we both nodded in agreement.

"Of course he didn't, Gabi," Juliana said.

"Sure," I agreed.

We both watched her scurry back into the kitchen, then looked at each other again.

"Who's her dad?" I asked nonchalantly.

"Chris McCormick. He's run the café since his wife died a couple of years ago." Juliana paused to take a sip of her Coke, but her eyes watched me beadily. "He didn't kill Joel Mackenzie," she added firmly.

"I never said he did," I replied, but in my head, I added Chris McCormick to my mental tally of potential suspects.

We both sat in silence for a little while before she said abruptly, "You wanted to know about Joel."

I nodded. "Yeah. What killed him, and when?"

Her eyebrows went up. "Straight to the point, huh?"

I shrugged.

"Okay." She pursed her lips as she looked down at the table. "I heard back from the medical examiner in Campbell River this morning. In fact, I was next door telling Jack about it before I stopped in here. Joel Mackenzie was hit on the back of the head by something heavy and irregular in shape. They found dirt in the wound, so they believe it was a rock picked up off the ground."

Leaning forward in my chair, I nodded.

"There was water in his lungs, so technically he drowned in your aunt's pond, though the blow to his head would have been fatal all by itself if he hadn't fallen in." She shook her head. "It was a bad way to go."

I took a moment to absorb this. "Do they know *when* he died?"

"That's a little trickier to determine. It was unseasonably cold that night, so the window during which he might have expired is larger than usual. But they're reasonably certain that he died sometime between midnight and three in the morning."

I barely noticed when Gabi reappeared to take our lunch orders; when prompted, I mumbled something about a grilled cheese until she went away again. The rough timeline provided by the medical examiner fit with my being awakened around one in the morning, so maybe I really had heard the attack. The idea gave me chills. "If someone just grabbed a rock from the ground and hit him with it," I mused, "that suggests it was a crime of opportunity rather than premeditated."

Juliana snorted quietly. "Someone's been watching too much *Law & Order*, I think."

I flushed but met her gaze defiantly. "Do you have a different opinion?"

"Probably not," she conceded after a moment's thought.

Fiddling absently with the silverware in front of me, I said, "It also suggests that anyone could have done it. I mean, it doesn't necessarily take a lot of strength to smack someone with a rock."

Juliana inclined her head in seeming agreement.

I continued to ponder this new information until our lunch arrived. The waitress looked composed, though she wouldn't meet our eyes as she asked if we needed anything else and then disappeared into the kitchen again. Juliana watched her go and shook her head grimly. "Poor kid."

I was inclined to agree. For someone who had been in Crescent Cove for only a couple of weeks, Joel had made a lot of very bad impressions.

"So how long have you lived here?" I asked, after taking a couple of bites of my excellent grilled cheese.

"Almost forty years, I guess. Came here straight after my residency." Juliana smiled wistfully. "I thought winding up in a small town would be the end of my career, not to mention my social life, but this place saved me."

"How so?"

"It wasn't easy being a female physician in those days, and especially so if you were . . . unconventional." I lifted an eyebrow, and she clarified. "Gay, I mean. I took a lot of flak from, well, just about everyone when I went through medical school in Ottawa. No one was interested in hearing from an outspoken female who also happened to be a *radical lesbian feminist*." She weighted those last words with wry scorn. "I expected torches and pitchforks when I moved to Crescent Cove, but instead I found a community that needed me and accepted me just as I was."

Juliana said all of this with a total lack of self-consciousness, and I found myself warming to her even more strongly. "It wasn't . . . lonely?" I asked delicately.

She laughed. "Not at all. There are a few like-minded folks in this part of the world. Not many, but enough." She popped a potato chip into her mouth and chewed vigorously before adding in a casual tone, "Heck, even the head of the Mountie detachment is one of us."

I stared at her. "Seriously? Jack is gay?"

She nodded, lips curved into a faint smile as she watched me.

Once again, I felt that funny little twist in my chest as I processed this startling news. "I . . . had no idea," I said slowly.

Juliana shrugged. "He doesn't fly rainbow flags from the detachment office, that's true. But it's common knowledge. That was one of the reasons he had such a hard time of it when he was younger."

I turned my head and stared out the plate-glass window, watching people stroll past outside. Jack had mentioned being bullied, hadn't he? I remembered the pair of us when we'd first found one another—two lonely kids, different from everyone else, desperate for a friend. *How lucky that we* did *find each other*, I thought. *Until I abandoned him.*

Juliana shattered my moody reverie by asking if I was going to finish my chips. Then, once she'd devoured them, we headed up to the counter, where she insisted on paying. After a half-hearted protest, I subsided and instead studied the tall, athletic-looking man who rang us up. Chris McCormick, I guessed, and sure enough, Juliana greeted him by name. He looked more than capable of teaching Joel Mackenzie a fatal lesson, I reflected, and I was so deeply mired in my suspicions that I barely returned his friendly nod of farewell before hustling Juliana out of the café.

"Listen," I muttered to her on the sidewalk, "are you sure . . . ?"

"He didn't kill anyone," she interrupted firmly.

"Yes, but . . ."

"Luke, stop." Juliana suddenly radiated authority, and I got the distinct impression that she rarely had to instruct her patients to do something more than once. "I know these people. Chris is one of the gentlest people you'll ever meet. He dotes on Gabi, that's true, but he would never hurt anyone. Never."

I nodded once and let it drop, though as far as I was concerned, Chris remained a potential suspect. *Someone* had murdered Joel Mackenzie, after all, and it was probably someone Juliana thought she knew.

She gave me a beady stare before switching gears. "Will I see you at Evelyn's soiree tonight?"

I groaned. "That's today? Ugh." At her expression of amused surprise, I added, "She insisted I go, but I really don't feel like it. It'll be a whole party of people wondering if I killed someone and gossiping about it endlessly."

"Oh, cheer up. It's a chance to reconnect with people you haven't seen in years, and the food at these things is first class." She patted my shoulder with a twinkle in her eye. "Plus, Jack always wears his dress uniform. It makes Evelyn happy."

I was immediately intrigued, which was why Juliana had mentioned it, of course. I gave her a wry look. "I'll see how I feel," I told her forbiddingly, and she went on her way with a smile that was entirely too knowing for my taste.

Chapter Eleven

A s the doctor disappeared down the sidewalk, I found
myself rather suddenly at loose ends. My day so far had
been a whirlwind of investigation, beginning at the Seahorse
Motel and then following a chain of clues to the library. And
now . . . well, I was fresh out of clues, though at least I'd accu-
mulated a larger pool of suspects than just me. I stood there
and eyed the RCMP detachment office next door to the café,
wondering if I should tell Jack about what I'd uncovered so
far, but I discarded that idea almost immediately. The problem
was that I didn't have enough information to make a definitive
conclusion about anything at this point, and Jack wouldn't be
interested in mere supposition.

I turned and started back toward the spot where I'd parked
my car. It was another glorious day, the sun shining overhead
in a sky devoid of clouds, and since it was now the weekend,
the center of town was even more crowded than it had been
yesterday. It looked like the businesses of Crescent Cove were
doing well, and I was happy to see it. Pausing in front of a

2

gallery that specialized in blown glass, I admired a few of the pieces in the window before continuing on my way. Then, on a whim, I turned left and crossed the street, following the gentle slope down toward the water. I had a lot of thinking to do, and I didn't want to return to the cottage just yet.

As I walked slowly along the sidewalk, my mind buzzed with half-formed ideas. I could feel Joel's blackmail note in my pocket as if it had real weight. Surely that note alone narrowed the potential suspects at least somewhat. There had to be people in Crescent Cove who could afford to pay out fifty thousand dollars, but there were also plenty who couldn't. The problem was that I didn't know if Joel had actually attempted to blackmail someone, or if he had just considered doing so. And even if he *had* blackmailed someone, I couldn't be sure that that person was the murderer. I'd already found at least two people who might have wanted Joel dead, for reasons that had nothing to do with money, and something told me they weren't the only ones. He hadn't been a very likable person.

I shook my head in frustration, only then noticing that I'd stopped outside a long, low building with green awnings that stirred and snapped in the breeze. Mounds of fruits and vegetables were displayed outside, along with a colorful selection of cut flowers. I turned to glance through the enormous windows and saw *Crescent Cove Greengrocers* etched in big gold letters on the glass. Aha. As luck would have it, I needed to buy a couple of things . . . and if I ran into the teenager who'd witnessed my tussle with Joel, I had a few questions for her as well.

The wooden door had been propped open and I wandered inside, pausing to take in the cheerful bustle of a store that was clearly doing well. The air was filled with the smells of spices, oranges, and freshly baked bread, as well as the occasional *ding* of the two cash registers that stood at the front of the shop. Vivid clumps of green veggies were arranged enticingly to my right, accompanied by an impressive selection of berries and apples, and at the back of the store, past the neat rows of wooden shelves, I spied what looked like a small bakery section. I felt like I'd stepped back in time, to a moment when independent grocery stores were the norm rather than the rare exception, and I loved everything about it.

Grabbing a plastic basket from the stack next to the door, I set out on a hunt for one or two things I'd need if I was going to be staying in town. It was difficult to tell, but I suspected that many of the people slowly circulating through the store were locals rather than tourists—they weren't sunburned and wearing flip-flops, at least, and there were blessedly few over-excited kids. The selection arrayed on the shelves was impressively broad, even if some of the prices made me wince a little. Fortunately, I didn't really need stuffed olives from Spain or gourmet pesto from Italy. Fancy food had always been more Bryce's thing than mine.

I had just secured a jar of peanut butter when I spotted a familiar figure heading in the opposite direction. Hurrying to catch up, I called out, "Excuse me," as I neared her, and Aleesha Perkins turned to face me. I pegged her at around fifteen or sixteen, with dark skin and thick hair in a cloud around her head. Her eyes widened slightly when she recognized me. "Hi," I continued, giving her a smile. "Sorry to bother you. I just had a question . . ."

"Uh, I'm busy, actually," Aleesha mumbled, dropping her gaze. "I should go and . . . do something." She started to turn away.

"Wait!" I blurted out. "Please."

Hesitating, she gave me a wary look.

"Look, I know I probably seemed violent and crazy when you saw me the other day. And I know you've spoken to the police about what you saw." She looked vaguely guilty at that, but I shook my head. "I don't care about that. You told them what you witnessed, and yeah, it looked bad, but . . ." I paused and she watched me wordlessly, her expression somewhere between relief and suspicion. "But I'm not a murderer," I finished, lamely.

Both of Aleesha's eyebrows went up. "Okay," she said slowly.

I felt like an idiot. This teenager didn't care if I was innocent—why would she? She just thought I was mentally unstable, and now I was bothering her at work.

Letting out a sigh, I said, "I just wanted to know if you'd ever seen that other guy before. Joel Mackenzie."

She studied me for a long moment, stepping to one side as an older lady trundled past with her shopping cart. "I'd seen him around," she acknowledged at last. "Normally, I don't really notice tourists or visitors, but he was everywhere. Always trying to talk to people, asking questions. He cornered my mom when she was outside arranging the produce display."

"What did he ask about?"

Aleesha shrugged. "Boring stuff. History. Though he also asked my mom about Marguerite's shop. It's just up the street from here, and he was mad that it wasn't open." She snorted. "Like my mom could do anything about that."

I listened closely. Joel's interest in history sure seemed to dovetail with his wanting to see the town archives.

Her expression darkened as she continued. "Then he grabbed Gabi McCormick at the Bluebird. She was super upset about it. I mean, he touched her *butt*. It was gross. After that, I think people stopped talking to him as much."

"Yeah, he didn't seem like a nice guy," I murmured, nodding.

"He was a straight-up creep," she corrected me.

I couldn't argue with that. Taking a moment to consider what she'd told me, I said, "Did you see my aunt? Marguerite, I mean. Before she died."

Aleesha nodded slowly, her expression of disgust giving way to a faint frown. "She came in here the day before it happened. I remember because she looked bad. Like, upset. Or scared. Normally, she was so friendly, always smiling. But not then. She grabbed a few things and hurried out to her car."

Turning over this information in my mind, I almost didn't hear when Aleesha said quietly, "I was really sorry when she died. I liked her."

"Yeah," I mumbled huskily. Clearing my throat, I said, "Thanks for talking to me. Sorry again for acting like a crazy person."

Eyeing me with the nonchalant lack of interest perfected by teenagers, she said, "It's okay. Like I said, that guy was a creep. He had it coming." I didn't know if she meant my pushing him off the porch or someone bashing his head in with a rock. Maybe both. After a brief hesitation, she added, "Talking to the police was kind of lame of me, but Cassie is my older sister and when she told me and my mom about the murder, I just kind of . . . blurted it out. And then she made me go and talk to Jack." She looked a little embarrassed about it.

Strangely, that cheered me somewhat. At least Aleesha hadn't sold me out to the Mounties on purpose. "I forgive you," I told her solemnly, and she rolled her eyes while trying not to smile.

An older Black woman appeared at the end of the aisle, wearing a green apron over a plaid shirt and jeans. "Aleesha, I need your help unloading this shipment," she called, and the teenager rolled her eyes at me once more before turning away.

Another teenager with enormous braces that reminded me of Jack's rang me up at the front of the store, and then I stepped back outside with a newly purchased cloth bag hanging from one hand and a brain buzzing with new information.

Chapter Twelve

As I turned and started to walk back to my car, parked in front of the library, I ran through what I'd learned. I now had a better picture of what Joel Mackenzie had been doing in Crescent Cove before his death. His interest in the town's history was strange but might be related to his attempts to blackmail one of the residents here. His note had mentioned a secret—it wasn't a stretch to imagine that secret was hidden somewhere in the past. It also seemed fairly clear that he'd wanted to get into Forget-Me-Not Antiques, and that Marguerite had been keeping a low profile in an effort to avoid him. Why else would she have closed up shop at the height of the summer season?

As my car came into view, I once again considered the uncomfortable possibility that Joel had been involved in my aunt's death. Perhaps her efforts to avoid him had led to his running her down out of frustration or anger. It was a horrible thought, but if the police could tie Joel's missing truck to what happened to my aunt, it would provide some closure, at least.

Having her gone was bad enough, but not knowing who had killed her and then driven away made it worse.

I cast a glance at the library's sandstone facade as I unlocked my car, then drove back to the cottage with only some of my attention on the road. Sparked by seeing the library again, the rest of my brain was replaying Samuel Beckinridge's strange reaction to my visit. No one enjoyed being connected to a murder victim, I supposed, but Samuel had behaved very cagily as soon as I mentioned that Joel was dead. It was odd, because his alibi appeared to be a good one; there were probably dozens of people at this meeting in Victoria who could confirm he was there. So why had he become so nervous?

I was still pondering this question as I drove slowly down the driveway to the cottage and parked my car. There was no one waiting for me, I saw with considerable relief as I wandered around to the front of the building and stood for a minute to take in the view. Then I let myself inside, finding as I did so that someone had pushed a square envelope under the front door. Within was an invitation to the Collingwood party, noting the time at which it would start as well as the formal dress code. Well, Evelyn was going to be disappointed in my attire, I thought to myself. My tux was back home in Toronto.

Scrawled on the back of the invitation was a note from Evelyn herself: *Looking forward to seeing you.* I sighed and pushed the expensive card stock back into the envelope. So much for hoping I was off the hook.

I checked my watch and found that I had several hours before the soiree began. Wandering slowly through the cottage,

I opened several windows to let in the sea air, though I hesitated on the threshold of my aunt's bedroom at the front of the building. I hadn't been able to bring myself to go in there since I arrived. The beautiful old four-poster bed was still there, arranged so that its occupant would have a perfect view out the bay window to the ocean. Framed photos, small bottles of perfume, and pieces of jewelry had been scattered across the top of the matching dresser in the haphazard array my aunt had left on the day she died. Sadness welled up in me, and I turned away without entering yet again.

After a little more dithering, I decided to go for a long walk in the Ravenwood. The deep silence and solitude of the woods seemed very appealing all of a sudden, so I changed into a T-shirt and shorts, grabbed a bottle of water from the fridge, and headed out the French doors at the back of the cottage. Carefully locking them behind me, I gave the ornamental pond a wide berth on my way to the back gate, then across the graveled area where I'd parked my car and into the trees.

There was a narrow path here, created by decades of my aunt's near-daily walks in the woods, and I followed its gentle turns as it wove between the Douglas fir that clustered close to the cottage. The air was markedly cooler beneath the trees, heady with the sweet scents of loam and crushed fir needles, and almost completely silent except for the occasional croak of a distant raven. I squinted up into the shafts of sunlight that speared through the canopy, drew in one deep breath after another, and started to feel the tension and sadness of the past couple of days slowly leech out of my body. Then, with a smile, I set off into the forest.

I walked for almost two hours, and with almost every step my surroundings seemed more familiar, more welcoming. Twenty years was a long time to be away from a place, but by the standards of the rain forests that covered this part of the island, it was a mere blink of an eye. The Ravenwood had changed very little in that time, if at all. Everything was just as I'd last seen it: this sharp turn in the path and the ancient oak that towered overhead; this narrow little stream that babbled and sang its way over a jumble of rocks on its way to the sea; this sudden clearing filled with tall grasses and wildflowers bending and bowing in the wind. It was all here, every glorious summer I'd spent with my aunt, the long, lazy afternoons and my solitary travels through these trees. I felt my heart expand to take it all in, and long before I'd made my circuitous way back to the cottage, I felt simultaneously more alive and more at peace than I had in a very long time.

I was probably no more than ten yards from the picket fence surrounding the cottage when my foot came down on something hard. Pausing, I peered at the ground and saw that I'd stepped on someone's phone, almost entirely hidden beneath the spreading fronds of a large fern. I stooped to pick it up and then brushed dirt from its cracked screen. It was an iPhone, older than mine, its corners scuffed and nicked by hard use and lacking a case or other identifying features. I looked up from the phone and tried to estimate how far I was from the cottage's back garden. Not far at all, I decided. I could hear the soft burble of water trickling into the pond from where I stood. Certainly close enough that someone could have thrown this here.

Wondering if I'd literally stumbled across Joel Mackenzie's missing phone, I pressed the home button and watched it flicker to life. There had been several missed text messages and calls, I saw, but when I tried to open the phone I found myself stymied by a requested passcode.

Clutching it in one hand, I hurried through the back gate and across the garden. It wasn't until I went to unlock the French doors that I remembered, all of a sudden, my confusion of the morning before. I'd found the doors unlocked just before I stepped outside and discovered Joel's body, hadn't I? At the time, it struck me as strange because I had made sure everything was locked before I went to bed. I'd forgotten all about it after seeing Joel's body lying in the pond, but now . . . I stared down at the key in my hand. Now I was convinced that someone had unlocked these doors. The murderer? The thought of someone creeping into the cottage while Joel's body cooled in the night air sent a shiver through me. Joel had been convinced that something he wanted was inside. Maybe the murderer wanted it as well.

The feeling of serenity I'd acquired in the Ravenwood evaporated. I needed to get these locks changed right away.

Less than half an hour later I had a locksmith there, a wiry man who kept up a friendly stream of chatter while he worked to replace the locks on both the front and back doors. I barely heard him. I was too busy brooding over the possibility that a murderer had been inside the cottage. Had I been their next target? The very idea made me feel sick. How many people had keys to my aunt's cottage? Probably a lot, I thought ruefully. That was one of the advantages of living in a small town, wasn't it? The idea that you could trust your neighbors.

I wasn't sure I trusted anyone now.

With the locks replaced and a shiny new key in my hand, I started to feel slightly better, but no sooner had the locksmith left than I had another person on my doorstep, this time a young woman with a suit bag hanging from one hand. *Velvet and Silk* was emblazoned across the front of the bag, and beneath it *Formal wear for any occasion.*

"Delivery for Mr. Tremblay," the woman announced as I opened the front door.

"Uh," I replied.

She thrust the suit bag into my arms without another word, offered a polite smile, and then disappeared.

Utterly bemused, I took the bag into the living room and unzipped it enough to reveal a gleaming tuxedo jacket and, attached to the hanger, a handwritten note:

For the party.
- E. C.

I slowly shook my head as I pulled the tuxedo free of the bag and held it up. There was also a snowy dress shirt and even a pair of polished black shoes in a plastic bag suspended from the hanger. Thanks to Evelyn Collingwood's largess, it appeared I would be wearing formal attire to her soiree after all.

With a glance at the clock ticking quietly on the mantel, I decided to take a quick shower before getting dressed. Not long after that, I was fiddling with the provided cuff links and growling in the back of my throat as I tried to fasten them properly when I heard a jangling, unfamiliar ringtone from the kitchen. The abandoned phone! I raced in and scooped it off the counter. The name *Leona* was visible on the cracked screen as I pressed the green phone icon and held it up to my ear.

"Hello?"

There was a long pause. "Who is this?" a woman finally asked.

"Oh, uh, I'm a friend of Joel's," I hazarded, before holding my breath.

"Well, where is he?" she asked, sounding annoyed, and I let out my breath in a rush.

"He's, um, in the bathroom." I winced at the falsehood, but until I knew who this person was and what she wanted with Joel, I didn't want to give anything away. "Is this Leona? He's talked about you a lot."

A snort came down the line. "Yeah, I bet he has. Look, if you're one of Joel's drinking buddies, you need to give him a message from me, okay? You tell him that he's three months behind on his child support payments, *again*, and this time I'm going to sue his broke ass to make sure I get every penny of what he owes. You got that?" Her voice rose as she said this, her tone becoming more and more irate. "And where the hell is he, anyhow? I went by his apartment today, and his neighbor hadn't seen him in weeks."

"Oh, he's out here in BC," I told her, and she gave a hard, throaty laugh.

"BC? Lemme guess: he's chasing that 'big score' he found, right? What a load of crap."

I listened closely. "Big score? Nope, Joel sure hasn't mentioned anything about that."

"Yeah, well, because it's crap, like I said," Leona snapped. "Joel worked at a nursing home in Toronto—well, until they fired him a couple of months ago for stealing from people's rooms—and he met an old, old lady there. I think she had dementia or something. She told him she was from a little town out west, and she used to go on and on about some shameful family secret. Someone died, she said. They were murdered."

I felt a tingle of excitement work its way down my spine. "Murdered? You're sure about that?"

"That's what Joel said," she replied, sounding weary now, as if trying to maintain her constant indignation was exhausting. "Sometimes she got confused, thought he was her son, and she would mention this secret and how it would ruin everyone if it came out. And then she died. But right before she did, she told Joel there was evidence of what happened. It was hidden away somewhere, and she was desperate to get it back. She still had family out west and she wanted to protect them. Or so she said. I think she was nuttier than a fruitcake."

Pressing the phone to my ear, I said quickly, "Did Joel ever tell you *where* this evidence was hidden?"

"The old lady kept going on about some antique box," Leona said dismissively. "Look, Joel always has some get-rich scheme going, and none of them's ever come to anything. Joel's a loser, okay? He's always been a loser and he always will be a loser."

"Yes, but this secret . . ."

"You know what's really sad?" she interrupted me. "He thinks if he can find this evidence, he might be able to persuade the old lady's family to cough up some cash. He's gonna threaten them like he's some kind of gangster. What kind of a plan is that? He's out there, spending the money that he owes me and our little girl, instead of looking for a real job!"

Yeesh. "I, uh, don't know if that's—" I started to say, but she cut me off.

"Look, just tell him that he's in serious trouble." And then Leona hung up.

I stared at the phone in my hand. Well, she wasn't going to be getting any payments from her deadbeat ex ever again. Was there *anyone* that Joel Mackenzie hadn't screwed over?

It sure seemed like the object Joel had wanted from my aunt was this mysterious box. I knew I had to share this with Jack, so I quickly finished dressing and found that Evelyn had done an excellent job of guessing my measurements. The tux fit perfectly. I dropped the cracked phone into a Ziploc bag before hurrying out to my car.

The Collingwood estate stood atop a ridge that looked out over the entire town, its extensive grounds bordered by a decorative wrought-iron fence that was almost eight feet tall. Evelyn's forebears had liked their privacy, apparently. This evening, however, the massive arched gates at the front of the property stood open, and I drove between them along with several other cars. We made our way down the long graveled drive, lined with mature maple trees, before swinging around the circular drive in front of the house and handing our vehicles over to a series of valets in red jackets.

I watched my rental drive off around the back of the house before pausing to take in the building itself, a mansion built in the Georgian style. It was made of pale brick and rose only two stories below its steeply gabled roof but sprawled elegantly into wings at either side. Imposing chimneys stood at both ends of the central part of the house, while a series of tall, narrow windows, trimmed in white, looked out across the expertly manicured grounds and the ocean beyond. As expensive houses went, the Collingwood mansion was relatively restrained, eschewing showy touches for a more refined sophistication, but everyone knew that a vast fortune propped up that simple facade. The Collingwoods had made their money first as timber barons in the late eighteenth century and then as shrewd investors in the railroads and other miracles of the Industrial Revolution. They could have lived anywhere in the world, and in fact the family did own properties elsewhere, but generation after generation they'd opted to stay in this quiet, beautiful part of Vancouver Island that they had built up practically from nothing.

I walked up several stairs and onto the rounded portico, supported by two columns on either side, before stepping between the front doors and into the entrance hall. A white marble staircase covered in a wide blue runner swept grandly up one side, while ahead of me I could see a number of people making their way down a wood-paneled corridor toward the rear of the house. I trailed along in their wake, feeling distinctly ill at ease as I cast quick glances into several richly appointed rooms along the way: a library, a games room with a billiard table at its center, an enormous dining room that looked like it could seat fifty people comfortably. I'd visited this house when I was young, brought along by my aunt, but I didn't remember any of this. Right now, when I didn't really want to be here, I found it all a bit overwhelming.

The Body in the Back Garden

Drifting aimlessly along with the other guests, eventually I found myself outside again, standing on a wide terrace that ran along the back of the house and looked out on a beautifully landscaped garden. I'd found the party, I realized, as I gazed down at what had to be two hundred people milling around in the warm glow of innumerable paper lanterns strung overhead. The soothing babble of dozens of conversations competed with a jazz quartet playing an energetic bit of music from a small stage off to one side, while attractive and smiling servers circulated through the crowds of well-dressed guests with silver trays holding food and drink.

Slowly, I descended a wide set of stone steps to the garden below and almost immediately snagged a crystal flute of champagne from a passing server. It felt like everyone was staring at me, though in fact I'm sure no one knew who I was. I knocked back the champagne in two swallows and then went hunting for more, squeezing my way through the clumps and drifts of well-heeled partygoers who stood and chattered to one another on the manicured lawns and flagstone paths. The air was fragrant with the smell of roses as well as a dozen different perfumes, and I found it all quite heady as I cornered a hapless server and swapped my empty flute for a full one.

I had some vague idea that I would wander around for half an hour and then leave, hopefully without having to talk to anyone, but then the crowds parted and I saw Jack.

Chapter Thirteen

H e was easy to spot in his dress uniform. His Red Serge tunic almost glowed in the lantern light, its buttons gleaming above midnight-blue jodhpurs with a golden stripe down the outside seam of each leg. The breeches were tucked into brown leather riding boots that matched the brown belt worn over his tunic, and the whole ensemble was completed by the traditional campaign hat with its wide brim that threw Jack's eyes into shadow. I stopped in my tracks and goggled at him. Everyone in Canada knows what the Mounties look like, but I'd never seen a dress uniform in person. Particularly not one that was as perfectly fitted to a set of broad shoulders as Jack's was.

I wasn't sure what kind of greeting I'd get, since we hadn't exactly parted on the best of terms, but there was no way I wasn't going to wander closer and get a proper eyeful. Jack stood at ease with his hands clasped loosely behind his back, solid and capable and terribly dashing, as I sidled through the crowds toward him, and as I approached his head swiveled in my direction. One side of his mouth curled upward in a wry little smile that made me think he was calling a temporary truce.

"You look . . . wow," I said rather helplessly as I reached his side.

"You clean up nicely yourself," he responded as his smile briefly widened. This close, I could see his eyes beneath the brim of his hat as he examined my outfit. "Do you always travel with a tuxedo?"

Self-consciously giving the jacket a tug, I said, "Evelyn sent it over. Presumably so I wouldn't embarrass her with my wrinkled chinos and scuffed shoes."

Head tilted thoughtfully, Jack murmured, "That's a nice gesture."

I motioned to his uniform. "I heard that she insisted on this as well."

"I don't mind," he said with a shrug. "This shindig is practically the only excuse I have to wear the Red Serge. It's nice."

"It really is," I agreed with feeling, surreptitiously eyeing the way those jodhpurs fit his legs like a glove. Then, before I could embarrass myself by drooling visibly, I added, "I found something that I need to give you. It's Joel Mackenzie's phone."

Jack's smile vanished, and after a pause he nodded once and put a hand under my elbow to steer me away from the people surrounding us. We drifted toward an unoccupied corner of the garden, and then he took his hand away and watched me expectantly. Transferring my champagne to my other hand, I reached into the inner pocket of my jacket and drew out the phone in its Ziploc bag. "I found it this afternoon, not far from the cottage," I told him as I passed it over. "It was close enough that someone could have thrown it into the trees. I knew I'd see you here, so I brought it along."

Jack listened in silence as he took the phone from me and examined it through the clear plastic. "How do you know it belonged to Joel Mackenzie?" he finally asked, looking back up at me.

"Because it rang while I was getting ready for the party. It was a woman named Leona—Joel's ex, apparently, and the mother of his child." I don't think I imagined the look of disapproval on Jack's face, so I hastened to add, "I didn't tell her anything. But she told *me* something. Joel used to work at a nursing home in Toronto, and while he was there met someone from Crescent Cove. An elderly woman. She told him that her family had a shameful secret, *and* that it involved a murder. After she died, Joel told Leona there was a 'big score' here. A chance to make some serious money."

I watched as Jack's mouth curved downward in a thoughtful little frown. "A murder? When did this happen?"

"I don't know. Probably a long time ago, if this woman was as old as Leona said." Thinking about it for a moment, I then said excitedly, "Maybe that's why Joel stole a bunch of old newspapers from the town archives! He was looking for articles about this murder."

Jack's eyebrows drew downward as well. "How do you know he stole from the archives?"

Whoops. "Um. It was just something that Samuel Beckinridge mentioned in passing," I mumbled, looking down at my brightly polished shoes. "You know. When I dropped by the library. For a book."

Jack let out a sigh. "Luke, c'mon. What are you doing?"

"I'm not doing anything except stumbling across evidence and handing it over to the police," I retorted. For a brief moment, I was tempted to confide in Jack, to tell him the other things I'd discovered about Joel's death, but I still wasn't sure he would listen with an open mind. "Am I still your chief suspect?" I asked instead, looking up into his hazel eyes.

He studied my face for a moment. "We're exploring several different angles," he finally said, a noncommittal response that I found less than comforting. Still, he hadn't clapped me in handcuffs yet, so that was something.

With a grimace, I quaffed the rest of my champagne. "Great."

Jack shook the phone gently in its plastic bag. "Hopefully this will give us some answers, though we'll have to send it away to be analyzed. That will take time."

I nodded moodily and started looking for more champagne, but at that moment a strange figure materialized beside us. If not for the piercings, I might never have recognized Barnabus beneath the dark-blue frock coat and actual powdered wig. "Whoa," I mumbled.

"Good evening, Sergeant Munro," Barnabus intoned, before giving Jack a courtly bow with one hand pressed to his silken cravat.

I snorted, and Barney shot me a filthy glare.

"Uh, hi," Jack responded, his bemusement obvious as he took in the younger man's outfit.

"You look very dashing in your uniform," Barnabus told him as he inched closer. "I've been looking forward to seeing it ever since Mrs. Collingwood's last summer soiree."

I watched, speechless, as Barnabus flirted with Jack Munro. It was amusing for about two seconds, and then I found myself unaccountably irritated. "I already told him that," I interjected.

Jack looked at me, the corners of his eyes crinkling slightly. "Did you? I must have missed it."

"I did," I insisted, flustered. "When I first saw you." Then I paused. Maybe that particular comment had been in my head. "Didn't I?"

Barnabus, meanwhile, sneered at me before turning back to Jack. "Would you care to accompany me on a stroll of the grounds, Sergeant?" he asked in portentous tones.

"He can't," I said loudly. "We're discussing the case. You know. The *murder*." I saw heads turn in our direction and cursed myself silently.

Jack looked from one of us to the other, probably trying to decide who was acting more crazed. "Um," he said.

"In that case," Barnabus declaimed, "I'll go get us a drink while you finish up with your *suspect* here." He practically spat the word *suspect* at me, and in response I bared my teeth in something approximating a smile. Then, turning smartly on his patent-leather slippers, Barnabus moved off with the tails of his frock coat flapping behind him.

"What a weirdo," I muttered.

"He's interesting, at least," Jack said, and I gave him a sidelong glance. Did he have a thing for Barney? I found the possibility extremely irksome.

"Let's go this way," I said abruptly, grabbing Jack's arm and propelling him to another part of the extensive gardens. We ended up standing beneath the curving branches of an enormous sequoia tree that had to be well over a hundred years old, its lower limbs strung with paper lanterns that glowed gold and pink and green. Looking at the crowds between us and the house, I edged us about halfway around the massive trunk until I judged that Barney would have a hard time finding us again.

"What are we doing here?" Jack asked after a few moments, giving me a puzzled little smile.

"Oh, you know, I just thought we could . . . talk."

"Talk. Okay. About what?"

I shrugged, suddenly awkward. "I don't know. Stuff." Inspiration struck and I added, "Samuel said that your mom stepped down as town librarian."

His smile slowly faded as he nodded. "Yeah. She got sick about three years ago. Pancreatic cancer." He looked away from me, off into the darkness of the estate. "She died ten months later."

"Oh, Jack." I moved closer and put a hand on his arm. "I'm so sorry. I had no idea."

"How could you?" he asked with a brittle kind of briskness as he turned his gaze back to me. "You've been gone."

And there it was: the thing that loomed between us, that had fractured our friendship and left us strangers to each other. My heart ached as I looked up into his eyes and saw the challenge there. Then I took my hand off his arm and stepped back a couple of paces, as if preparing myself for some kind of grueling ordeal. In a sense, I was.

"When high school ended," I said, fighting to keep my voice steady, "before I went away to university, I came out to my parents. I was tired of hiding who I was, of pretending to date girls.

I thought, *I'm an adult now, they'll understand.* But they didn't."
I looked down at my shoes. "They disowned me. Kicked me out
of the house. Told me never to contact them again, or anyone
else in the family. I . . . I was lucky, I guess, that I had a place
at Dalhousie waiting for me. At least I had somewhere to go. I
blew most of my savings on the trip from Edmonton to Halifax.
I hitchhiked at first, took buses when that stopped feeling safe.
And then I just . . . tried to survive. I worked as many jobs as I
could to pay my way. It was really, really hard." Slowly, I lifted my
gaze back to Jack's square, handsome face. "I wrote to my aunt,
that first summer I was out there. Asking if I could come here
and stay with her. All I got back was a letter saying that I couldn't
visit. That was it. No explanation. Nothing. It broke my heart."

I stopped for a moment, then cleared my throat. "Evelyn
told me that my aunt had been pressured by the rest of the family to keep me away. She'd made a mistake, and she regretted
it for the rest of her life. For twenty years, I thought I had no
family left and that I would never be welcome back here. I was
wrong, on both counts."

I stared off blindly in the direction of the house, my vision
blurred with unshed tears. And then I felt Jack's big, strong arms
wrap gently around me as he pulled me into a hug. I pressed my
face into the wool of his Red Serge and smelled cedar as well
as traces of his aftershave. He was solid and warm, and for a
few moments I allowed myself to lean against him and feel the
regret and pain that had always lurked just beneath the surface.

"I'm sorry," he said quietly, and I could feel his baritone
voice rumbling through his chest. "If I'd known, I wouldn't
have been so harsh with you in my office."

"How could you have known?" I asked with an attempt at lightness. "I've been gone." His arms released me, and I was unsettled to realize that a part of me wanted him to keep them there forever, or at least for the rest of the party. "You weren't wrong to be angry with me. I *did* abandon you, and I'm sorry I did that. I was young and selfish and in a lot of pain. I should have realized that you were in pain too."

He nodded as he gazed stoically over my head. "But you came back."

"I did," I agreed, a little shakily. "Too late, maybe, but I did come back."

Jack looked down at me, but before he could say anything, a woman's voice interrupted. "*There* you are!"

We both turned to find Evelyn Collingwood approaching across the grass, a young man at her side. She looked lovely in a gown of green silk that shimmered in the lantern light, a fur stole wrapped around her shoulders in deference to the cool evening air, while the man with her wore a tuxedo that seemed to have been exquisitely tailored. He looked vaguely familiar, and as they neared us, I saw he had the same unusual turquoise eyes that she did.

"I've been looking everywhere for you, Luke dear," she said as she leaned in to press a kiss to my cheek. "I see you got my little present," she added as she adjusted my lapel. "You look very handsome."

"Yes, thank you," I said. "It was quite a surprise. You really shouldn't have gone to all this trouble."

Diamonds flashed from a bracelet encircling her slim wrist as she waved a hand. "Oh, it was nothing. I thought you deserved a lovely night out, that's all." Half turning, she indicated the man with her. "And I'm sure you remember Kieran."

I smiled politely and nodded, though I didn't really remember him at all. He was an extremely handsome man with incredible cheekbones and an aquiline nose, and his teeth were a dazzling shade of white as he grinned and offered a hand for me to shake.

"It's fantastic to see you again, Luke," he told me. His hand was firm and warm, and he held mine for a heartbeat longer than necessary. I felt more than a little flustered as he looked earnestly into my eyes and said, "I was devastated when I heard about Marguerite."

"Thank you," I murmured. "That's very kind."

"Good to see you too, Munro," Kieran added, giving the other man a casual punch on the bicep.

"Kieran," Jack said stiffly. "Evelyn." There was a slight pause. "The party seems to be going well."

Evelyn laughed indulgently as she turned to gaze at her guests. "Oh yes, it's always such fun. What do you think of the band? I brought them over from Vancouver, you know."

Jazz tended to occupy the same realm as elevator music for me, so I hadn't registered the quartet at all since I'd arrived. Nonetheless, I nodded and said, "Oh, they're great, yeah." I noted Kieran giving me an amused look and flushed slightly, but fortunately his mother was oblivious to my lack of musical appreciation.

"We need more champagne," she decided, before waving over a server and then handing around delicate crystal flutes to all of us. Jack tried to demur, but Evelyn was implacable, and in due course we were all raising our glasses in a toast. "To happier times ahead," she proclaimed, and I found myself echoing her wish with genuine sincerity as our glasses clinked together with a loud crystalline chime.

"Now tell me, Jack," she said, after we'd all taken a sip. "Have you made any progress on solving this horrid murder?"

"We're still hard at work," he replied blandly.

"They're pursuing several angles," I added helpfully, which earned me a stern look from him.

Evelyn shivered and pulled her stole more tightly around her shoulders with one hand. "I wish we could all just move on. Let the dead rest." Kieran put a comforting arm around her, and she leaned against him for a moment. "And I know it's under dreadful circumstances," she went on, turning to me, "but I'm glad you're staying here a little longer."

"I'm glad too," I told her, a little surprised to realize it was the truth.

We all stood there in silence for a few moments, sipping our champagne, until the jazz band started playing a tune with a languorous tempo. Jack cleared his throat, and when I glanced over, I saw him looking at me, but it was Kieran who spoke up. "Would you care to dance, Luke?"

I blinked a few times. "Uh, sure," I said. Evelyn beamed as Kieran offered me his arm, and feeling more than a little ridiculous, I let him escort me across the lawn and toward the flagstone patio where several couples were already dancing. We left our empty champagne flutes with a convenient server, and then before I quite registered what was happening, Kieran was holding me close as we swayed slowly to the music.

What the hell is going on tonight? I wondered. *I've gone from the arms of one attractive man to another in the space of ten minutes.* As innocent as it was, it was still more action than I'd gotten in a long time.

Kieran danced with an easy confidence, and after a little while, I forced myself to relax and let him lead. He smelled incredible, something masculine that wasn't overpowering, and I couldn't help feeling a little thrill as I looked into his eyes. "I haven't done this in years," I murmured. "I hope I don't step on your toes too often."

"You're doing great," he assured me, his hand warm on my back as he pulled me into a gentle quarter turn. I had no idea what the people around us thought about two men dancing together, but it was obvious that Kieran didn't care. He gave me his full attention, and it made me feel all tingly inside as he studied my face while we moved.

"I remember you, you know," he said, after a little while. "There weren't a lot of kids my age in Crescent Cove when I was growing up, so I noticed when you arrived in town." His smile was mischievous as he added, "I thought you were cute."

"Me? Cute?" I spluttered. "I don't think so. I was the nerdiest, pudgiest kid who ever lived, with Coke-bottle glasses and acne."

He tilted his head to one side, curious. "Is that really how you saw yourself?" At my uncertain nod, he said, "To me, you always seemed like you were off in your own world, someplace more exciting and interesting than this one. I remember wishing I could go with you." I looked away, embarrassed, and he laughed quietly. "Also, I have a thing for red hair."

As someone who'd grown up hating my unruly curls, I found that hard to believe. "I'm surprised to find you still in Crescent Cove," I said, trying desperately to change the subject.

"Oh, I'm just visiting. I live in London. In the UK," he clarified, in the way that all Canadians do so as not to confuse one of the world's great cities with the distinctly smaller municipality of London, Ontario. "But I try to come back here as often as I can. Mother always appreciates it when I attend her summer soiree." His mouth curved into the faintest of frowns. "Especially this year. She's been out of sorts ever since . . ." He paused, and I knew he was thinking of my aunt's death.

The song gradually wound to an end, and as the last notes faded away, we stayed where we were, watching each other. "Do you sometimes wish," he murmured, "that you could go back in time, to when things were simpler?"

I thought of Jack and the painful distance that had sprung up between us. "Yes. Sometimes."

Kieran released my hand, but only so he could rest his fingers under my chin and tilt my head back. Then he kissed me on the lips, just a quick brush of his mouth against mine. I felt sparks ignite in my brain and cascade through my entire body, and I stared at him, incapable of speech.

"I'm sorry if that was too forward," he said quietly, his eyes searching mine. "I don't even know if you're with someone."

"I'm not," I croaked. Then, clearing my throat, I repeated for emphasis, "I'm not."

"Lucky me," he murmured.

We stood there like a couple of fools as the band struck up a much livelier tune, and when Kieran finally released me, we both left the patio, his shoulder brushing mine. My legs felt rubbery. Then I turned and saw Jack walking away from me through the crowd, impossible to miss in his uniform, and an icy feeling of regret doused the butterflies fluttering in my stomach. Had he been watching us dance? He was probably disgusted that I was drinking and dancing with rich, handsome men while under suspicion for murder, as if I didn't have a care in the world. But as I watched him retreat, I felt anything but carefree.

Suddenly, any enjoyment I might have taken in the party evaporated. Kieran was very solicitous, keeping up a bright stream of chatter as he grabbed more champagne for us, and Evelyn was all smiles as she introduced me to an endless succession of locals whose names I forgot as soon as she said them. I encountered a few familiar faces as well—Samuel Beckinridge, who pretended not to see me as he brushed past; Juliana, dapper in a brocade vest and matching trousers, clearly several sheets to the wind; Aleesha Perkins, looking bored and uncomfortable in a sleeveless tunic dress. But Jack was gone, and I stayed as long as seemed polite before deciding to leave as well.

Kieran walked me to my car like a consummate gentleman and pressed a kiss to my cheek in farewell, but as I drove away, somehow I felt lonelier than I had when I arrived.

Chapter Fourteen

I awoke the next morning with a bit of a hangover, which I cured with copious amounts of coffee and a brisk walk along the foggy beach below the cottage. Then, feeling slightly more human, I showered before deciding to have breakfast in town. Leaving the rental car parked behind the cottage, I set off on foot, making my way along the tree-shrouded curves of Ravenwood Lane and then turning east until I reached Shoreside Drive, which followed the long, sweeping, crescent-shaped cove for which the town was named. The fog started to lift as I meandered along, and shortly before I turned onto Main Street, patches of blue sky started to appear overhead.

Three blocks up from the water, I paused outside Forget-Me-Not Antiques and studied its window display with a feeling of melancholy. Normally my aunt would open late on Sundays so she could enjoy a long breakfast, but now . . . well, now it would never open again. That realization, though not surprising, hit me hard for some reason. I laid my hand on the rough bricks next to the window and thought about how proud my aunt had been of this shop. Many of the stores and restaurants and galleries that lined the street had changed over the years, but Forget-Me-Not had weathered countless storms and emerged unscathed. It struck me as profoundly sad that its time had come to an end.

With a curt shake of my head, I banished these gloomy thoughts and turned to continue up the street. What choice did I have? I certainly had no interest in taking over the shop myself. Selling it off, along with the cottage, would net me enough money to buy out Bryce's half of our townhouse. Without that, I didn't have enough cash of my own to afford something in Toronto's insane real estate market. My aunt wouldn't begrudge me that, I told myself, and hoped it was true.

Another block up Main Street I found a little coffee shop called the Java Jolt that looked to be doing a brisk business, so I decided to stop in and grab a breakfast sandwich to go. Standing in line with a couple of other customers, I gazed around at the mediocre art on the walls before absentmindedly studying the man in front of me. He was wearing a thin fleece jacket and a pair of running pants, and it wasn't until he spoke to the man behind the counter that I recognized his voice: it was Chris McCormick, owner of the Bluebird Café. I watched him out of the corner of my eye as he paid and then wandered over to wait for his order next to an unoccupied table. This might be an excellent chance to ask a few careful questions about a possible run-in with Joel Mackenzie.

Once I'd ordered my sandwich and paid for it, I casually strolled over to Chris and hovered nearby. He was gazing down at his phone, but when he put it away and looked around, I happened to catch his eye and offered him a friendly smile. He blinked once at me, and then I saw his jaw clench.

"I know you," he said bluntly, in a voice that lacked the warmth I'd been hoping for.

"Yeah, I had lunch in your café yesterday. It was really good."

The compliment bounced off his stony expression without making a dent. "Gabi was really upset after she waited on you," he remarked, folding brawny arms across his chest. He had a boyish face and his sandy hair was thinning a little in front, but he looked like he could snap me in half without too much trouble.

I remembered his daughter and how mortified she'd been when she confessed to Joel's grabbing her. "Oh. I'm sorry to hear that," I started to say, but he cut me off by moving directly into my personal space.

"It makes me angry when customers upset my daughter," he told me, his voice rising until a few of the people at the tables around us started to look over.

Taking a hasty step back, I lifted my hands in a placating gesture. "We didn't mean to upset her. She overheard us talking, and . . ."

"So now you're accusing Gabi of eavesdropping?" he demanded belligerently.

"No! Not at all. We mentioned Joel Mackenzie, and she . . ."

Chris's face twisted into a scowl. "That scumbag. What, was he a friend of yours?"

I stared at him with my mouth hanging open. How had this conversation gone so completely off the rails? "No, he wasn't. If you would just let me explain—"

The backs of my legs hit something as Chris loomed even closer. "Joel Mackenzie touched my Gabi and got his brains bashed in with a rock," he growled, his voice soft now as he thrust his face next to mine. "Take the hint." Then, before I could respond, he brushed past me so roughly that I almost fell into the elderly couple whose table I'd backed into.

"Sorry," I muttered to them. Everyone in the place was staring at me, I realized, some of them with forks suspended in front of their mouths. I was too busy watching Chris McCormick stride out the door and down the sidewalk to care, though. Once he disappeared from view, I ran a shaking hand across my face and thought to myself that I was very lucky to still have all my teeth.

A wide-eyed employee materialized at my elbow with my order, which I took as a polite invitation to leave immediately, so I grabbed it with a word of thanks and then cautiously made my way outside. There was no sign of Chris, thankfully, and I just stood there for a while feeling shell-shocked. I'd never been threatened like that before.

Juliana had claimed that Chris McCormick was a gentle man who would never hurt anyone, but I had firsthand evidence to the contrary. There was no doubt in my mind that he'd been prepared to hit me—in fact, he probably would have if we hadn't had an audience—and all I'd done was upset his daughter. What might he have done to the man who assaulted her?

My appetite was gone, but I clutched the brown paper bag holding my breakfast as I turned and retraced my steps back toward Shoreside Drive. This time, though, I decided to cross to the narrow little park that ran between the road and the beach, a thirty-foot-wide strip of grass and flowering shrubs interspersed with benches and picnic tables. It hadn't existed twenty years ago, but I was glad it was there now. I needed a quiet place to think.

Settling myself on a bench, I stared out at the water. The morning sun laid a wide stripe of molten gold across the rolling waves, its reflection a little muted by the lingering fog. A couple walked along the paved path in front of me, pulled along by a pair of energetic little dogs, followed a minute later by someone jogging. That made me think of Chris McCormick and his running clothes. I turned my head to peer around, half afraid I'd find him headed in my direction, but he was nowhere to be seen.

WWJFD? I wondered to myself as I turned my gaze back to the sea. *What would Jessica Fletcher do?*

For one, Jessica Fletcher would never be intimidated by a suspect. Chris might be in superb shape and overflowing with testosterone, but I wasn't going to let him stop me from trying to solve Joel's murder. I ran through our encounter again in my mind, then paused.

He'd known that Joel had been hit with a rock.

How could he have known that? True, Juliana and I had been sitting in the Bluebird Café when she shared that information with me, but we'd been speaking quietly, and I was certain that Chris—who'd been back in the kitchen, more than twenty feet away—hadn't been able to hear us.

So how did he know?

I felt a chill that had nothing to do with the breeze coming off the water. It was the kind of careless slip that murderers made on TV all the time. Granted, this wasn't TV . . . but it was still incredibly suspicious. Chris certainly had a motive to attack Joel, and he was more than strong enough to grab a rock and break someone's skull with it. Add to that his specific knowledge of the murder . . .

My phone started vibrating in my pocket. It was a call from an unfamiliar number, and I answered cautiously. "Hello?"

"Luke? This is Jack." Hearing that deep voice in my ear made my heart jump a little. "Sorry to call you on a Sunday morning, but I thought you'd want to know that we've found Joel's truck."

All thoughts of Chris evaporated. "Where?" I asked hurriedly.

"A hiker spotted it early this morning, parked in the trees off a tiny access road less than five hundred meters from your aunt's cottage. It was a lucky find. The closest property has been empty for a while, and that truck could have sat there for months with no one the wiser."

I mulled this over in silence, Jack waiting patiently on the other end of the line, before I said, "Anything interesting inside the truck?"

"We're still combing through it, but so far all we've found is the usual detritus."

"Okay. Thanks for letting me know." I paused again, then made a snap decision. "Hey, do you think you'll have time to meet today? There's something I need to tell you."

He sounded wary as he replied, "Sure. Cassie can handle the truck on her own for now."

"Are you at the office?" When he confirmed that he was, I said, "Okay, I'll be there in ten minutes."

Chapter Fifteen

I found the door to the RCMP detachment office unlocked but the front desk empty when I arrived. In fact, the whole place was spookily deserted. They were probably closed on Sundays, I thought as I made my way past the darkened workspaces and toward Jack's office. Another perk of living in a small town.

I knocked on Jack's open door, and he looked up from behind his desk. He was wearing civilian clothes—a blue-and-white checked shirt, jeans, and a fleece vest—and I realized this was the first time I'd seen him out of uniform. He looked good. Less intimidating, for sure. But I didn't think I was imagining the dark smudges under his eyes.

"You look tired," I greeted him as I stepped into his office and grabbed a chair.

He grunted. "I didn't get a lot of sleep last night." His gaze veered away from mine.

"I was sorry you left early," I told him quietly, and he shrugged those big shoulders of his.

"I had work to do."

I watched him for a moment, but when he stayed silent, I said, "I just had a very tense encounter with Chris McCormick."

His eyes found mine. "When?"

"Less than an hour ago. I stopped at the Java Jolt for breakfast and ended up behind him in line." I hoisted my grease-stained paper bag as proof. "He recognized me from yesterday. Juliana and I had lunch in the Bluebird Café next door. And we discovered that Gabi, Chris's daughter, had a bad encounter with Joel Mackenzie."

Jack's eyebrows lowered in concentration as he grabbed a pen and started noting this down. "What kind of encounter?"

"He grabbed her inappropriately. She's still pretty traumatized by it. So this morning, Chris got in my face about upsetting her. He said that customers who upset his daughter made him angry. And then he threatened me." I leaned forward in my chair. "Jack, he knows that Joel was hit with a rock."

Jack frowned as he listened, and his gaze was sharp as he looked up at me. "Wait a minute. How do *you* know he was hit with a rock?"

"Juliana told me." He let out an exasperated huff, and I added quickly, "I know, I know, but she thought I had a right to know." I decided not to mention that I'd asked her point-blank for information. "So unless she's telling the whole town every detail about Joel's murder . . ."

He shook his head. "Jules loves to talk, but I was very clear with her that forensic details were to remain confidential." He snorted. "Of course, look how well she managed that."

"So it's possible she's told other people?"

Jack thought about it for a few moments. "I doubt it," he finally said. "I can see her telling you—she and your aunt were close, and she's made it very clear that she doesn't believe you're a suspect—but she knows better than to spread these details around."

I leaned back, warmed by Juliana's faith in my innocence. "Meaning Chris shouldn't know how Joel was attacked."

I watched as Jack mulled this over, jotting down a couple more things on the notepad in front of him. "I'll bring Chris in for an interview," he finally said. "You're right: something here doesn't add up."

I felt a little thrill of triumph, but then I steeled myself. "There's something else you should know." And I told him about the rest of my investigation: my rummaging through Joel's motel room and finding proof that he was blackmailing someone; his public argument with Samuel Beckinridge at Sal's and then Samuel's odd behavior when I'd asked him about it; my realization that someone had been in the cottage on the night of the murder.

By the time I finished confessing my sins, Jack's expression had darkened. "Are you serious?" he growled at me. "You stole evidence from a potential crime scene?"

"It was stupid, I know," I fired back defensively, "but you were ready to lock me up for murder! I needed to exonerate myself!"

"No, you needed to trust me to do my job!" Jack replied heatedly. He brought a hand down on his desk with a loud thump. "You realize that I could charge you with obstructing an inquiry, right? Hell, I *should* charge you! Maybe a couple of days in jail would knock some sense into you!"

I bit back a stinging retort and took a deep breath instead. "Look," I said evenly, "I still have the note I found in Joel's room. It's back at the cottage. I can bring it to you whenever you want."

"Forget it," Jack muttered. "We're going there right now." He got to his feet. "You need a ride, or am I meeting you there?"

I mumbled that yes, actually, a ride would be nice, and we exited the back of the building to a small parking lot where Jack's Wrangler was waiting. He was still fuming as he got behind the wheel, and I decided it was best to say nothing as I climbed into the passenger seat and fastened my seat belt.

The interior of his Jeep was very tidy but carried the unmistakable odors of damp fur and peanut-butter breath.

"I didn't realize you have a dog," I remarked as he started the car and drove out of the parking lot.

He was silent for a long time before saying gruffly, "His name is Bentley."

I nodded and then held my tongue until we reached the cottage, which took about five minutes. "How long are you going to give me the silent treatment?" I finally asked as we both exited the Jeep.

Jack gave me a repressive stare as I walked around the front of the Wrangler and unlatched the back gate. "I don't want to say something I'll regret."

"Really? I wouldn't have thought that would stop you."

I heard him snort as he fell in behind me, and together we wended our way through the garden and to the French doors at the back of the cottage. "I changed the locks," I noted as I opened them with my new key, "since it seems like there might be a murderer running around with one of my aunt's old keys."

134

Jack said nothing as he stepped into the kitchen and paused to look around. Leaving him there, I made a beeline for the study and grabbed the blackmail note in its Ziploc bag off the desk before finding that Jack was now in the living room, peering at the framed photos on the mantelpiece.

I paused in the doorway from the foyer and watched him for a moment. "Is any of it familiar?" I finally asked, and he wheeled around to face me.

"It hasn't changed much," he conceded. "I used to love visiting here," he added, his gaze turning to the bay windows and the sweeping view of the sea.

"A lifetime ago," I murmured, and he exhaled slowly.

"Yeah."

I approached and handed over the note. "This is all I found. It was in the trash can in his room."

He took it from me and studied it for a time. "It definitely looks like he thought about blackmailing someone," he said at last.

"He *did* blackmail someone," I insisted, but Jack shook his head.

"We don't know that. Maybe he got cold feet and never sent a note after writing this."

"Oh, c'mon," I said, hands on hips. "Everything I've learned about Joel Mackenzie suggests the guy didn't have a conscience. We know from his ex that he came here looking for money, and I'm certain that's why he was killed."

Jack shrugged. "It's plausible, but this"—he brandished the note—"doesn't prove anything except that he was *considering* blackmail."

He was right, and that really annoyed me. "Fine," I muttered, before throwing myself onto the sofa in a fit of pique.

Jack waved the note at me and said, "We're not done talking about this, Luke. I told you specifically to stay put and leave this investigation to me and my people. Breaking into Joel's room—"

"I didn't *break in*," I interrupted. "Someone had already shot out the lock on the door."

He lifted his eyes skyward as if importuning a higher power for help. "Exactly. Someone *with a gun* could have been in there. In fact, it seems likely that they *were* there shortly before Cassie arrived. That door was undamaged less than an hour beforehand when the motel manager walked past."

"But there wasn't anyone there," I pointed out reasonably.

Jack's shoulders slumped in resignation. "You need to leave this alone. Okay? Otherwise, you're going to put yourself in the way of someone very dangerous."

I watched him from where I slouched on the sofa. "At least you're no longer convinced I did it."

He shook his head. "You're not completely out of the picture yet, so you can stop looking at me with that smug expression." I hastily rearranged my features into a semblance of outrage. "And I was serious when I said I could charge you with interference. I know you think you're being helpful, but you're actually just making things harder for us."

Some small part of my brain conceded that he might have a point, but rather than admit that aloud, I said, "I worked as an investigative journalist for a long time, Jack. Remember? This isn't the first violent death I've come across."

"You may have covered actual police investigations," he responded sharply, "but that's not the same thing as trying to solve a murder yourself."

I folded my arms and settled for a nonverbal *hmph*.

With a long, low sigh, Jack walked over to stand in the pool of sunlight that slanted through the window. He stood there for a while, his back to me as he stared outside, before saying quietly, "You looked like you were having fun with Kieran Collingwood last night."

"I guess I did," I agreed cautiously, wondering where this was coming from. "For a little while, at least."

"Is that your type? Rich guys?"

He asked that in a neutral tone, but I felt my face heat as if he'd accused me of something terrible. "No," I snapped. Then I thought of Bryce, who wore $1,000 shirts made in Milan and owned an espresso machine worth more than most cars. I'd be lying if I said his wealth hadn't made him more attractive, at least at first, and I'd certainly enjoyed the lifestyle—dining at expensive restaurants, jetting off on lavish holidays, all the accoutrements of the life Bryce felt he deserved. All that money hadn't stopped him from cheating on me, though, and it certainly hadn't softened the blow when our relationship imploded after nearly four years together.

"I danced with Kieran because he asked me," I went on, shaking off thoughts of Bryce. "Maybe I'd have danced with you too, if you hadn't bailed."

"I had to go home and feed Bentley."

"I thought you said you left because you had work to do."

Jack turned his head until I could see his face in profile. "That too."

The silence stretched.

"Well," I finally said, my voice soft, "that was probably your only chance. I don't think I'll be attending Evelyn's soiree next summer."

He bowed his head before turning on his heel and moving toward the front door. "I need to get back," he said stiffly.

I stood up from the sofa and awkwardly shoved my hands in my pockets. "You'll let me know if you find anything in Joel's truck?"

Jack gave me an unreadable look. "We'll see." Then he unlocked the door and stepped outside, shutting it firmly behind him.

Chapter Sixteen

After Jack left, I felt very much at loose ends. The fog out-side had lifted entirely and it was turning into another beautiful day, but I didn't feel like going anywhere. I was still a little shaken by my encounter with Chris McCormick and half convinced I would run into him again. So I pottered around the cottage for a while, watering the plants that filled every room, before finding some empty cardboard boxes in the tiny storage space off the kitchen. Then I made a slow but thorough circuit, taking everything that looked like it belonged in my aunt's shop and packing it away so I could bring them all back to Forget-Me-Not. Barnabus would need them for his inven-tory, I reasoned.

I paused on the threshold to my aunt's bedroom, still reluctant to enter. Then, struck by a thought, I pulled out my phone and dialed the number Jack had called from earlier that morning. It rang several times before he picked up with a terse, "Munro."

"Hi again," I said. "It's Luke."

I don't think I imagined the faint sigh on the other end of the line. "What's up?"

"While you're examining Joel's truck, could you . . . could you check to see if there's any evidence that it struck someone? Like my aunt?"

There was a long pause before Jack said quietly, "That's the sort of thing the forensics people would check for anyhow, but yes, I'll make sure they examine it thoroughly for evidence of a hit-and-run."

I felt a sense of relief as I murmured, "That's great. Thanks."

Jack hesitated again before saying, "By the way, when I got back to the office, there was a message waiting for me. It seems that several people in town received blackmail notes late last night or early this morning. Notes demanding an awful lot of money in exchange for keeping secrets."

My ears perked up at that. "What? Really? That's a weird coincidence."

"It is, yeah." His tone turned wry as he added, "I thought I'd tell you myself so that maybe this time you won't go running off half-cocked."

I rolled my eyes. "You think that's going to stop me?"

"Behave, Luke," he told me warningly, before hanging up.

I stared down at my phone for a moment, then had another idea. After scrolling through my contacts, I dialed a number with a Toronto area code and listened as it rang several times. It was a Sunday, so there was a chance no one would answer, but if I knew Tony . . .

Sure enough, the line clicked and a deep voice said, "Anthony Eriksson, *Toronto Star*."

"Hey, Tony," I said, trying to inject a brittle cheerfulness into my voice. "It's Luke Tremblay. Still working Sundays, huh?"

There was a brief pause before Tony said, a little cautiously, "Hey, Luke. Wow." He paused. "Uh, yeah, you know, I like it here when it's quiet. Long time, huh?" He and I had been colleagues at the *Star* for years, until a change in editors precipitated my embarking on a new career path. Let's just say my departure hadn't been exactly . . . amicable.

"Yeah, it has been. How're you?"

"I'm good, man."

"That's great. And Jessica and the kids?"

"They're good too." He paused once more. "What's up?"

"I was wondering if you could do me a favor." Feeling awkward, I started pacing slowly around the living room. "I'm looking into something, and I need help tracking down a name."

I could hear papers being shuffled around as Tony thought about it. His desk had always been a disaster, covered in documents and Post-it notes half a foot deep, but he'd still been one of the best reporters I'd ever known. We'd both done investigative work at the *Star*, and there wasn't anything that Tony couldn't find once he put his mind to it. "Sure, Luke," he said at last. "I'll see what I can do. What are you working on?"

Letting out a long, quiet breath, I said, "I'm trying to chase down a former employee at a nursing home in the GTA. His name is Joel Mackenzie and he lives in Hamilton."

"Okay," Tony said. "Which home did he work in?"

"Yeah, that's the problem. I don't know."

A long, slightly incredulous silence was my only response until he said, "You don't know? Do you have any idea how many nursing homes and assisted living facilities there are in the Greater Toronto Area?"

I winced. "I know, Tony, I know. This is a big ask."

"It's not just big, Luke. It's impossible."

"There's more, though. This guy was fired from his job something like two months ago. He was stealing from residents. That's got to narrow it down, right?"

A long, weary sigh came down the line. "A little," he conceded, "but not much."

My voice sped up as I said, "You're the best at finding stuff like this, Tony. Way better than I ever was. And you've got access to records that I don't, now that I'm freelance." I paused and listened to the silence at the other end. "This is really important," I finally told him. "You have to believe me."

Another sigh. I could picture Tony leaning one elbow on his desk, pinching the bridge of his nose the way he did when he was annoyed. "Fine," he muttered. "I'll take a look. But I have no idea how long this will take."

My relief was profound as I said, "Thanks, Tony. I really appreciate it. What I need is a list of every resident who died in the facility where Joel Mackenzie worked. Specifically, residents who died in the last year. Okay?"

"Okay, okay," Tony said irritably.

I gave him my email address and, after thanking him again, hung up the phone. It was a long shot, but if Joel had learned of a dark secret from an elderly woman in a nursing home, then maybe her name would point me toward whatever family she had left here in Crescent Cove. Since I'd told Jack what I'd learned from Joel's ex, it was possible that the RCMP was now trying to trace the same thing, but I would bet everything I owned on Tony finding the information first. He was a blood-hound in a journalist's body.

Feeling vaguely satisfied, I picked up the box full of knick-knacks and carried it into the library next door, ready to continue tidying. Before I could even set it down on the colorful carpet in the middle of the room, however, there was a brisk knock at the front door. Uneasily wondering if it might be Chris McCormick, ready for round two, I peered cautiously through the living room window. But it wasn't Chris standing on the front porch—it was Kieran Collingwood.

Opening the front door, I said, a little awkwardly, "Hi."

He straightened from his casual lean against one of the porch posts and gave me a dazzling smile. He was dressed in khaki shorts that ended well above the knee and a pale-green polo, and as he removed his aviator sunglasses, I was treated to those unusual turquoise eyes gazing earnestly into my own. He looked like an Abercrombie & Fitch model who'd grown up and become fabulously wealthy, and I couldn't decide whether that appealed to me or not.

"I'm glad I caught you," he said as he stepped forward and brushed a kiss against my cheek. I had to fight the urge to back away as he got right up in my space. "Would you like to head out on the water? I've got a little boat anchored at the marina, and it's an absolutely beautiful day." He glanced up at the bright-blue sky and then spread his hands to either side as if to say, *Check it out!*

Hesitating, I stared at him. Part of me wanted to stay put in the cottage with the doors locked and the curtains drawn. Another part of me thought Kieran was ridiculously attractive, and hey, how often did I get invited by millionaires to hang out on their boats? "Sure," I said at last, with an enthusiasm that was at least partly genuine. "That sounds great. Give me five minutes to get ready?"

He nodded. "I'll wait in the car."

Hurriedly throwing on a different shirt and grabbing a sweater, I let myself out the back and found Kieran standing next to the ornamental pond in the middle of the yard. He was gazing down at the water lilies . . . or, perhaps, at the dark gap in the greenery where Joel had died.

Turning his head as I appeared, he said, "So this is where you found him, huh?"

I nodded tersely as I approached, though I kept my gaze on him rather than the pond. "That's the spot."

"That must have been incredible," Kieran mused.

"Strange choice of words."

He flashed me another smile. "Well, it's a once-in-a-lifetime thing, isn't it?"

I fervently hoped so. "Shall we go?"

With consummate chivalry, Kieran opened the passenger door of his sporty BMW convertible and waited for me to settle myself inside before closing it. Then, sunglasses back in place, he put the car in gear, and we spun out of the parking spot and down the driveway almost before I knew what was happening. The wind tossed my hair in every conceivable direction as we made our way north to the other side of town, then east toward the water, Kieran waving to a few people here and there as we sped along. All of them waved back with big smiles on their faces. The town certainly loved its Collingwoods.

The marina was where the town's older and wealthier residents kept their expensive toys, which meant I'd never been there before. It was small as these things went, with berths for no more than twenty boats, and more than half of those were empty. The boats that were there bobbed gently up and down, their white masts swaying, while sea gulls dove and spun overhead and called raucously to one another. The marina sat in a protected little cove, with the shoreline curling around it on one side and an artificial breakwater on the other, but beyond that stretched the deep-blue water of the Georgia Strait, glittering with a million reflected points of sunlight.

I'm not a boat person, something that became increasingly clear to me as I followed Kieran down the wooden dock. I mean, they're fine to look at, and in theory I enjoy the idea of sailing, but there was something about venturing out onto the open sea that sparked some deep, atavistic fear in the more primitive parts of my brain. As we came to a stop in front of a small, sleek sailing vessel, I swallowed convulsively and asked myself why I'd agreed to this madness in the first place.

"Here she is," Kieran announced with obvious pride. "What do you think?"

I gazed at the boat and nodded reflexively. "It's, uh, really nice," I mumbled. And it was, I suppose. The gleaming white hull curved appealingly from stern to bow, and as we moved to the right side, I saw the word *Intrepid* written in bold red letters. But the vessel also looked very small, with an intimidating number of ropes everywhere, and as I watched, the whole thing heaved aggressively in response to a particularly large swell. "Do you go out often?" I asked weakly, desperately hoping for reassurance.

"All the time, when I'm in Crescent Cove," Kieran responded cheerfully. With a graceful leap, he sprang aboard and then turned to offer me a helping hand. "Let's get you settled and then I'll cast off."

It took a few minutes for me to clamber awkwardly aboard, don my life jacket, and then tuck myself into the spot Kieran indicated toward the rear of the boat. Once he'd untied the mooring ropes, he settled himself nearby, at the tiller, and said, "This is a single-handed dinghy. It's rigged so that I can operate everything by myself, from right here. So you don't have to worry that I'm going to suddenly shout at you to pull a line or anything like that. The only thing I might ask you to do is move to the opposite side of the boat if we need to redistribute our weight, and if that happens, I need you to move fairly quickly. Okay?"

I nodded mutely and tried to loosen my death grip on the narrow wooden bench I was sitting on.

It took remarkably little time for him to hoist the sail and then use the wind to maneuver us out of our berth. He kept one hand on the tiller while the other tugged and released various ropes, and though it all looked ridiculously complicated, he was clearly an expert. In no time at all, we were accelerating out into open water as the town shrank slowly behind us.

"I'm glad you came to Mother's soiree last night," he said as the sail snapped and billowed overhead. "I don't usually meet anyone interesting at those things. It's just a lot of shaking hands and smiling at people."

"And champagne," I reminded him.

He laughed. "That too." I couldn't see his eyes behind his aviator sunglasses, but I got the impression that he was watching me. "You seemed friendly with Jack Munro," he said at last, his tone casual.

I shrugged uncomfortably. "Jack and I used to be friends. A long time ago. And of course I've been seeing him a lot lately, what with the dead body in the backyard."

Kieran glanced up at the sail and pulled gently on the rope in his left hand. "Right," he said. "The dead guy. What was his name? Joel something?"

"Joel Mackenzie."

"That's right. He was a real piece of garbage, wasn't he?"

I hesitated, struck by the nonchalant way he said that. "From what I've heard, he wasn't the nicest person," I allowed.

Kieran shook his head slowly. Behind him, the town had shrunk to a few smudges of color surrounded by dark-green trees. "I think he was worse than that. He was a cancer. A virus. Spreading sickness, polluting our home." His voice was cold now, his words edged with anger. "I caught him snooping around the estate, you know. He had binoculars, if you can believe that."

Feeling increasingly uncomfortable at this sudden change in tone, I said cautiously, "Do you know what he was doing there?"

"The same thing he did everywhere in Crescent Cove. Snooping. Spying." He gave a hard tug to the rope in his hand, and the sail swung rapidly to one side, causing the boat to pitch sharply. I grabbed for the bench as Kieran said, "We weren't the only people, you know. He was spying on everyone. Or he did, until I took his binoculars and smashed them into little pieces." His mouth curled into a satisfied smirk.

I tried to calm the bubbles of anxiety that were rising in my stomach. "When was this?" I asked, my voice a little higher than usual.

He didn't seem to notice my discomfort. "A few days ago," he said with a shrug. "He snarled and whined about it, until I explained what I would do to him if I ever saw him near our house again." He smiled. "That little creep got the message, believe me."

Maybe the message he'd gotten was a rock to the back of the head. My fingers tightened around the wooden bench until they ached. Was I in the middle of the ocean with a murderer? Kieran's polished, easygoing demeanor was gone, replaced by something hard and, frankly, a little scary. I had no doubt whatsoever that this person was capable of killing someone in cold blood if he thought it was necessary. Would killing me become necessary if I asked too many questions? If I discovered what Joel had been after?

Kieran, meanwhile, had become preoccupied with adjusting the sail again, seemingly unaware that he'd said anything unusual. I took several deep breaths of cool air as I considered my situation, then said in a voice that shook ever so slightly, "I'd like to go back to shore now, please."

He focused his concerned attention on me at once. "Are you sure? There's a really beautiful little island I wanted to show you. We'll be there in a few minutes."

"I'm sure. I'm really not feeling well. Seasickness."

He looked disappointed, but then nodded and said, "Okay, no problem. Just hang tight. I'll get us back as soon as I can." Moving the tiller and adjusting the sail, he turned us smoothly in a long arc until the bow pointed back toward the Island and we sped over the waves.

It was really too bad, I reflected as I held on for dear life. Kieran was handsome, fabulously rich, and clearly into me. In another world, he might have swept me off my feet. Now, though . . . even if he hadn't killed Joel, there was a darkness to Kieran that unsettled me. It might be nothing more than the uncompromising confidence of a man used to getting what he wanted, but after four years with Bryce, that was a quality I'd come to despise. And no matter how I tried, I couldn't shake the conviction that, if someone threatened his interests in some way, Kieran Collingwood would be capable of a drastic, even brutal response.

The awkward distance that had sprung up between us lasted all the way back to shore and then to the cottage. As he pulled up next to the picket fence and parked his BMW, however, he turned to look at me.

"Are you sure you're all right?"

Nodding, I plastered on a sickly smile. "I'll be fine. I just need to settle my stomach. But, uh, thanks for taking me out on the water. It was a lovely idea."

He reached over and took my clammy hand in his strong, warm grip. "It's strange, seeing you after all these years. I found you so intriguing when we were kids, and I still do."

I said nothing. I'd encountered Kieran maybe twice in my whole life before this week, and he'd made zero impression on me then. I felt kind of bad about that. At the same time, I was genuinely stymied by the idea that this ridiculously attractive person would find me "intriguing." I usually felt about as interesting as wallpaper paste.

The silence stretched for a few uncomfortable moments before Kieran released my hand. "A friendly word of advice?" he said in a markedly cooler tone of voice. "Watch yourself with Jack Munro."

I stared at him. He was gazing through the car's windshield at the cottage. Or was he once again studying the pond where Joel Mackenzie died? I couldn't tell. "What does that mean?" I asked.

Kieran shrugged, still not looking at me. "Jack's got something of a reputation around here, that's all. He's a heartbreaker. A real jump-'em-and-dump-'em kind of guy."

I sat there and digested this startling statement. "It sounds like you know this from personal experience," I said cautiously.

His mouth curved into a mirthless little smile as his gaze veered back to me. "You could say that."

Almost more unsettled by this revelation than the idea that Kieran might be a murderer, I fumbled at my seat belt and finally managed to extricate myself from his convertible. "Thanks again," I said loudly as I slammed the door behind me. "Take care."

With a final wave, he put the car in reverse and then sped away, leaving a cloud of dust in his wake.

Chapter Seventeen

After Kieran left, I wandered slowly around to the front of the cottage with my mind spinning. Evelyn's son was now at the top of my list of suspects. Other people might have had their reasons for killing Joel, but to me, Kieran was the only one who seemed genuinely capable of it. I had no problem imagining him creeping up behind the other man and bashing in his skull. Had Joel tried to blackmail Kieran? It was possible, certainly, though the Collingwoods lived very public lives. They'd been scrutinized and profiled for decades, and that would make it very difficult for them to hide a secret big enough to kill for. Not impossible, though.

Stepping up onto the front porch, I turned to gaze blindly out across the glittering ocean as my mind continued to work. The problem was, there was no proof that Joel had actually tried to blackmail anyone. Jack had been right about that. And without that as a motive, did Kieran really have a reason to murder . . . ?

My brain lurched to a halt midthought. *Jack.*

I couldn't deny that Kieran's claims about Jack had shaken me, which was stupid. I barely knew Jack. And besides, he hadn't exactly endeared himself to me since I'd returned to Crescent Cove. He'd practically accused me of murder. He'd been ready to toss me in jail and throw away the key!

And yet . . .

The hug he'd given me last night had felt . . . nice.

Then, five minutes later, I'd been in Kieran's arms on the dance floor. Talk about a wild ride. No wonder my emotions were veering all over the place today.

I didn't like the picture of Jack that Kieran had not-so-subtly painted today. I wanted to believe he was better than that, if only because we used to be friends. No other reason, I told myself sternly. None.

But what if it was true?

I stood there for a few moments longer, watching the sea, before my phone rang with jarring suddenness. "Hello?" I mumbled.

"It's me." Jack's deep voice made my heart jump ever so slightly, a habit that I was starting to find irritating. "Our forensics people just finished going over Joel Mackenzie's truck."

"Did you find anything?"

"Not really." He sounded regretful. "It was full of junk, mainly. A few gas station receipts from his drive here from Hamilton and a lot of fast-food wrappers."

I stifled my surge of disappointment. It had been too much to hope that a vital clue would just be sitting in the truck.

"The only fingerprints we recovered were Joel's," he went on to say. "But there's evidence that some parts of the vehicle were wiped down, including the glove box. Someone else was in there."

"Someone very careful," I observed.

Jack let out a long sigh. "Yeah, unfortunately."

"How are you holding up?"

"I'm okay." He paused for a moment, then said carefully, "They also checked the front of the truck for damage. There were a few dings and scrapes, the kind of thing you'd expect to see on a vehicle this old, but nothing consistent with hitting something large and solid."

I hadn't realized I was holding my breath until I exhaled slowly. "Okay," I said around a curious tightness in my throat. "Thanks for checking. I just thought that maybe . . ."

"Yeah, I know." His voice had taken on a gentle tone. "But it doesn't look like he was involved in Marguerite's death."

I nodded, then realized he couldn't see me. "Okay," I said again.

There was a brief pause, and then Jack said, "I also spoke with Chris McCormick."

I perked up at that. "And?"

"He's not in the frame for Joel's murder."

"But he knew about the weapon," I protested.

"Yeah." His voice sounded grim. "As it happens, Cassie and Ranjit were in the Bluebird Café yesterday. They sat at the counter and discussed the case practically in front of Chris. That's how he knew that Joel was hit with a rock. I've already spoken with the two of them about their unprofessional behavior."

I felt oddly disappointed at the news that McCormick was out of the picture. "You're sure?"

"I'm sure. His alibi for Thursday night is solid: he was in the emergency room in the North Island Hospital in Courtenay. He has type 1 diabetes and suffered a bad episode. His daughter drove him there and stayed with him the whole time."

I mulled this over. "Well, he still has serious anger-management issues," I muttered at last.

"Yes, and we had a long conversation about the way he behaved with you." Jack's voice had taken on a faintly belligerent tone. "It won't happen again."

Strangely warmed by his indignation on my behalf, I said quietly, "Thanks."

Silence fell. Finally, Jack said, "I'm about to check on those blackmail notes, so . . ."

"Can I tag along?" I blurted out.

There was a startled pause before Jack said, "What? Why?"

"I . . . just don't want to be alone right now." I winced even as I said that—it sounded ridiculously lame—but it was the simple truth. Between my run-in with Chris and Kieran's unsettling behavior, I was having a disquieting day. A couple of hours in Jack's company sounded . . . oddly comforting right now.

After another lengthy pause, Jack finally said, "Okay. I'll pick you up in ten minutes."

I was waiting behind the cottage when Jack pulled in, driving his white Jeep emblazoned with the red, yellow, white, and blue stripes shared by all RCMP vehicles. He checked his phone while I buckled my seat belt, then said, "Cassie just texted the addresses where people received notes."

"How many are there?" I asked as we reversed and then headed back down the driveway.

"Three reports came in today, though there could be more. People are sometimes reluctant to report things like this."

Right, I thought to myself, *because the assumption is that there's no smoke without fire.* No doubt that was particularly true in a small town like Crescent Cove, where even a minor scandal might tarnish your reputation for decades.

There was relatively little traffic on this bright Sunday afternoon as we drove past downtown and then turned west. "All three addresses are in this part of town," Jack said as we slowed and then turned onto a quiet, tree-lined street.

"Do you think this might be Joel, somehow?" I asked. "Did he mail out a bunch of blackmail notes before he died?" It sounded a little implausible to me, but then, everything I'd learned about Joel suggested he'd had a rapacious appetite for money matched only by a deep aversion to paying what he owed.

Jack shook his head. "It's the weekend, remember? No mail delivery. These notes were each taped to the front door."

"Not particularly subtle," I noted. "Even if they weren't mailed by Joel, though, it's definitely a weird coincidence. Unless there's a lot of blackmail in Crescent Cove."

Jack grunted.

On a whim, I switched gears and asked casually, "How well do you know Kieran Collingwood?"

I didn't think I was imagining the way his shoulders tensed as he turned to look at me. "Why do you ask?"

"I, uh, saw him earlier today. After you left the cottage." I could feel his scrutiny even though I trained my own gaze on the road ahead. "He was acting . . . strange."

"Strange how?"

I shrugged uncomfortably. "He said some things about Joel. About how glad he was that Joel was dead. That he had it coming." I hesitated before adding, "It freaked me out a little."

The silence stretched long enough that I glanced over at Jack and found him gripping the steering wheel with both hands, his knuckles white with strain. "Kieran and I had a fling," he finally said, staring straight ahead. "A couple of years ago. It didn't last. I mean, how could it?" His gaze veered back to mine, and I saw a surprising bitterness there as he went on, "I'm a half-breed cop from the plebian side of town."

I winced before I could stop myself. "I wish you wouldn't say that," I told him quietly.

"Lots of other people say it," he responded curtly. "Including Kieran Collingwood."

I didn't really have a response to that. At least this history explained Kieran's trying to warn me away from Jack. It sounded like there wasn't much love lost between them.

"Do you think Kieran might be involved in Joel's death?" Jack asked.

"Maybe." I thought about it for a moment. "I don't know. His behavior this morning was . . . off. Creepy. I wouldn't be surprised if we found out he'd done it—let me put it that way."

Jack didn't say anything to that, and we drove along in silence for another couple of minutes until we pulled up outside a regal-looking mock Tudor house surrounded by well-kept gardens. "This is Vivian and Ken Liu," he told me as he switched off the Jeep, his tone brisk. Apparently we were no longer discussing his ex-boyfriends or the fact that one of them might be a crazed murderer. "She runs a beauty salon downtown. I'm not sure what he does."

"Something that might warrant a little blackmail?" I suggested, and he grunted noncommittally in response before exiting the car.

I trailed along behind him on the flagstone path as Jack walked up the elegant stone steps to ring the doorbell. The people inside had clearly been waiting for us, because the heavy wooden door opened almost immediately to reveal a well-dressed couple in their middle years, both of Asian heritage.

"Mr. and Mrs. Liu? I'm Sergeant Munro with the local RCMP detachment." Their eyes flicked to me, standing a couple of paces back, and he added, clearly as an afterthought, "This is Mr. Tremblay."

"I'm a consultant," I put in, and Jack gave me a long-suffering look before turning back to the couple.

"I understand that you received a note recently that caused some concern."

Mr. Liu handed over a rectangular piece of paper that looked to have been folded and crumpled several times. "We found this taped to our front door this morning," he said, sounding a little angry. Shooting a look at his wife, he then added, "We weren't sure whether or not to call the police."

"You definitely did the right thing," Jack assured him as he reached into a pocket on his tactical vest and withdrew a plastic baggie. "If you wouldn't mind sliding that note in here . . . thank you." After sealing the evidence bag, he turned it over to read the note, a small line appearing between his eyebrows as he did so. Wordlessly, he handed it over to me.

The note was not what I would have called a professional job, its one sentence hastily scrawled in black Sharpie. "*Give me a milion dollars or else evryone will know you're secret,*" I read, then paused. "Wow. That's . . . really not spelled correctly."

Jack took a moment to study the couple. "Do you know what the note is referring to?"

"No, Officer. It's a complete mystery." Vivian Liu said this with absolute conviction, and yet my journalist's instincts told me something was fishy here. She seemed appropriately bewildered, but I was looking for the indignation that comes from being falsely accused and not finding it.

"And you have no idea who left this?"

"We don't," Vivian replied with an emphatic shake of her head. "It was very alarming." Her voice lowered to a tremulous whisper. "Do you think we might be in danger?"

"I think that's pretty unlikely," he told her, "though of course we'll take this note seriously."

Twisting her hands together, she looked up at him and said, "Would you mind examining our property? I don't like the idea that someone was here."

Jack nodded once. "Of course, ma'am. I'll walk the perimeter and see if I can find anything." Giving me a quick glance, he retreated down the front steps and started walking around the garage, headed for the side of the house.

As soon as he was out of view, Vivian's entire demeanor changed. She stopped wringing her hands, and her shoulders straightened as she rounded on her husband, saying something softly but fiercely in what I thought was Mandarin. He responded in kind, raising his hands defensively. *Well*, I thought to myself, *this is interesting*. Easing forward a couple of steps, I cleared my throat, causing them both to look at me in surprise.

"*Are* you lying about something?" I asked curiously, brandishing the poorly spelled note in its protective baggie.

The Lius looked at each other. He was tight-lipped with disapproval as he nodded meaningfully in my direction, and she gave him a disgusted stare before turning to me and asking suspiciously, "You're not with the police, right?"

"I'm not with the police," I agreed.

Lifting a hand to rub between her eyebrows, she sighed and muttered, "Fine." With brittle defensiveness, she added, "I run a beauty salon here in town, but I also have a side business which is strictly off the books. Cash only, payments under the table, that sort of thing."

"It's illegal," her husband muttered.

"It paid for your fancy car," she hissed back. Regaining her composure, she said to me, "I sell health and beauty supplements. It's not hurting anyone, and I earn a little extra income that isn't taxed. I don't know how this person found out, but I would have handled it on my own if Ken hadn't panicked and called the police." She shot her husband a glare.

"Handled it how?" he yelped. "Paid them off? We don't have that kind of money!"

She folded her arms and shrugged eloquently, refusing to dignify the question with a response. He, in turn, shook his head and muttered fiercely under his breath.

I looked from one to the other. "And you're sure you haven't seen anything unusual? Strangers hanging around, unfamiliar cars always parked nearby, someone talking to your neighbors?"

Vivian shook her head, then hesitated. "There *was* something," she said slowly, a faint frown on her lips. "An old, rusty pickup truck kept appearing at the top of the hill." She gestured to the road in front of the house. "I do a lot of sales out of our garage, and I remember seeing it up there several days in a row while I was meeting with clients. The only reason I noticed it was because there was always someone sitting inside, which seemed odd to me."

I nodded encouragingly. "Okay, great. Do you remember when you last saw it?"

She thought about it for a moment. "I'd say about a week ago."

Before Joel Mackenzie was killed, I thought to myself. And her description sounded vaguely like Joel's truck. Interesting.

At that moment, Jack appeared from around the other side of the house, stepping carefully along the decorative paving stones placed among the shrubs and flowers. "All clear," he called to us as we watched him approach. "There's no sign of anyone entering or leaving your property, Mrs. Liu."

"Oh, thank you, Officer," she fluted, playing up the nervous-citizen routine for all she was worth. "I feel so much better now."

"We should get going," Jack said to me. Nodding to each of them, he added, "We'll be in touch if we learn anything. Thanks for your time." He turned and headed back toward his Jeep.

"Thanks," I echoed before following Jack, the blackmail note still clutched in my hand.

"So," Jack said as he closed his door and fastened his seat belt, "did you get the truth out of them?"

I paused in the act of putting on my own seat belt. "What do you mean?"

He snorted as he put the Jeep in gear and pulled away from the curb, giving the couple still standing in the doorway a small wave as we cruised past their house. "They were obviously hiding something. And you seem to have a knack for getting people to talk to you."

Studying his profile as he turned the Jeep down another quiet street, I said at last, "Look at you, all observant and stuff."

One side of his mouth quirked into a sardonic smile. "You remember that this is my job, right?"

"Sure, of course." I looked down at the note in my hand for a moment. "Someone was watching the Liu house for a while. Someone in a truck that sounds an awful lot like the one I saw Joel driving."

Jack was silent as we pulled up to a stop sign. "Watching them doing . . . what exactly?"

I thought about obfuscating a little—maybe I could get a sweet discount on some off-the-books collagen supplements if I kept her dealings to myself—before saying, "Mrs. Liu is running a side business out of their garage. Cash only, under the counter."

"Hardly earth-shattering," Jack noted as we eased forward.

"No. But possibly enough to get the Canada Revenue Agency involved. That could end up being pretty costly, to say nothing of the embarrassment if it becomes public."

"Still," Jack muttered, shaking his head, "it's not the kind of thing that someone pays a million dollars to keep quiet."

"It's not," I agreed. "And if it was Joel who was watching them, then who hand delivered these notes?" I scanned the note in my hand again. "I just realized that this doesn't include instructions about how or where to pay the money."

He nodded. "I noticed that as well. Either this person is planning to deliver a follow-up note with those instructions, or . . ."

"Or we're dealing with someone who didn't really think this through," I finished.

"Or both."

I conceded the point with a tilt of my head. "So are you going to stake out the Lius' house and wait for the blackmailer to come back?"

Exhaling slowly, Jack said, "No. I don't have the people to spare for something like that. Especially since there isn't really a credible threat here."

It made sense. Staring down at the note, I finally said, "Something about this doesn't add up. The note I found in Joel's motel room was different. I mean, it was just a fragment, but the handwriting was a lot neater than this one. Its demands were also more reasonable than 'a million dollars.'"

"You're suggesting that someone else wrote this?" Jack asked as he glanced over at me. "I'm inclined to agree. Though it does raise the question of why we have *two* potential blackmailers operating in a small town at the same time."

It certainly did. In my mind, it also raised the uncomfortable question of whether Joel had an accomplice and, if so, where they were right now.

The other two addresses were just a couple of minutes from each other, and in both cases we found people who were quite upset about the notes that had appeared on their front doors. The first was a widower who told us that he had started seeing a *much* younger woman, a student at Vancouver Island University, a few months ago. He still wore his wedding band, even though his wife had died more than two years ago, and he was terrified at the thought that his wife's family would learn about his May-December romance. The other recipients were a well-to-do couple who staunchly insisted that they had nothing to hide, though they seemed awfully worried for people with no secrets. In both cases, they had received notes identical to the one sent to the Lius, abysmal spelling and all.

I was thoughtful as we pulled away from the last house. All three blackmail notes rested in my lap, each encased in its own evidence bag.

"We've learned two so-called secrets this afternoon, and both were things that someone could have picked up just by listening to local gossip," I mused as we made our way back down toward the water. "I'm guessing the same is true of whatever those last people are trying to hide."

"What do you mean?" Jack asked, glancing over at me.

I tried to put my thoughts into words. "Like you said before, these aren't terrible or even particularly scandalous secrets. They're the kind of fairly trivial thing that people in a small town might relish discussing with one another—embarrassing maybe, or noteworthy, but we're not talking literal skeletons in literal closets here."

Jack was silent as we turned the corner onto Sanderson. "You're thinking that anyone could have learned this information just by keeping an ear to the ground."

"Exactly! How many people buy supplements from Vivian Liu? A lot, probably. And Mr. Mancini told us that he was only trying to conceal his new relationship from his in-laws so that he didn't hurt their feelings. I wouldn't be surprised if at least some of his friends and neighbors already know what's going on. Why try to blackmail people over things that are, if not common knowledge, then at least not exactly secret?"

We drifted past the library, and I was distracted momentarily by a memory of Samuel Beckinridge's odd behavior when I'd questioned him the day before. Someone else with secrets, perhaps?

"Because it might not be common knowledge to an outsider," Jack said slowly as we turned onto Ravenwood Lane.

I grinned at him, briefly delighted that he was following my own thoughts. "Right. Take Mr. Mancini, for example. He still wears his wedding band, but to someone who doesn't know he's a widower, it sure looks like he's cheating on his wife in a clandestine and scandalous affair with a younger woman. And that would definitely be fodder for blackmail."

Pulling the Jeep into the graveled area behind the cottage, Jack turned off the ignition before looking at me. "So it's an outsider. Possibly Joel Mackenzie, someone who we know at least contemplated blackmailing someone. Except he couldn't have delivered these notes himself, and you think they were written by another person. So do we have another outsider staying in town who also happens to be another would-be blackmailer?"

Sighing in frustration, I said, "I know, I know. Something's not adding up."

"You'll get there eventually, Nancy Drew," Jack said dryly, and I gave him a moody poke in one very hard bicep.

"Thanks for letting me tag along," I said, after a brief silence. "This was interesting. And I think we're onto something with the outsider theory."

"Having you there was . . . fine," he conceded grudgingly. "You didn't completely mess everything up."

"Wow, what a compliment." Handing over the notes, I opened the passenger door and slid to the ground. "Keep me posted about this, okay? I want to know what shakes out."

He gave me an ironic salute before I closed the door and stepped back, watching as he drove away. Then I slowly walked back into the cottage and locked the door behind me.

Raindrops started to tick softly against the window as I wandered back into the library, where I spent another couple of hours sorting my aunt's papers into several piles and clearing out her desk. By the time I was done, the rain was falling in earnest and my stomach was rumbling, so I retired to the kitchen to make myself some dinner. Outside, the Ravenwood looked especially forbidding in the dreary gloom. I leaned disconsolately against the countertop and munched my sandwich, watching silvery trails of water meander their way down the windows. Then I wandered around the cottage, turning on lamps and closing windows, before standing in the living room and watching the gray waters of the sea heave dully in the failing light. It seemed like a good evening to curl up on the sofa with one of the books I'd brought with me and try to forget about mysteries, murders, and long-ago scandals. So that's what I did, falling asleep at last to the soothing sound of rain drumming against the roof.

Chapter Eighteen

I was up bright and early the next morning, ready to tackle clearing out my aunt's bedroom, when my phone rang and Jack's number popped up.

"You just can't leave me alone," I greeted him.

"We've got a problem," he said in response, his tone serious.

"Besides a murderer on the loose? Great," I sighed, leaning back into the old sofa where I was finishing my coffee.

"Someone broke into your aunt's shop early this morning."

I sat up straight. "Did they take anything?"

Jack's voice was grim as he replied, "Yes. And they assaulted Barnabus."

"Crap." I thought for a moment. "Is he okay?"

"Mostly. He was there earlier than usual and obviously surprised the perpetrator, who did a number on him. He's shaken up and has a couple of bruises, but he was lucky. Whoever this was, they meant business."

I chewed my bottom lip as I squinted through the bay window at the sun rising over the ocean. "Do you think it was the murderer? Looking for this box that Joel was after?"

Jack sounded tired. "I do, yeah. It's too much of a coincidence otherwise. Why else would someone break into a store at the center of a police investigation?" Then he paused as my words registered. "Wait a minute. What box?"

I winced. "Didn't I mention that Joel was looking for a box?" I asked weakly.

"No, you didn't." His voice was sharp with exasperation as he added, "How do you know this?"

"Leona mentioned it when I answered Joel's phone. She said the evidence of this scandalous secret was hidden inside a box of some kind." I paused. "Sorry, Jack. I really did think I'd told you."

I listened as he let out a long breath. "Fine," he said at last. "So we're looking for a box."

"Are you at the store now?" I asked, rising to my feet and moving toward the back door.

"Yes."

"Okay. I'll be there in ten minutes."

"Luke . . ." He trailed off with a sigh. "You should just stay put."

I shook my head, even though he couldn't see me. "No way. That's my aunt's store. Technically, in fact, it's my store now. So I'm coming down there to assess the damage and see how Barney is doing."

Another sigh. "Fine," Jack muttered, and I disconnected the call with an unreasonable sense of triumph. Then I hurried out to my car and made a beeline for the center of town, managing at this relatively early hour to secure a parking spot just around the corner from the shop.

When I arrived at Forget-Me-Not Antiques, a small crowd of curious onlookers was standing outside, murmuring excitedly and peering through the windows to try to see what was happening inside. *Nothing like someone else's misfortune to enliven a small town*, I thought to myself, a little bitterly, as I shouldered through them on my way to the shop's door. The tone of their murmuring escalated to near-frenzied levels of agitation at my appearance, no doubt thanks to the presence among them of a real-life murder suspect.

Ignoring the hysterical buzz, I approached the door and found the very young RCMP constable standing there, thumbs hooked casually behind his tactical belt. He gave me a big smile as I approached.

"Hey, Mr. Tremblay!" he said with the friendly enthusiasm of a puppy. "Sarge said you might be by." A name badge that read CARSON gleamed on his chest as he shifted to one side and gestured me closer. "You can see where the perp gained entry," he told me as he pointed to the splintered doorjamb with the somber gravity of a seasoned pro, though I suspected this was probably his first break-in and, quite possibly, his first week on the job.

"Wow, you sure can," I responded dutifully, eyeing the deep gouges that had been left in the green-painted wood. "What was it? A crowbar?"

He blinked uncertainly. "Sure," he said, after a small pause. "Yeah. That's exactly what it was."

Nodding solemnly and giving him a pat on the shoulder, I squeezed past him and into the shop, shutting the door behind me to keep the onlookers out. At first glance, the interior looked unchanged since my last visit, the usual clutter homey and somehow reassuring. As I moved farther into the store, however, broken glass crunched under my shoes, making me wince. My gaze tracked toward the back of the shop, where I saw that a display case had been smashed to bits. Jack was standing next to it, his big arms folded across his chest as he watched Juliana Kestenbaum attend to a battered-looking Barnabus, who was sitting in what I judged to be quite a fine Hepplewhite chair.

All three of them looked at me as I scraped and grated my way through the field of glass shards, my wince deepening with every step. "Sorry," I muttered as I finally reached them. As beat-up as he was, Barney still managed to curl his lip at me, while Juliana shook her head and then returned her attention to her patient. For his part, Jack heroically refrained from rolling his eyes, but I could tell he wanted to.

I really wanted to ask about what had been taken, but instead I squared my shoulders and said to Barnabus, "I'm glad you're okay." He didn't *look* okay, I had to admit—one corner of his mouth was bleeding where, I surmised, someone had punched him, and the skin around his right eye was beginning to bruise. His round little glasses rested in his lap, one side of them mangled. He also had a long but shallow cut across his forehead, which the doctor was closing up with a series of butterfly stitches.

He gave me a flat stare in response before pressing a small gauze pad to the side of his mouth.

"What happened exactly?" I asked, turning to Jack.

"A single individual forced his way into the shop through the front door sometime around six thirty this morning," he replied, nodding his head toward the entry. "He used a small crowbar"—I gave myself a mental pat on the back for my deduction skills—"but clearly wasn't expecting anyone to be here. As it happened, though, Barnabus *was* here—"

"I couldn't sleep," the other man mumbled through his busted lip.

"—and he surprised the perpetrator just as he was about to smash the display case here." Jack motioned to the case next to him, which normally would be full of rare and valuable coins. Now, though, it contained nothing more than dark-green velvet covered in pieces of broken glass.

I stepped closer to examine what was left. "It looks like he cleaned us out," I said, unable to keep the dismay out of my voice.

Jack nodded once. "After subduing Barnabus, the perpetrator grabbed everything in the case and stuffed it into a cloth bag."

"A shopping bag," Barnabus chimed in. "From the greengrocers."

"At least they're eco-friendly," Jules murmured as she applied the last butterfly stitch to Barney's cut. Jack glowered at her, clearly unamused, though I had to fight back an involuntary smile.

"Did they take anything else?" I asked, once I'd regained my composure, looking from Jack to Barney.

At this, Jack turned his attention to Barnabus, who said sullenly, "He wanted to know where we kept our boxes."

I gave Jack a triumphant look. "I knew it. This person is looking for the same thing Joel was. I'm sure of it."

Jack's mouth curled into a small frown. "Maybe," he conceded. "It's possible that he grabbed the coins because he saw literal money sitting here and decided to take it, but what he really wanted was an antique box."

Thoughtfully, I turned in place to survey the rest of the shop. There were all kinds of valuable objects on display, crowding the desks and tables and armoires that my aunt had used to showcase them. And of course, there was also a lot of inexpensive stuff, objects that might attract a buyer who didn't particularly care about provenance or historical significance. It often took a discriminating eye to tell the difference, and I could understand a would-be robber demanding that Barney show him the most valuable pieces so he could grab them. But just boxes? No, this guy had been looking for something specific. Looking back at Barnabus, I asked, "What did he take exactly?"

The younger man lifted a slender hand and counted them off. "Three vintage cigar boxes. A very pricey ebony jewelry box. Another jewelry box in walnut with some damage to the edges. A lovely music box from the turn of the twentieth century. And a plain oak box with a broken clasp."

"And was that every box in the store?"

He shook his head wearily. "Just what I could find in the two minutes he gave me. He kept shouting at me to hurry up."

Jules waited until he'd finished before soaking a clean gauze pad in sharp-smelling antiseptic and then pressing it gently to Barney's lip. He hissed in momentary pain but otherwise remained silent as she dabbed at the small wound with brisk efficiency before leaning in to get a closer look.

"I'm going to grab some ice from the Sand Dollar across the street, okay?" she said quietly, giving his leg a pat as she stood up from the Shaker-style wooden chair she'd been using. "That'll help take the swelling down." He nodded mutely and she strode outside, more glass crunching underfoot as she went. Through the window, I could see her trying to shoo away the small crowd still gathered on the sidewalk, her scowl evident.

Taking Jack by the elbow, I tugged him toward the jewelry cases, all of which had survived unscathed. Allowing himself to be pulled away, he lifted both eyebrows in silent inquiry as he looked down at me.

"You said on the phone that this can't be a coincidence," I said quietly, "and I agree. Joel was desperate to get in here before he died, and my aunt closed up shop for almost two weeks rather than let him in. Now we have someone searching for a box. It has to be the thing that Joel was after."

"I'm with you so far."

"Well, who else would want it except the person who killed him? Assuming Barney can provide a description of the person who attacked him, we have our murderer!"

Jack tilted his head to one side. "Possibly," he allowed, after a moment's thought.

"C'mon, Jack. Think about it. Assuming Joel was black-mailing someone about a mysterious secret—"

"We have no proof that he actually blackmailed anyone. Remember?"

I let out an exasperated sigh. "Fine. But we *do* know that someone in Crescent Cove has a secret that Joel *also* knew. Moreover, the thing he wanted from my aunt is connected somehow to that secret. Ergo, the only two people in town who wanted said object were Joel himself and the person with the secret."

Jack's mouth curved into a wry little smile. "*Moreover? Ergo?* You sound like a fancy lawyer now."

"Shut up," I muttered. "Well?" I then demanded. "It fits, doesn't it?"

He looked away from me, through the window behind the jewelry cases. "Maybe," he said at last, grudgingly.

"Ha. You're just mad that I'm putting these things together faster than you are."

Jack turned back to me at that, and there was no trace of a smile now. "I've already asked you to keep out of this, Luke," he rumbled warningly. "I called you about this break-in as a courtesy, not because I needed the investigative skills of a hotshot Toronto reporter."

My eyebrows went up at that, but I decided to let the remark slide. "Someone murdered a person in my backyard and then entered the cottage while I was sleeping, probably looking for the same thing Joel was after," I said evenly. "And now my aunt's beloved shop—her legacy in this town—has been trashed. I'm sorry, but 'keeping out of this' doesn't appear to be an option for me." My voice rose until I was speaking louder than I'd intended, my jaw thrust forward belligerently as I glared up at Jack's disapproving expression.

The cheerful sound of the bell hanging over the door broke the tension between us, and I turned away to see Juliana enter with a couple of tea towels wrapped around handfuls of ice. Barney was watching us from where he sat close to the wrecked numismatics case, but he accepted the ice packs from her with a wan smile and then pressed one to his eye and the other to his mouth. The doctor folded her arms and looked around the shop, shaking her head.

"Marguerite would have been so angry," she said, a little sadly, as I approached her. "Nothing like this ever happened in all the years she ran this place. And now . . ." She trailed off and shook her head again, more forcefully this time. "It isn't right."

"It isn't," I agreed. "But we'll find the person who did this." Turning to Barnabus, I said, "I'm sorry to ask, but . . . can you describe your attacker for me? Every detail you can remember."

He lowered the ice pack resting against his mouth and muttered, "I've already told the police what I saw."

Jack drew closer. "Let's go over it one more time," he suggested, shooting me an unreadable look.

Barnabus sighed wearily. "Fine. The guy was big. Not tall, but bulky. He was wearing a red-and-black plaid shirt over an olive-green T-shirt, jeans, heavy work boots spattered with mud. And a black ski mask over his head. I couldn't see what color his hair was."

"And his eyes?" I prompted.

"I don't know. Blue, maybe, or green."

I nodded. "Any tattoos you could see? Scars on his hands? Any distinguishing marks at all?"

Barnabus gave me a withering look. "No."

Turning to Jack, I said, "There can't be that many men in town that fit the same general description. Right? So let's start bringing them in."

One side of his mouth quirked sardonically. "You're assuming this guy is local. I'm not so sure."

"Why?"

He shrugged. "This isn't the first robbery we've had on Main Street. More often than not, they're perpetrated by opportunists passing through the area, trying to make a quick score in a town with relatively little security." I opened my mouth to protest, and he raised a hand to forestall me. "I know you have your theories about who was behind this, but my job is to consider every possibility. And I'm not going to start dragging every man who owns a pair of work boots down to the detachment office for questioning."

I bristled a little at his tone, but I had to concede that he wasn't wrong. Not entirely, anyhow. Before I could formulate a response, however, Carson, the boyish constable stationed outside, pushed his way through the front door and approached Jack, holding out one gloved hand as he did so.

"Cassie found this about a block from here," he said quietly. Edging closer, I could see that the young man was holding a gleaming coin in the palm of his hand. "She said there were a few small pieces of glass, too, that the perp might have tracked out of here. All of it leads north down Rosewood."

Rising slowly to his feet, Barnabus shuffled over and then leaned down to get a good look at the coin. "It's an American silver dollar," he told us after a moment. "A Peace dollar, in fact.

Good condition. Not the most valuable coin we had, but not the cheapest either."

Impressed in spite of myself at Barney's level of numismatic knowledge, I watched as Jack ordered a door-by-door canvassing of the streets north of the shop. Then, with a last look around at all of us, he strode outside to continue doing . . . supervisory things, presumably. Juliana gave Barnabus's shoulder a squeeze and said, "I have some house calls to make, but I'll stop by later to take a look at those injuries. Keep icing them and try to get some rest, okay?" At his nod, she followed Jack outside, leaving me and Barney surrounded by broken glass and awkward silence.

"I'm going to clean this up," he finally mumbled around the ice pack pressed to his mouth. I noticed for the first time that he was wearing a plain white T-shirt and sweatpants rather than his usual historical attire, and somehow that made his battered appearance even more pathetic.

"No, you're going to lie down and rest," I said firmly. "I'll tidy up and call around to find someone who can repair the door." Barney looked like he was about to object, so I added, "I've got it covered. Go. Shoo."

Barnabus gave me a cool stare, then turned and shuffled into the back room of the store. A moment later I heard the soft creak of an ancient staircase as he made his way up to the small apartment over the shop. I hadn't realized that's where he lived, but I supposed it made sense now, why he'd been down here after being unable to sleep.

It took me a few minutes to locate the tiny closet where my aunt had kept practical things like brooms and mops and about a million adhesive price tags, and then I got to work sweeping up the broken glass littering the old wooden floors. Every time I thought I was done, I stepped on another shard, which got really annoying. Once I'd hunted down the last speck of glass, I had a moment of inspiration and called Daisy Simpson to ask about repairs to the shop. She was suitably horrified to hear about the robbery but promised to send someone round to see about fixing the door. Then, at something of a loss, I slumped against the jewelry case and stared around me.

Forget-Me-Not Antiques had never been organized in the traditional sense of the word. My aunt had created a veritable labyrinth out of clutter and assorted knickknacks, encouraging her customers to drift through its many twists and turns before finding that one unique item that they suddenly needed to have. For all its apparent chaos, however, she had known where to find every single thing. I smiled as I remembered her uncanny ability to pull exactly what someone wanted seemingly out of thin air. This shop had been such an important part of her life, and as my gaze drifted to the splintered remnants of the smashed display case, I couldn't help but agree with Juliana's assessment: my aunt would have been furious to see this happen to the store she'd built from nothing.

I was angry, too, but more than that, I felt a deep, cold determination to find the person who had done this and make them pay. Jack was being too cautious, too careful, with this robbery—I knew, without a doubt, that the person who had barged in here was the same person who had murdered Joel Mackenzie. I was certain as well that it was a local, someone who knew that the center of town would be deserted at six thirty in the morning despite the sun being up. Nothing opened on Main Street before at least eight AM.

The real revelation, though, was that the murderer was looking for the same box that Joel had been after. Might have it already, in fact, along with the secret it contained.

But what if he didn't?

Newly energized, I spent most of an hour hunting through the store for boxes, eventually accumulating a small collection on the counter next to the cash register. Then I remembered the storeroom where my aunt kept her overflow inventory—items that she'd acquired that didn't end up on the shop floor for one reason or another—and located another four boxes in there. Once I had them all arranged, I inspected each carefully and found . . . nothing. Just a lot of empty boxes. There were no false bottoms or hidden compartments that I could find, even after an exhaustive regimen of shaking, tapping, and prying at each one of them.

Disappointed and more than a little frustrated, I slumped into the Hepplewhite chair that Barnabus had used earlier. Short of taking a hammer to each and every box in there, I was pretty sure I hadn't missed anything. So either the murderer now had the box he wanted or it hadn't been in the shop in the first place. Either way, I was no closer to discovering why Joel had died and who might have done it.

Leaving the boxes where they were in case Barnabus or someone else wanted to examine them, I decided to step outside for some fresh air. The crowd of nosy onlookers had moved on, thankfully, and the sidewalks teemed with tourists and locals alike, enjoying another beautiful summer day. The shop's door was too damaged to latch properly behind me, and I was just considering how to keep it closed when a van pulled up next to me and a tiny, energetic woman with short-cropped red hair hopped out. She was wearing a white tank under a pair of dark-blue overalls, and I couldn't help noticing that her tattooed arms were impressively muscled.

"Hey." She greeted me with a nod. "I'm Eve. Got a call about some restoration work . . . ?" She trailed off as she peered around me to examine the splintered doorframe with professional appraisal.

"Uh, right, yes." I shifted to one side so she could take a closer look. "Thanks for coming. As you can see, it's sort of a mess." I gestured rather helplessly to the damage.

Eve nodded absently as she ran her fingers across the door's scarred edge. "No problem. I can have this cleaned up and the lock replaced in a couple of hours."

"That's awesome, thank you." Tilting my head back to glance up at the apartment windows on the second floor, I added, "Barnabus runs the place and he's just upstairs, if you need anything."

She gave me a quick smile. "No sweat. Barnabus and I go way back. We used to be in Medieval Chaos together."

"Oh. Is that a band?"

"Nope. LARPing. Or, technically, HARPing." At my look of incomprehension, she added, "High-action role playing. We dress up and hit each other with swords."

"Ah." I watched her studying the damage for another moment until something across the street caught my eye. On an impulse, I said, "I need to head out for now, but, um, thanks again for this." She offered a wave without looking at me, and I hurried across the street and into the Sand Dollar Café, in hot pursuit of the two Mounties I'd seen strolling inside.

Chapter Nineteen

Hovering next to the café's door, I had to crane my neck to see around the people lined up ahead of me until I spied my quarry settling themselves at a small table at the back of the room. Edging my way through the crowded space and its muted cacophony of murmuring voices and the clink of silverware, I approached Constable Cassie Perkins from her left. She was wearing her RCMP uniform minus the hat, her hair in thick twists that fell to just under her jaw, and across from her was another Mountie, a Sikh man wearing a dark-blue turban with his uniform. They were chatting to each other and looking at the menu when I cleared my throat and said, "Uh, hi there."

Simultaneously, they turned in their chairs to give me the same evaluative once-over. Cassie's eyes brightened with recognition after a moment, though her colleague just watched me curiously. "Mr. Tremblay, isn't it?" she said. After sharing a knowing glance with the other Mountie, she added, "How can we help you?"

"I don't want to interrupt your meal. I was just wondering if I could talk to you." With a look at her colleague, I amended hastily, "Both of you."

They shared another wordless glance before Cassie said, "Sure. Pull up a chair." I did so, my knees bumping theirs as I sat down, and she gestured to the other officer. "This is Constable Ranjit Singh. I don't think you've met."

He gave me a small nod, expressionless, and I offered a faint smile in return. "You found something that the robber dropped on his way out," I said, turning to Cassie. "A coin. Did you find anything else? Did anyone see anything?"

She shook her head, and the twists of her hair swayed gently. She bore a strong resemblance to Aleesha, her younger sister, but her demeanor was more straightforward and open. "Ranjit and I knocked on every door within a three-block radius. Most of the people we talked to weren't even awake when the robbery took place this morning. A couple of people thought they heard an engine revving and tires screeching, but that's it."

I nodded, disappointed but not entirely surprised. The person who did this had been counting on being able to get away unseen. "Okay. Uh, do you mind if I ask you both about something else?"

Cassie shrugged in a friendly fashion, flashing me a crooked smile. "Ask away, so long as we can eat something. I'm starving."

"You're always starving," Ranjit interjected with a rueful shake of his head.

"Shut up, Ran."

A rather harried-looking man appeared next to me, pen and notepad in hand, and I took a few seconds with the menu before adding my order to that of the other two. As he scurried off, Cassie tilted her head to give me a curious look. "So what is it you want to know?" she asked. After a moment's hesitation, she exchanged a wary look with Ranjit and added, "We can't discuss the murder case with you, if that's what you're after. Not here, anyhow."

Remembering that Jack had just disciplined these two for blabbing in front of Chris McCormick, I nodded solemnly. "It isn't about the case," I assured her. "It's about Jack. I mean, Sergeant Munro."

They both looked at me so intently that I felt my face heating. "What about him?" Ranjit finally asked, his deep voice laced with suspicion.

Now that I was actually having this conversation, I wondered what the hell I was doing. "You may not know this," I began, playing nervously with my silverware, "but Jack and I were friends when we were kids. But then I stopped visiting Crescent Cove, and now . . ." I lifted my shoulders in a small shrug. "Now I'm not sure who he is. He's . . . different. Like, *really* different."

They stared at me.

Is he a heartbreaker? I almost asked, Kieran's words from the day before swirling through my mind, before remembering who I was talking to. "Is he a good guy?" I asked instead, a little weakly.

Once again, the two officers glanced at each other. Then Cassie leaned back in her chair and folded her arms. "Sarge is the best," she told me. "This town would fall apart without him."

"He's a real hard-ass, though," Ranjit volunteered. "Crazy-high expectations."

"Whatever expectations he has for us, they're twice as high for himself," Cassie objected, and Ranjit nodded after a moment. "True."

I looked from one to the other. "He said some stuff the other day, about having a tough time here when he was younger."

Slowly, Cassie shook her head. "I was just a little kid when he was in high school, but . . . yeah. I've heard stories. This town used to have a small but vocal minority of ignorant people. You know the type, probably: racists, homophobes, all of that. They were tolerated, unfortunately, if not exactly welcomed, until their behavior started crossing some lines. Kiara, Jack's mom, was the only First Nations person in town for a long time, and she was bullied for years. Those same people didn't like the fact that she'd married a white man. Eventually, the rest of the town made it crystal clear that those racist idiots were no longer welcome here. Most of them moved away, thankfully, but not before they made Jack's life really difficult for years and years. He was a shy, nerdy kid, and that probably made him seem like an easier target." Her mouth quirked in a wry little smile. "Hard to believe, looking at him now, but my mom told me once that Jack spent more time in the library or off by himself than he ever did with kids his age." She looked thoughtful. "Even in small towns like Crescent Cove, shy people can end up being ostracized, relegated to the periphery of things."

As a former shy kid myself, this was something I knew all too well. "It probably didn't help when people figured out he was gay," I murmured. "When did he come out?"

Cassie thought about it for a moment. "University, I think? He went to UVic and majored in . . . something." She waved a hand. "One of those subjects that everyone thinks is useless. He'd come back during the summers, and I remember there was a commotion of sorts because one year he brought a boyfriend to meet his mom." Shaking her head with a grimace, she looked away, out the window of the café. "Jack got a lot of grief for that. Crescent Cove is a pretty enlightened town these days, but it sure wasn't always that way."

"I've only been here a couple of years myself," Ranjit chimed in, "but yeah, I've heard that some folks made life hell for Jack until he went away to Depot for cadet training. He came back from Regina tougher than anyone in this town, though. Managed to land a spot at the detachment office here, which was lucky, and then started laying down the law." A smile creased his bearded face. "The way I hear it, the people who'd bullied him all those years started crossing the street when they saw him coming. And then most of them moved away."

"That's true," Cassie agreed with a sharp nod. "Jack cleaned up this town almost single-handedly. Before he became an officer, the detachment here tolerated a lot of bad behavior. But then the more senior officers retired or were reassigned, and Jack stepped up. He stopped the underage drinking at places like Sal's, made life uncomfortable for the worst offenders in the area, and generally turned things around. It helped that his mom was well respected and that he had the support of people like Evelyn Collingwood."

I cleared my throat. "And have there been other boyfriends?" I asked casually.

Ranjit coughed into his hand, but I was pretty sure he was smothering a laugh. For her part, Cassie gave me a long, steady look. "Sure. One or two. He had a thing with Kieran Collingwood for a little while too. But Jack lives and breathes this job. Always has. He doesn't strike me as the type to settle down and grow roses or whatever."

I nodded and stared out the window at the sun-drenched sidewalk, lost in thought. Around us, the bustle of the café had faded somewhat as the lunch hour passed and people wandered off to enjoy their afternoons. Cassie and Ranjit checked their phones and murmured to each other until the server returned with our food, and then all three of us tucked in with gusto. It was easy to see why the Sand Dollar was so popular—they definitely knew how to make a sandwich—and we ate in companionable silence, punctuated once or twice by a muted crackle from Cassie's walkie clipped to the shoulder of her tactical vest.

When I was almost too full to move, I leaned back in my chair with a long sigh. "Thanks for letting me join you," I said to them both as they finished up their meals. "And for telling me more about Jack. For whatever it's worth, I'm sorry I wasn't around more, when things were tough for him."

Cassie tilted her head and gave me a shrewd look. "You two were friends, you said?"

"Once upon a time."

"Interesting position he's in, then, being the one in charge of investigating a murder on your property."

I laughed hollowly. "I don't think Jack cares that we used to know one another."

"Maybe," Ranjit said with a small shrug. "Maybe not. He's tough, but there's a heart buried somewhere in there."

I looked from him to Cassie, who just raised an eyebrow at me.

"Well, I'm leaving again as soon as this case is solved," I told them both. "And Jack will have one less problem in his life as soon as I'm gone."

"Oh, the Sarge thrives on solving problems, believe me. He might miss you more than you'd think." Cassie's walkie crackled again, and this time I heard Jack's distinctive voice asking her to call in. "We gotta go," she said to Ranjit as she got to her feet, adjusting her sidearm and vest. Flashing her dimples at me, she added, "Lunch is on me. You have a good day, Mr. Tremblay."

I watched them leave. Ranjit gave me a little smirk as he headed out the door, and I wondered what to make of that.

Chapter Twenty

I felt restless and out of sorts as I left the café. Across the street, I could see Eve hard at work on repairing the doorjamb, drifts of sawdust eddying around her feet. She definitely didn't need me getting in her way. Shoving my hands in my pockets, I turned and started to walk slowly up Main Street, past the brightly painted stores selling ice cream and T-shirts and fudge. People strolled along in the sunshine, laughing and chatting, their lives untroubled by murder or violent robbery. I envied them. Heck, just a few days ago I had *been* one of them, preoccupied by trivial concerns like selling my aunt's cottage and the article I was supposed to be writing for a popular science website. My life back in Toronto, such as it was, seemed like a distant memory, as inaccessible as the carefree existence of the people walking past me.

Pausing at the corner of Main and Douglas, I almost jumped out of my skin when someone's hand grasped my shoulder. Wheeling around, I found myself staring into the concerned face of Evelyn Collingwood. She was wearing a slim pair of black leggings with an oversized red sweater that matched her ballet flats, her silver hair pulled back into a simple ponytail.

"Oh dear, did I startle you? I'm sorry." She gave my shoulder a little squeeze before saying, "I was shopping in Claire's little shop here when I saw you pass by and rushed out to grab you." Her other hand gestured absently to the charming boutique on the corner, its windows occupied by mannequins modeling tasteful women's wear. "How are you, Luke? I just heard about the terrible business at Forget-Me-Not." Her fine-boned features bore a look of deep distress as she examined me from head to toe. "You're not hurt, are you? Claire said that someone was injured."

"No, I'm fine," I assured her. "Barnabus wasn't as lucky, though. He was roughed up pretty badly."

Clucking her tongue in dismay, Evelyn steered me back toward the boutique and through its open door. I didn't bother resisting. "How awful! Will the young man be all right?"

"He should be okay," I told her, keeping my voice low. Nonetheless, one or two of the women browsing nearby looked over at us curiously as Evelyn guided me toward the counter at the back of the shop. "Eventually."

"Was the store damaged at all?" she asked me, glancing over at a curvy, striking-looking woman with a slash of white running through her dark hair who stood waiting next to the cash register. "Thank you, Claire, I'll just get those things there," Evelyn murmured, nodding to a pile of what looked like cashmere sweaters neatly folded on one side of the counter's wooden surface. The woman nodded and flicked me a quick glance as she started ringing up the purchases.

A little uncomfortable at discussing the robbery in front of other people, all of whom were obviously listening to our conversation, I murmured, "A display case was smashed, and some things were taken."

Evelyn shook her head and sighed as she paid for her sweaters. "You'll let me know how I can help," she told me, and I nodded mutely, though I had no intention of asking for assistance. Then I found myself carried along in Evelyn's wake as she left the shop once more with a cheerful farewell to the proprietor.

"I truly don't understand what's happening to this town," she said with another sigh as we paused outside. "So much death and violence." After looping the shopping bag over her arm alongside her purse, she wrapped her other arm around mine and pulled me into a companionable stroll along the sidewalk. "What did this person take from Marguerite's store?" she asked, after a few moments.

"A lot of valuable antique coins, along with some other items. Boxes, mainly."

"Boxes?" she repeated, turning her head to look at me. "How strange."

"It is," I agreed.

Having crossed Douglas, Evelyn steered me away from Main Street and toward a small, narrow building halfway down the block, sandwiched between a bustling bistro and a hair salon. The sign hanging above the door read *Paper Moon*. "You don't mind if I stop in here, do you?" she asked, though she didn't really give me an opportunity to refuse. I found myself propelled at her side into the cozy shop, a bell chiming cheerfully as we pushed through the door. She released me long enough to purchase a ream of thick, shockingly expensive paper and an assortment of thank-you cards, keeping up a steady stream of chitchat with the youngish man behind the counter. Then, before I could do more than glance around the store's tidy interior, we were back out on the sidewalk.

"I try to do as much of my shopping as possible here in town," she informed me with an unselfconscious air of noblesse oblige. "My father always taught me that the Collingwoods must support the people who live and work in Crescent Cove."

"That was generous of him," I said diplomatically.

"He was a great man," she assured me, patting my arm before looping her own around it once more. "Now," she continued briskly, "I think I'd like a cappuccino, and you can tell me how much you enjoyed your outing yesterday with my son."

Oh boy. Giving her a nervous little smile, I allowed her to steer us another block or so and into a tiny coffee shop that smelled like dark roast and cinnamon. After placing our orders with a teenage barista sporting magenta hair and several eyebrow piercings, we settled ourselves at a table next to the window. Jazz played in the background, punctuated occasionally by the loud hiss of the milk steamer, as Evelyn fixed me with an implacable gaze.

"Kieran said you two had a lovely time out on the water."

"We did," I hastened to assure her, determined to lie through my teeth for the rest of our conversation. "It was very nice of him to take me out on his boat. I hadn't been sailing in years."

Evelyn smiled indulgently. "He's always been generous that way," she murmured, then paused as the barista shuffled up to our table with two enormous porcelain cups. I watched as

Evelyn took a dainty sip of her cappuccino and dabbed at her lips with a paper napkin before turning her attention to me once more.

"It's a shame you're not planning to stay in Crescent Cove, Luke dear. It might persuade Kieran to spend more time here. I think he's quite smitten with you."

I laughed, though it sounded strained to my ears. "That's good to hear, but I just got out of a four-year relationship. My heart is still a little bruised."

Her lips turned downward. "I'm sorry. That's very sad. Whoever he is, he's a fool for letting you go." She spoke with good-natured fierceness, and I warmed to her even more.

"Thanks for saying that." I stared down into my mocha for a few moments, lost in thought. "This break-in at the store has made me really miss my aunt," I said at last. "I keep asking myself what she would do."

Glancing up again, I saw Evelyn nod slowly. "I think about her every single day," she said softly. "And I find myself asking the same thing. Marguerite was an amazing woman. I've tried to live up to her example for years." Her striking turquoise eyes filled with tears and she looked away, out the window.

Once I'd given her a moment to collect herself, I said, "I'd like Forget-Me-Not to stay in business, after I've gone back to Toronto. I was planning on selling it along with the cottage, but today . . ." I sighed. "Today made me realize that I want it to stay on Main Street for another forty years." She turned her head to face me, her thin eyebrows lifting. "Would you . . . keep an eye on it for me?" I asked, a little awkwardly. "Barnabus is very capable, but it would mean a lot to me—and, I'm sure, to my aunt—if you could, I don't know, stop in once in a while. Make sure it stays afloat."

"Oh, Luke." Reaching across the table, she grasped my hand tightly between both of hers. "Of course I will. What a wonderful way to honor Marguerite's legacy in this town. I promise you that nothing will happen to that store as long as the Collingwoods are here."

I smiled at her, my heart lightening a little. Even if the sale of my aunt's store would have made my life much easier back in Toronto, the thought of closing its doors for good was just too much to bear. I wanted to know that it was still there, keeping my aunt's memory alive, for years to come.

There wasn't much to say after that. We finished our coffees, Evelyn chattering about how much she'd enjoyed Saturday's soiree, and then we parted ways on the sidewalk outside. She flitted off to run more errands while I walked the two blocks back to Forget-Me-Not to check on Barnabus. I was pleased to find that the door had been repaired and was now firmly locked.

After knocking for a while and peering through the two big windows, I finally heard someone fumbling with the new lock. When the door opened a crack, I couldn't stop an involuntary wince when I saw Barnabus's face. The bruise around his eye was now a brilliant purple, and his upper lip had swollen around the split left by his attacker's fist. The neat row of butterfly stitches closing the cut on his forehead seemed to glow in the gloom of the shop's interior.

"Oh, it's you," he muttered. With obvious reluctance, he stepped back and swung the door open so that I could enter.

Then he closed it behind me and snapped the lock back into place with a loud click.

"Hi," I said awkwardly, as I watched him shuffle toward the back of the store. "How are you feeling?"

"Not great," he replied bluntly. "Jules was just here, though, and she thinks I'll recover fairly quickly."

I nodded mutely. The shattered display case was still there, though the last remnants of broken glass and splintered wood had been tidied up. It would take at least a couple of people to haul it out of there. "Can I get you anything?" I finally asked. "I can walk over to the greengrocers or the pharmacy or . . ."

"I'm fine, thanks," he cut me off. Without his glasses and dressed only in sweats and a T-shirt, he looked very young. "I just need to go back upstairs and rest."

"Okay. Sure." I shoved my hands in my pockets. "Look, uh . . . I wanted to let you know that I'm not selling this place. I want it to reopen—whenever you feel up to it, obviously—and I'd like you to run it." He stared at me, expressionless. "Does that sound okay?" I ventured.

Lifting a slender hand, he twirled his finger in the air. "Whoopee," he intoned sardonically.

I felt my jaw clench and forced myself to relax. *He's just been assaulted and is probably in a lot of pain*, I told myself. *Cut him some slack.* Before I could say anything, though, my phone vibrated in my pocket, and I pulled it out to glance at the screen. There was a text from Jack: *Call me.*

"I should go and leave you to your rest," I mumbled. "Let me know if you need anything, okay?" Barnabus didn't respond;

he just watched me leave the shop, and as soon as I'd stepped outside I heard him locking the door behind me.

Dialing Jack's number, I turned and started walking back up Main Street, absent-mindedly dodging tourists gawking at window displays or trying to decide where to find a midafternoon snack. "Hey," I said when he answered. "What's up?"

"We've got a lead on the man who robbed the antiques shop," he responded tersely. "I thought you'd want to know."

I felt a little thrill of excitement at the news. "That's great! I'll be there in less than five minutes." I hung up on him telling me not to bother and then jogged the rest of the way up to the detachment office. I was more out of breath than I'd have liked when I staggered through the door and found Jack standing next to Carson, who was seated behind the front desk. Jack's expression was grim, and his eyes flicked to me as a faint line appeared between his eyebrows.

"You don't need to be here," he said as I drew closer.

"Yes, I do," I shot back. "What have you found?"

"I sent Cassie and Ranjit up to Campbell River a couple of hours ago. There are two or three pawnshops there that have a reputation for fencing stolen goods. Cassie called me right before I texted you: earlier this morning a man matching the rough description Barnabus gave us tried to sell a bunch of antique coins at one of those pawnshops. The owner was smart—she knew trying to move goods like that would be more trouble than they were worth and that law enforcement would come down on her like a ton of bricks if we found out she had them. So she got the guy to give her his name and promised to check with 'an expert' who could value the coins. Cassie reported that he gave her the name Marek Andrzejewski."

"Okay, that's great. Do you know who that is?"

Jack didn't reply. Instead, he turned on his heel and strode to his office, his back ramrod straight.

Giving Carson a look, I followed and found Jack putting on his tactical vest. He looked . . . angry. Kind of scary, actually. "You do know this guy, don't you?" I guessed, and he looked over at me with an icy gaze.

"I know Marek, yes," he allowed after a lengthy pause, during which he adjusted his belt and checked his sidearm. "We went to school together. He was popular. Played hockey, baseball. Got into all kinds of trouble when we were kids." Tugging his vest sharply into place, he added, "He also made my life a living hell for years. He was the first person to call me *half-breed*. Taunted me with racist slurs about my mom." The strong lines of his face had arranged themselves into a bleak expression. "He almost drove me out of Crescent Cove for good."

My heart ached as I looked at him. "Oh, Jack," I murmured, stepping closer. "That's awful." I stared up into his face and he gazed back at me, imperturbable.

"It was a long time ago."

Clearly not long enough, I thought to myself. "I'm coming with you," I said.

"No, you're not," he growled. "It's absolutely out of the question. This could be dangerous."

"You need me," I argued. "You have two constables still up in Campbell River, and that kid sitting out there looks like he couldn't investigate his way out of a paper bag. *And*," I went on, raising my voice to forestall his imminent objection, "this matters to me. If this is the person who smashed up my aunt's shop and smacked Barney around, then I want to be there when he goes down." I gave him a challenging stare, fully prepared to throw myself bodily in front of his Jeep if he tried to drive off without me.

He held my gaze for a long moment, clearly struggling with himself, before letting out an exasperated breath. "Fine. You can come. But I want you to stay in the Jeep. Is that clear?"

"Crystal."

Muttering something under his breath, he moved past me and out of his office. "Carson," he called, "gear up and meet us out back. We're going to pay Andrzejewski a visit."

The young man bolted to his feet. "Do you need an address, Sarge?" he called after Jack, who was already heading for the parking lot.

"Don't bother. I know where he lives."

Chapter Twenty-One

"Do you know if he'll be . . . wherever we're going?" I asked from the back seat of the Jeep. Constable Carson got to sit in the passenger seat, of course, so I had to speak through a metal grille that divided the two halves of the Jeep. It felt awkward, like I was a kid being chauffeured by his dad—if, you know, his dad was a cop—and I didn't particularly like it.

"No," Jack responded, tilting his head to look at me in the rearview mirror. "But my guess is that he's going to lay low. Traveling to Campbell River was a significant risk when people were out looking for him. His instinct now will be to hole up somewhere safe and wait to hear back from that pawnshop."

Nodding to myself, I turned to stare out the window as trees and houses whizzed past. We were making a beeline for the old two-lane highway that snaked its way out from the north edge of town and along the coastline, Jack driving swiftly but with obvious skill. As we left Crescent Cove, the trees closed in around us like a dark, quiet tunnel through which shafts of sunlight occasionally slanted. Once in a while I saw a house off in the distance, lonely looking amid the towering firs.

Less than five minutes later, we turned off the road and past a painted wooden sign that read *Forestview* before finding ourselves in a large, well-maintained trailer park. Mobile homes were dotted throughout, surrounded by gardens and lawns, and paved roads wound their way between stands of trees. Eventually we turned down a narrow street that took us toward the edge of the park. The character of the homes we passed started to change; they became smaller and narrower, surrounded more often than not by unkempt yards or gravel. I saw one or two people watch the RCMP vehicle pass by with sullen, suspicious faces, and wondered how often the police were called out to this little corner of the world.

At the end of the road sat a lone trailer, maybe forty feet from the wooden fence that held back the surrounding forest. As we pulled up in front and parked on a large patch of dead grass, I saw that the trailer was pretty dilapidated, its vinyl siding that had once been a pale blue now dulled with grime, its narrow windows covered by filmy curtains. A rusted-out lawn mower crouched nearby, next to a couple of metal folding chairs with empty beer cans scattered between them.

Jack took a long moment to study the property before saying, "Be ready for anything." Carson, seated next to him, nodded determinedly. Then they both got out, putting on their uniform hats as they looked around.

"Hey," I called before they could shut their doors, "can I at least sit in the front? I'm locked in back here."

With an obvious show of patience, Jack obligingly opened the back door and allowed me to settle myself in the passenger seat. "Stay put," he warned me before closing the door and striding toward the trailer. Three steps made from concrete blocks led up to the battered vinyl door, and Jack climbed to the topmost step before banging repeatedly on its dingy surface. Carson took up a position at the bottom of the stairs, one hand resting on his sidearm.

Fortunately, the Jeep's window was rolled down, so I could hear when someone hollered from inside, "Go away." Jack pounded again, and eventually someone flung open the door and stepped into view.

Marek Andrzejewski was a stocky man who stood a couple of inches shorter than me, with the barrel chest and wide torso of someone whose muscles were turning to fat. He had short blond hair in messy spikes and small, squinting blue eyes over a nose that looked to have been broken several times in the past. His irritated expression changed to one of surprise as he saw the two officers standing at his door, and then his eyes narrowed.

"Well, well. If it ain't Munro, the golden boy." He screwed up his mouth and then spat meaningfully onto the concrete step next to Jack's boot. "Here to give me another parking ticket?"

Jack looked past him, into the grimy little trailer. "Mind if we come in? I just have a few questions for you."

"You know what? I do mind." Marek squared his shoulders as if preparing for a brawl, or maybe to shove Jack bodily down the steps. I could see Jack's whole body tense. Things were about to get ugly.

Hastily opening the passenger door of the Jeep, I scurried over to the steps. "I'm so sorry," I said urgently, "but I *really* need to pee."

All three of them turned to stare at me, Carson's eyes looking about as wide as they could go. Clenching my hands together in front of myself, I hopped from foot to foot as I turned a pleading stare on Andrzejewski. "Please, man. Just let me in there to use the bathroom," I begged. "This is a genuine emergency."

"Who the hell is this?" Marek asked of no one in particular, his brow furrowed. Up close, I could see that his olive-green T-shirt had several small holes around the bottom and that his feet were bare.

"Luke," Jack said in a warning tone.

"I have a medical condition," I babbled, rocking back and forth. "Please let me in, or else I'm going to have to pee in your yard, and you definitely don't want that."

Marek's expression went from incredulous to disgusted. "Fine," he snapped. "Get in here." Without a word, I clambered up the steps and squeezed past first Jack and then Marek. "The bathroom's back there," he told me, gesturing to my left. "Hurry up."

I headed off as, behind me, Marek said in a belligerent tone, "Hey! I didn't say *you* could come in!" Hoping that Jack was trying to capitalize on my unorthodox means of entry, I made a beeline for the back of the trailer, stepping around piles of clothing, empty pizza boxes, and discarded beer cans as I went. The old carpet was dotted with stains and cigarette burns, and a pile of dirty dishes moldered in the small kitchen sink. The air smelled of pot and BO and unwashed clothes. All in all, it was pretty horrifying.

So this is what happens to popular high school jocks, I mused as I glanced over my shoulder and saw that Marek had been pushed back into the middle of the living room by Jack's larger frame. Carson hovered in the doorway, eyes still wide but expression determined. *Then again, maybe it's just this particular jock*, I amended as I took one look into the tiny bathroom and kept moving with a shudder, pausing only to slide shut the accordion door so it looked like I was in there. Then I took two more steps and found myself in Marek's bedroom at the rear of the trailer.

It was pretty much what I'd expected. Most of the room was filled by an enormous waterbed covered in cheap satin sheets and a chipped dresser with an old TV resting on top. Weak sunlight streamed through the half-drawn blinds on the window, enough to illuminate more piles of discarded clothing and an overflowing ashtray on the bedside table. From the other end of the trailer I could hear Jack speaking in his calm, deep voice, followed by Marek responding in an aggravated tone. I didn't have much time before one or both of them came looking for me.

The bed's base went all the way to the floor, so I didn't bother looking there. Instead, I hurried over to the closet and pulled open another accordion door. It was a mess inside, the floor heaped with shoes and clothes and God knew what else, so I dropped to my knees and plunged my hands into the pile. Almost immediately I heard a soft clinking sound as things shifted, and my heartrate spiked. That definitely sounded like coins to me. Sure enough, moments later I withdrew a heavy cloth bag identical to the one in which my groceries had been delivered, its contents plinking together melodiously. A glance inside revealed dozens of coins, probably a small fortune in all, jumbled carelessly together.

Elated, I surged to my feet and left the bedroom. In my preoccupation, I'd failed to notice the raised voices coming from the other end of the trailer. Now I saw that Jack was standing in the middle of the shabby living room with a hand outstretched toward Marek, who looked like he was ready to start throwing punches. "I want you and your *associate* out of here now!" Marek hollered.

"Calm down," Jack growled, "before you do something you'll regret."

"Jack!" I called out, lifting the cloth bag in one hand. "Look what I found!"

Everyone froze for a moment, all eyes trained on the stolen coins. Then, with a wordless snarl, Marek lowered his head and bull-rushed Jack, trying to tackle him or maybe just push past him to the door. Carson shouted something and Jack braced himself, his big arms wrapping around Marek's shoulders as the shorter man barreled into him. There was a brief flurry of movement, and then Jack hooked a foot behind Marek's and upended him onto the dirty carpet. Moving quickly, he rolled the other man onto his stomach and planted a knee in the middle of his back before snapping at Carson, "Restraints!" The constable fumbled a set of zip ties from his belt as Marek shouted a steady stream of profanities and dire threats, his body thrashing uselessly as he tried to dislodge Jack. Moments later, his hands were secured behind him and Jack was able to relax a little.

My heart, meanwhile, was trying to pound its way through my rib cage. That had been . . . intense.

"Get him in the Jeep," he told Carson as he rose back to his feet, and the young man sprang into motion with alacrity. He might have looked like a high schooler, but he was more than strong enough to lift Marek off the ground and then propel him toward the door, one hand on the back of his neck. The erstwhile burglar was whining that the restraints were too tight as Carson expertly maneuvered him down the concrete steps, but I barely noticed. I was more concerned about what Jack was going to say.

"Barging in here like that was dumb," he told me bluntly as he stalked closer. "You know that, right?"

"I'm sorry," I said as steadily as I could. "I thought things were about to go sideways, and I wanted to give you an opportunity to get in here."

"That's not your job, Luke," he said with some asperity.

"Maybe not, but if I can help you, I will." I held out the bag containing the stolen coins, and he took it from me after a moment's pause.

"I just don't want you getting hurt," he muttered as he turned away.

I didn't really have a response to that, so I just followed him outside, where both of us watched Carson manhandle Marek into the back seat. Carson then had the unenviable task of sitting next to him as we made our way back to the detachment office, and Marek didn't stop complaining and swearing at us the whole way.

It was not a pleasant ride.

When we arrived, Carson took charge of Marek again and hustled him into the detachment. I watched as Jack handed over the coins to Ranjit—back from Campbell River, obviously—and then spoke quietly to Cassie. Both of the constables had watched with bright-eyed interest as Marek was steered into the interview room, and now they gave Jack sharp nods before turning away.

"I want to be there when you question him," I said before Jack could follow Carson and Marek.

Jack turned on his heel to stare at me. "Fine," he said at last. "Maybe you'll see something I don't."

Buoyed by his seeming faith in me, I trailed behind as Jack opened the door to a small room that was barely big enough to contain all four of us. Carson stood next to the door, thumbs tucked behind his belt, while Jack and Marek sat opposite each other across a small metal table. I took up a position behind Jack, leaning against the pale-gray wall with my arms folded.

"I have rights," Marek insisted. His hands were now restrained in front of him, and a plastic cup of water rested within reach on the table.

"You do," Jack agreed evenly. "That's why you've been provided with legal representation. Your lawyer will take a while to get here from Courtenay, though, and in the meantime, we're going to have a chat."

"I'm not saying anything," Marek muttered, looking away from Jack and out the small window placed high up on the wall.

"That's up to you," Jack agreed, as if he didn't particularly care what Marek did. "Though if I were you, I'd be trying very hard to explain how you ended up with a collection of stolen coins in your home."

"I've never seen those before," Marek snapped, immediately contradicting his previous assertion. "I don't know what you're talking about."

Leaning forward slightly, Jack said, "We have a witness who can confirm that you tried to sell these coins in Campbell River. We also have footage from security cameras that show the same thing."

Marek's shoulders rose a little, and his narrow eyes flicked back to Jack's face. "So what? Maybe I found them. Maybe I didn't know they were stolen when I tried to sell 'em."

"*When* you tried to sell them? That sounds like a confession."

Marek hunched over even further. "It's not a confession," he said loudly.

"Okay." Jack shrugged as if it didn't matter to him in the slightest. "We also have people on their way to your trailer right now. I'm willing to bet they're going to find clothing with blood on it. Blood belonging to Barnabus Delacruz."

Shifting in his chair, Marek muttered, "I don't know who that is."

"No? He's the young man you beat up this morning."

Mouth curling in a sullen sneer, Marek didn't respond, but his gaze darted around the room as if looking for an escape.

"Why did you murder Joel Mackenzie?" The question burst out of me before I could stop myself. Jack turned in his chair to give me an incredulous look, but I was focused on Andrzejewski, who turned his attention to me with a puzzled expression.

"Who *are* you?" he asked.

Striding to the table, I placed my fists on its surface and leaned down toward him like this was an episode of *Law & Order*. "We're asking the questions here," I shot back. "Now tell me: why did you murder him?"

Marek's voice went up in pitch as he said, "I didn't kill Joel. I didn't do that. I swear." His already pale features looked positively bloodless now. Being accused of theft was one thing, but being accused of murder was something else entirely. "We were buddies! Why would I hurt him?"

Jack watched him closely. "You knew Joel Mackenzie?"

Licking his lips nervously, Marek looked at him and nodded. "We met at Sal's a couple of weeks ago. Joel was in town to earn a little money. He was a real entrepreneur, you know? He had all kinds of plans."

"Like what?" I demanded.

Marek squirmed a little in his chair and looked down at his restrained hands. "He said there were people in this town with secrets. Things they'd pay good money to keep quiet. He said he had proof, but he offered to cut me in if I did a little snooping for him, dug up more. There's always secrets in towns like this, he said. And I thought, yeah, why not? What did Crescent Cove ever do for me?" He raised his head and gave Jack a belligerent stare. "*Nothing*, that's what, because I'm not some bootlicking wonder boy."

"This town handed you everything you could want on a silver platter," Jack said in reply, his voice hard. "I was there, remember?" Marek snarled wordlessly and looked away again.

"So Joel was spying on people?" I asked, thinking of Kieran finding Joel outside the Collingwood estate and the old pickup truck parked outside the Lius' house.

"Yeah. He was a genius at ferreting out things that folks wanted to hide. He was charming, you know? Bought people a drink or two, then listened while they spilled the goods." He shook his head admiringly. "I've lived here my whole life, but Joel had this town eating out of his hand after less than a week."

"And he was planning to blackmail these people," Jack said. "Once he'd uncovered their secrets."

Marek shrugged a little uncomfortably. "Yeah. When he caught a whiff of something, he'd follow it up. He had a list of people who were up to no good, hiding things. Sometimes he'd send me to watch them, sometimes he'd go by himself. He had a pair of binoculars."

I thought about this for a moment before moving on to my next question. "Was Joel looking for a box? Is that why you stole them from the shop?"

Marek's expression darkened. "The people we were watching, they were small potatoes. Joel thought we could squeeze them and get a little money out of it. But he was chasing a big score, something that would set him up for years, he said. And yeah, one night, after a few beers, he told me there was some box that he needed to find. It had the proof he needed to really put the screws to someone here in town and get them to pay out."

"Who was this 'someone'?" I interjected, but Marek shook his head.

"I dunno. I asked, but Joel never told me. He was so focused on getting that box. He knew it was in that antiques shop downtown, but the old lady who ran the place had started avoiding him. It was really pissing him off. And then the old lady died, and I started wondering . . ." He swallowed audibly. "I started wondering if Joel had bumped her off. He said no, he'd needed her alive, but I wasn't so sure."

My throat closed up a little as I listened to my aunt's death discussed so callously.

"And then?" Jack said.

"And then *Joel* winds up dead, and I start to panic." Marek edged forward in his chair, fixing Jack with a wide-eyed stare. "Whatever secret he was chasing, whatever was in that box, it was big enough that it got him killed. So I decided to cut my losses and run. I wrote notes to the people we'd been watching—I remembered some of them from that list Joel was keeping—and told them to give me money. I figured if even one of them paid up, I'd be golden."

"But you forgot to tell them where to deliver it," I guessed, and he nodded, scowling.

"Yeah. I'd had a few beers when I wrote the notes. So then I decided to break into the antiques shop and find this box for myself. I don't know why Joel never did that. I saw the coins and thought, hey, those I could sell somewhere, so I grabbed them first. But then that guy showed up, and I freaked out. I hit him a few times and then made him give me every box he could find."

Silence fell as we all digested the fact that Marek had just confessed to everything—well, everything except Joel's murder. Several moments passed before this fact dawned on him too, his eyes growing wider and wider as the gears in his tiny little brain struggled to work. Then he dropped his head onto his hands with a groan.

Pushing off the table, I straightened and watched him for a moment before looking at Jack. His expression was stony as he met my gaze.

"What about the boxes?" I asked after a moment.

Marek's head came up, and he gave me a bleary stare. "What?"

"The boxes you took from the store. What did you do with them?"

He let out a sharp, dismal bark of laughter. "Oh yeah. Joel's big idea—the box full of secrets." Shaking his head, he muttered, "I tore those boxes to pieces as soon as I got them home. Took a hammer to them." I winced at the thought. "And you know what I found?" he demanded rhetorically. "Nothing. What a stupid waste of time."

Jack stood at that, then motioned for me to follow him out of the room, leaving Carson in there with Marek.

"Well, that's that," he said, a little wearily, as the door closed behind us. "Two cases solved."

I nodded slowly. "That all wrapped up surprisingly quickly."

"He was scared that we might pin Joel's murder on him. That's life in prison." Jack lifted his broad shoulders in a shrug. "Stakes like that tend to make people talkative."

"Plus he's dumb as a bag of hair." I looked at Jack for a moment before taking a deep breath and saying in a reasonable tone of voice, "I know I crossed some lines today, and I'm sorry about that."

He studied me without expression. "Are you?"

"Yeah, I am. I just . . . I wanted justice for my aunt, as stupid as that probably sounds. I hated seeing her shop wrecked like that. I needed to see someone pay."

Jack sighed and looked away from me. "Look, you should go," he said, after a pause. "We're going to be processing Marek for a while, and then I have a ton of paperwork to fill out. Just . . . go back to the cottage. Okay?"

"Okay." I hesitated, then walked away, making for the front door. I almost ran into a young, harried-looking woman in a skirt suit who was juggling a file folder and her briefcase as she barged through the door. She gave me a muttered apology as she hurried past, and I guessed that she was Marek's lawyer.

Boy, was she about to be extremely unhappy.

Chapter
Twenty-Two

That night, as I finished the last of the casserole Evelyn had brought, I reflected on the deep and insidious influence Joel Mackenzie had exerted on Crescent Cove. There were people like Gabi McCormick, who would probably remember her assault for years to come, and the others Joel had harassed, like my aunt. But then there were the ripples of Joel's influence that continued to spread through town even after he was dead, upending the lives of people like Ken and Vivian Liu, and poor Barnabus. How many others had listened to Joel's boasts the way Marek Andrzejewski had and admired him enough to follow his example, taking whatever they wanted from people and leaving them to pick up the pieces? How deep had the rot spread?

These were not happy thoughts. I finally gave up on the casserole and, feeling sick at heart, crawled into bed and stared up at the ceiling for a long time before sleep came.

The next morning was gray and rainy, perfect weather for pottering around the cottage. I decided to tackle the hundreds of books in the library as my next project. They would need to be sorted and then given away. I wondered if the town library would take them. If not, there was an excellent, if small, used bookstore just off Main Street that might want them.

The walls in my aunt's library were covered with built-in bookshelves, even around the huge picture window and comfortably padded window seat that looked out on the gnarled trunk of the oak tree outside. The only exception was the right-hand wall, where the rolltop desk stood—it had been decorated instead with a couple of framed movie posters and a few smaller pieces, mementos from my aunt's travels. I stood for a few minutes and gazed around the room. It was a beautiful space, perfect for curling up with a good book. An old rocking chair sat in one corner next to a bronze-plated stand lamp, and I nudged it with a hand until it started moving. Stepping closer to the wall of books in front of me, I ran my fingers slowly along their spines. Everything in here was ordered meticulously, I remembered, with fiction arranged by author and nonfiction by subject. My aunt's system had made it easy to find whatever you were looking for if you didn't want to just grab a book at random and fall through its pages into a whole new world.

I decided to start with the fiction section, and I had cleared almost half of the first bookcase when I ran into a strange problem—namely, a book that didn't want to move. It was a copy of Dickens's *Great Expectations*, and as I gave it another futile tug, I realized that it was part of a row of books that didn't belong in my aunt's shelving system. Next to Dickens sat *Alice in Wonderland*, then *The Great Gatsby*, *Catcher in the Rye*,

Rebecca, *Sense and Sensibility*, and *Gulliver's Travels*. They were all identical in size, though their colors differed, and I assumed they were part of a boxed set or something, several classics sold together to people who just wanted something to display in their living room. But *Great Expectations* seemed to be stuck to *Alice in Wonderland*. In fact, I soon realized that they were all stuck together, a big, immobile block of books.

Pushing and pulling at them with a mounting sense of frustration, I heard a faint click. Their spines swung out together on hidden hinges to reveal a secret compartment, a hollow space concealed within the seven fake books.

I stared. This was certainly unexpected. Crouching slightly, I peered into the shadowed recess and saw a rectangular object within. I reached in to pull it out and discovered a small wooden box.

I stopped and stared down at the box in my hands. Could this be . . . ? It had to be! I felt my heartrate accelerating as I realized I'd stumbled across the very thing that first Joel and then Marek had wanted so badly.

Carrying it over to the window, I held the box up to the light and examined it closely. It was small, maybe no more than eight inches by six, made of some dark wood that had been carved into elaborate curling designs along the top and sides. Four stubby legs protruded from the bottom. I tried to open it and found that there was no lid—in fact, there were no seams at all.

Stymied, I wandered slowly into the dining room and placed the box on the table before sitting in one of the mismatched farmhouse chairs. My mind began to work furiously.

Joel Mackenzie had learned about a terrible secret buried in Crescent Cove from a woman who used to live here. She'd told him, at the end of her life, that the secret was hidden in a box, and he'd decided that this might be his ticket to a lot of money. He must have known who this woman was—and who her family was, the people still living in Crescent Cove—but hadn't revealed that to Leona or to Marek.

That was where my aunt entered the picture, I guessed. Joel had known, somehow, that she had the box he wanted. Had it been as simple as him walking past the antiques shop and seeing it in the window? Maybe, though I still wasn't sure how he would have recognized it. How else might he have found it? I thought about it for a while before experiencing a flash of insight. Grabbing my phone, I did a quick Google search and . . . there it was. My aunt's shop had a website, filled with professional-looking photos of dozens of objects.

I sat back in my chair. I don't know why this possibility hadn't occurred to me sooner. I should have realized that my aunt would have modernized things a little over the past twenty years. A website made it easier to attract customers, especially outside the tourist season that normally accounted for most of her business.

It didn't take me long to search the inventory displayed on the shop's website and find the very box sitting in front of me. There were photographs taken from several different angles, including the bottom, and the accompanying description was simple enough: *Black walnut puzzle-box, circa 1900, possibly Spanish. Very fine high-relief carving on top and sides. Small mark (maker's mark?) on bottom.*

I turned the box over. Sure enough, something had been carved into the center of the dark wood. It looked like a small crest: a shield containing three stylized fir trees standing side by side, and below them a pair of nautical anchors angled so that their tops overlapped.

Slowly placing the box back on the table, I stared through the window at the forest outside as my mind worked through various possibilities.

Joel learns of a dark secret in Crescent Cove, hidden in an old box. He goes online, searches for local antique dealers to see if he can find anything useful, and stumbles across my aunt's website, filled with helpful photos.

But how had he recognized the box he wanted? I shook my head slowly as I thought it over. Maybe the old woman had described it to him; the carvings were pretty distinctive, after all. Or maybe the maker's mark was familiar.

Convinced that he's found what he needs, he drives all the way here from Hamilton, believing that if he can get his hands on the box, he can put the screws to whoever wants to keep this secret concealed. He settles at the Seahorse Motel, visits my aunt . . .

My thoughts trailed off. He'd visited my aunt, and shortly thereafter she was dead. She'd balked at helping him, finally sending Barnabus away and closing up her shop. Why?

An answer came to me almost immediately: because she'd known whomever Joel intended to blackmail. Of course she had. Crescent Cove was tiny, and Marguerite had lived here most of her adult life. She would have been outraged at the thought of Joel trying to harm someone in her community, and probably even more so because the box had been in her shop. So she'd tried to help . . . and wound up dead.

My hands were shaking as I dialed Jack's number. No response. With a frustrated grunt, I scooped up the carved box, headed out to my car, and made a beeline for Main Street.

Chapter
Twenty-Three

Less than ten minutes later, I was knocking firmly on the door to Forget-Me-Not Antiques. "Barnabus?" I called as I peered through the wavy glass panes in the door. "I know you're in there. Let me in. It's Luke!"

The door jerked open a couple of inches, and a gimlet eye stared out at me. Not the bruised one, at least, but the overall effect was almost as off-putting. "What do you want?" Barnabus demanded.

"I need to ask you something." Without waiting for him to let me in, I pushed the door open over his protests and squeezed through, the box cradled to my chest.

"You can't just barge in here!"

"Of course I can," I snapped. "I own the damn place."

The younger man stepped back and folded his arms tightly across his chest. His face was still puffy in places, the bruises a little more pronounced today than they'd been yesterday, but he'd forgone the sweats and T-shirt and was dressed in a white dress shirt, dark-red velvet trousers, and a paisley ascot. His dark hair brushed his shoulders, and he'd found another pair of glasses to replace the ones mangled by Marek Andrzejewski. "What do you want?"

"Do you recognize this box?" I held it out for his inspection. Around us, the shop was eerily silent.

Barnabus shuffled closer and peered down at the item in question. "Maybe," he finally admitted begrudgingly. "Why do you want to know?"

"Because I think this box is why my aunt is dead. And I think it's also why you were attacked yesterday." His eyes narrowed. "So it's really, really important that you try and remember everything you can."

He reached out and took the box from me, holding it delicately between both hands. "I remember this," he said slowly as he turned it from one side to the next. "Marguerite found it sitting in the back and decided it should be out here." He glanced up at me for a moment. "We have a ton of stuff back there, things that people bring in or that we find at estate sales. A lot of it isn't worth the space it would take up out front. But she liked the look of this. The only problem was that we couldn't figure out how to open it, or even if it's supposed to open at all. That's why she'd left it in the back for . . . however long she'd had it."

"Did she know who brought it in?"

He shook his head. "No, she couldn't remember, though she thought it had been jumbled in with a bunch of stuff." He shrugged. "It's a beautiful piece and in great shape, but without a way to open it, she wasn't sure it would sell. She asked me to photograph it and post it online, though, because you never know."

I chewed absently on my lower lip as I considered this. "Did anyone express an interest in it?"

Barnabus shrugged again. "She had it in the window. One day, right before I left to go to Saskatoon, I noticed it was gone. I asked her if it had sold after all, but she didn't really answer. There was no record of a sale in the books, so I assumed she'd decided to put it back in storage." With a flick of his wrists, he turned the box over. "It was funny, though. After I finished photographing it, I caught her studying this maker's mark."

"Right, I saw that as well. She was interested in it?"

"Maybe. I pointed it out to her while I was writing up the description, and she seemed . . . puzzled by it."

I peered down at the small crest. "Do you know what it is? What it means?"

Barnabus thrust the box at me so abruptly that I fumbled to grab it from him. "No idea. Are we done here?"

"Sure," I mumbled, only half paying attention as I stared down at the box in my hands. "Thanks."

A long, chilly silence fell. "You're not right for him, you know," Barnabus suddenly announced.

I blinked several times as I looked back at him. "Who?"

"Sergeant Munro." His tone had now veered toward openly hostile. "I saw the way you were all over him at the party. And in here, yesterday, the way you spoke to him. I saw that too."

"Wait . . . what? *All over him*?"

"Do you deny it?"

"Uh, yeah, I do." I stared at him, heat rising in my cheeks. "All I did at the party was talk to him."

Barnabus snorted so violently that he had to readjust his glasses. "Oh, please. You were practically drooling."

I paused as I tried to process what was happening here. "You're jealous," I finally said wonderingly.

"I am *not*."

"No, you totally are. You were making googly eyes at Jack at the party, weren't you?" A savage kind of glee rose up inside me. "Oh, wow. You're crushing on Jack and warning me to step back from your man. That's adorable."

He was practically vibrating with indignation as he snarled, "You shut up."

Cradling the box to my chest with one hand, I lifted the other in a gesture of surrender. "Jack and I are just friends. Or we were, a long time ago. I don't live in Crescent Cove, and I'm certainly not going to steal your crush. Okay?"

Barnabus gave me one last furious glare before turning and stalking away.

I watched him go and shook my head. The idea that Jack and I might . . . that he and I were . . . well, it was ridiculous. As soon as the authorities solved Joel's murder, I'd be on a plane back to Toronto while Jack and Barney settled down and adopted eight babies and spent the rest of their days gazing adoringly into each other's eyes.

My petty satisfaction at Barney's discomfiture suddenly evaporated, leaving me oddly bereft. He'd disappeared into the back room, and I thought briefly of trying to apologize—he'd had a rough couple of days, after all—but then decided that probably wouldn't help. So I exited the shop, the box still cradled against my chest, and considered my next steps.

I needed to identify the design carved into the bottom of the box; that was clear. And where better to start than the library?

Resolute, I pulled up the hood on my raincoat and walked quickly up Main Street to Sanderson Avenue, and in almost no time at all I was bounding up the front steps to the library. Inside, it was hushed and largely empty as rain tapped against the stained-glass windows set into the ceiling. There was only one young person working behind the circulation desk as I approached.

"Hi. Is Samuel in?" I asked.

They nodded and looked up at me through a pair of purple-tinted glasses. "He should be up on the second floor, doing some reshelving. There's just the two of us here most days," they added, a little apologetically.

"Great, thanks."

Trailing a hand along the polished wooden banister, I made my way up to the mezzanine that formed the second floor. I saw a couple of people sitting at tables and leafing through books as I wandered around, and it didn't take me long to find Samuel. He had a metal cart half-full of books next to him as he rearranged a shelf that stood beneath one of the tall windows.

"Hey there," I greeted him, and he gave a convulsive start, as if I'd fired off an air horn next to his ear. As he whipped around to face me, I saw that he was dressed in what probably qualified as casual attire, meaning that he'd forgone his bow tie.

"Oh!" he gasped. "Oh. It's you. Hello, Luke." He pressed a hand to his chest as if fearing a heart attack.

"Sorry to startle you. I just wanted to ask you a quick question." Holding the box in my hands, I turned it over. "Do you recognize this design?"

Samuel stepped a little closer and bent at the waist to peer at it. "It looks like a crest of some kind," he murmured. "But I can't quite make out . . ." He trailed off as he tilted his head to first one side and then the other. "Huh."

I waited expectantly.

His gaze shifted to meet mine before he turned back to the bookshelf. "I'm sorry, but no. I don't recognize it."

I studied the back of his stocky form. "You're sure?"

"Yes, yes, perfectly sure."

Well, I now knew one thing for certain: Samuel was a terrible liar.

"Okay, thanks for taking a look."

He waved a hand in an absent sort of way and I left him to his reshelving, walking back downstairs and then outside with the box still in my hands. I'd parked a couple of blocks away, and by the time I reached my car, I found myself at a metaphorical dead end. I believed that Samuel had recognized the mark, but for some reason he was reluctant to share what he knew. So, with a frustrating lack of clear answers, I decided to return to the cottage and continue the frankly depressing dismantling of my aunt's life. The cottage would need to go on the market eventually—assuming Jack ever allowed me to leave town—and I wanted to sort through her things myself rather than ask Daisy or my aunt's lawyers to do it.

Back at the cottage, I decided to relocate my aunt's clever fake books to one of the bookcases on the other side of her study, where it would be camouflaged, then stashed the box back inside. Better safe than sorry, I reasoned, since someone was still looking for it. I spent the rest of the afternoon packing up what remained of the fiction section, and by the time evening arrived, my back was killing me and I was too tired to worry about mysterious boxes or cryptic crests. After treating myself to a long, hot bath, I curled up in bed and was asleep almost before my head hit the pillow.

Chapter
Twenty-Four

The next morning dawned cool and clear. I stood on the front porch, a mug of coffee cradled in my hands, and contemplated the sweeping vista in front of me. A brisk walk along the beach was exactly what I needed to clear away the cobwebs, I decided, so after taking a few minutes to dress warmly, I descended the rickety stairs to the beach below and found it deserted apart from a few sea gulls. Waves lapped quietly against the dark sand as I paused for a moment to gaze out across the water.

When I heard the first gunshot, I didn't realize what it was. The loud *crack* reverberated across the beach, sending gulls spiraling into the air in a squawking panic. I thought the noise might have originated out at sea, perhaps coming from a passing boat, but when I shaded my eyes and looked eastward, I saw nothing. My brain was still processing this when the second shot came, and this time I heard the distinctive whine of a bullet ricocheting off a nearby rock. Chips of stone and a small cloud of dust exploded from where the bullet had struck maybe two feet to my left, and that's when I understood that someone was trying to kill me.

Without pausing to think, I hurled myself to the right, landing with jarring force on the rocky shore. My elbow hit something hard with a sudden spike of pain, but it barely registered. As I tried to scramble to my hands and knees, I threw a glance skyward and caught the barest glimpse of someone standing on the bluff above me, dressed in black and pointing something in my direction. Sunlight glinted on dark metal—a gun.

I threw myself forward, toward the face of the bluff itself, as another shot rang out. My fingers tangled in exposed roots and the few hardy plants that had managed to survive in near-vertical conditions, and I pressed myself against the dirt wall. My heartbeat thundered in my ears as I waited for more gunshots, but I was now out of sight to whoever was up there. They would need to either slide down the thirty feet of exposed soil to the rocky shore below—a near-suicidal feat—or take the stairs that led from the cottage. I stayed where I was, my gaze fastened on the stairs more than a hundred feet along the beach, listening for movement overhead, but I couldn't hear anything over my frantic breathing and the continued cries of the gulls still circling overhead.

I have no idea how long I stood there, pressed against the damp earth and shaking uncontrollably. It wasn't until an elderly man and his dog wandered past that I realized the danger was gone. He asked if I was okay, and that's when I collapsed onto a nearby log of driftwood and buried my face in my hands. His dog ambled over and snuffled at my ears, which I found oddly comforting.

Eventually, I managed to paw my phone out of my pocket and call Jack. "Please pick up, please pick up," I muttered as the line rang several times, and when he finally answered, I almost wept with relief. In a shaking voice, I told him what happened.

"Are you safe where you are?" he asked tersely, almost before I'd finished speaking.

"I . . . I think so."

"Good. Stay put. We'll be there in five minutes." Then he hung up.

The older gentleman, whose name was Henry, kindly offered to wait with me until the police arrived, and I spent the next few minutes hugging his very patient golden retriever while she licked my face. It wasn't long before we heard sirens approaching from somewhere beyond the top of the bluff, and then Jack's voice calling out a rapid series of instructions. Boots thumped swiftly against wood, and I turned to see him clambering down the steps from the cottage, the whole staircase vibrating under his weight.

"Are you all right?" he asked as he strode closer. He was wearing the tactical vest I'd first seen when he arrived to investigate Joel's death, and his firearm was holstered prominently on his hip.

In reply, I stood and stumbled over to him, throwing my arms around his solid, comforting bulk and leaning into him as hard as I could. After a momentary hesitation, I felt his arms encircle me in return. Part of me felt a little embarrassed—what would my new friend Henry think of me flinging myself at Jack like this?—but I was in desperate need of comfort, and once I got to my feet, I discovered that my legs were having a hard time supporting me.

"Sorry," I mumbled into his chest. "That was just . . ."

"Really scary," he finished quietly. "I know." One big hand made slow circles against my back. "Are you injured?"

I shook my head. "I banged my elbow, but that's all. They missed me. Though not for lack of trying."

He gave me a minute to collect myself, and then he gently disengaged himself and asked for a detailed account of the shooting. I was showing him where the second bullet had struck a large rock when a female voice called down from above: "Sarge? All clear up here."

I looked up and saw Cassie silhouetted against the sky. For just a moment, she looked so like my attacker that a visceral jolt of terror rushed through my body and my legs almost folded beneath me.

With a sincere thank-you to Henry and a final pat for Violet the golden retriever, I allowed Jack to escort me back up the stairs and into the cottage. I'd locked the front door when I left on my walk, and my hands were shaking so badly that it took me forever to get the new key into the lock. It looked like everyone from the RCMP detachment was there, and all of them were armed. Once I finally got the door open, they smoothly took charge of me, and I soon found myself sitting at the dining room table with a glass of water in front of me and Jack seated to my right. Cassie hovered nearby, notebook open and pen in hand as she took my statement. The other two had gone back outside to search the area.

"You're absolutely certain you didn't recognize the shooter?" she asked, her dark countenance solemn.

"I caught just a quick glance," I told her with a shake of my head. "I was too busy running for cover."

She nodded. "Good instincts. Could you tell if they were male or female? Short or tall?"

I thought about it, but everything was a confused blur. "I . . . don't know. It was hard to tell from my perspective down on the beach. They were wearing something dark and baggy with a hood, though." A flash of memory came to me. "And sunglasses. Big sunglasses."

Jack watched me in silence, his concern evident in the deep crease between his eyebrows, while Cassie jotted down a few notes. "Do you know why someone might want to attack you?" she asked eventually.

I glanced at Jack and then cleared my throat. "Possibly," I said, but before I could continue, Carson clomped through the front door and across the living room.

"We found some tracks in the tall grass close to the edge of the bluff, Sarge," he reported as he stopped next to the table. "Someone was definitely standing up there. It looks like they came out of the trees just to the north of the property here and went back the same way, but we had a hard time finding their trail in the woods. We did find these, though." He held out a latex-gloved hand in which rested three metal objects. It took me a moment to identify them as bullet casings. "All in roughly the same spot. I'd say they're nine-millimeter."

Jack tilted his head to study the casings, then nodded. "Any sign of a vehicle?"

"Nope. They probably parked on Ravenwood Lane and cut down through the trees. It would have taken them two, maybe three minutes to get from there to the edge of the bluff, and that stretch of road can't be seen from any of the nearby properties. Ranjit's gone to canvass the neighbors, though, just in case someone was out walking or driving or something."

With another nod, Jack turned his attention back to me, but before either of us could say anything, the walkie handset clipped to his tactical vest let out a burst of static and then something that might have been a word. He grimaced apologetically as he stood and headed outside through the French doors, leaving the two junior officers staring at me, but it wasn't long before he reappeared in the kitchen.

"We need to move," he said to the other officers. "One of you radio Ranjit and tell him we'll pick him up on the road." Both of them started toward the back door as I stood up from the table. It was clear from Jack's expression that something was wrong, but all he said to me was, "Stay inside and lock the doors. Don't open them to anyone but me. I'll be back as soon as I can."

I nodded jerkily and watched as he strode out into the back garden and then to the two RCMP vehicles parked on the other side of the picket fence. In moments they had reversed and then sped away, lights strobing, and I was on my own.

Dutifully, I made sure both the front and back doors were locked. Then I started pacing a nervous loop of the cottage's square floor plan, pausing occasionally to peer through the windows. I'd always liked the fact that trees enveloped the house on three sides; it felt cozy somehow. Today, though, I eyed their shadowed depths with suspicion and no small amount of anxiety. What if the mysterious shooter came back? Clearly, they were either brazen or desperate enough to attack me in broad daylight—I didn't think they would hesitate to hop over the fence and finish the job if they had the chance. My imagination swirled with black-clad figures skulking up to the cottage, kicking in the door, raising a gun . . .

I came to a dead halt in the middle of the living room and squeezed my eyes closed. "Stop that," I chastised myself aloud. "You're fine. Everything will be okay." I took several deep, albeit shaky, breaths and rubbed my sweaty palms on my jeans. Then I purposefully switched my mind back into investigation mode and got to thinking.

If someone really wanted to harm or kill me, they'd had plenty of opportunities to do so since I arrived in Crescent Cove. I'd gone on solitary walks before this morning. So why now? What had changed?

The box, I thought at once. I'd found the box. Except . . . finding it wasn't the issue, was it? I'd *showed* it to people. I'd asked both Barnabus and Samuel to look at that mysterious crest. If Barney was to be believed, he'd already seen it when he photographed the box for my aunt's website—though all I had was his word on that. I hadn't considered him a suspect before, but I had to now. Was it possible that he had recognized the box when it first appeared and then . . . what, persuaded my aunt to hide it from Joel Mackenzie? Eliminated her when she started asking questions, then decided to do the same to me when I showed up waving the box around? It was a chilling thought. Had he really gone to Saskatoon as he'd claimed? I doubted the police had bothered to check. And of course, he already disliked me. I could see him making the cold-blooded decision to kill me before I told anyone what I knew.

And then there was Samuel. He'd obviously lied when he insisted he didn't recognize the crest. He'd been humiliated and harassed by Joel, and I believed him as capable of an impulsive, violent act as anyone, sweater-vests notwithstanding. Similarly, despite what Jack had told me, I hadn't discarded Chris McCormick yet as a viable suspect. We'd only interacted once, but he'd proven himself to be both aggressive and angry. Put a gun in the hand of someone like that and they're going to use it. Maybe this morning's attack hadn't been about the box at all—maybe Chris had just wanted to make an extremely scary and violent point.

I shook my head slowly as I considered the possibilities. Without more evidence, any of them could be true, or none of them. I just had to hope that Jack would figure this out before one of these people succeeded in bumping me off.

Chapter
Twenty-Five

With that cheerful thought bouncing around in my skull, I flung myself onto the comfy old sofa and stared bleakly at the fireplace. All around me, the cottage was still and quiet. It was strange to think that, at one time, this place had been a refuge for me, somewhere I could escape the chilly, conditional beneficence that my parents thought of as affection. My aunt Marguerite had been cast from a different mold than her brother; she'd been a warm, loving presence in my life at a time when I desperately needed it. And now her home had become a refuge once again, a place of safety in a time of darkness. My heart ached from missing her.

I stayed there for a long time, alternating between fond memories of my summers in Crescent Cove and panic-inducing speculation about the whereabouts of my would-be killer. It was late afternoon, the skies beginning to cloud over, when I heard a brisk knock at the front door. I started and rolled off the sofa onto my feet, then padded quietly to the bay window and peered outside. Jack was standing on the porch, his expression grim. Hastening to the door, I unlocked it and pulled it open.

"Something's happened, hasn't it?" I greeted him.

Removing his hat, Jack nodded once and waited for me to move aside before stepping across the threshold. I shut the door behind him, briefly aware of his woodsy aftershave as we crowded close to one another.

Turning to face me, he said tersely, "Samuel Beckinridge is dead."

I felt my stomach plummet. "How?" I finally managed to ask.

"He was shot in his home this morning. A neighbor heard something and went to investigate. Someone killed him while he was eating breakfast."

I processed this as I looked up at Jack. He had dark circles under his eyes and a hard twist to his mouth, signs of the strain these past few days must have placed on him. "Come in," I said after a moment, touching his shoulder. "I'll make some coffee. And then I have a lot to tell you."

I led him into the dining room and gestured to the table, then went into the kitchen to brew a fresh pot of coffee. While the machine gurgled and steamed, I retrieved the box from its compartment in the library and deposited it in front of Jack.

"Is that what I think it is?" he asked, studying it with a faint frown.

"I think so." I left him to examine it while I waited for the coffee to finish brewing. He was still trying to open the box when, a few minutes later, I returned with two steaming mugs, milk, and sugar.

"Where did you find this?" he asked as he added milk to his coffee, and so I told him. It took me a while to relate everything I'd learned and now suspected, and as I spoke he just watched me, his hazel eyes thoughtful.

"Until you told me he was dead," I concluded, "Samuel was one of my chief suspects."

He snorted. "The librarian? The guy who had a different bow tie for each day of the week?"

I shrugged and met his sardonic gaze with a level stare of my own. "I don't think the person who killed Joel Mackenzie is an outsider. They've been living in this town for years, probably. Do you know anyone in Crescent Cove who looks or acts like a murderer?"

Jack conceded the point with a sour grunt. "And this?" He tapped the box in front of him with a finger. "You really think the key to all this is locked away in here?"

"I do, yeah. That box is why Joel Mackenzie died. And I think it's why someone ran down my aunt as well."

The stern line of his mouth softened a little at that. "Luke, we don't know that."

"We don't," I agreed, staring down at my hands where they clasped my coffee mug. "But I still believe it's true."

Silence fell. I looked back up at Jack and found him watching me with an unreadable expression. "Was Samuel shot with the same gun that shot at me?" I asked.

"We found similar casings at the scene," he said with a nod. "We need to do full ballistics testing to be sure, but my guess is that they're the same."

"And he was shot before his attacker came here?"

Another nod. "It looks that way. A couple of people saw a dark-blue or gray car driving away from his house early this morning. Those sightings are the first real break we've gotten." He offered me a flinty smile. "Our murderer is getting sloppy."

"Or desperate," I pointed out, to which he shrugged.

"The result is the same. They're starting to make mistakes, which means we have a chance to find them."

Hopefully before I wind up dead, I thought to myself.

Jack frowned at the box. "Do you have a hammer here?"

"Probably," I said slowly. "Somewhere. But we're not breaking open that box."

"Why not? You said it yourself: the answers we need are inside this thing."

I shook my head. "What if we destroy whatever's inside?" He sighed, and I added, "C'mon. We're two reasonably intelligent people. I'm sure we can figure it out between us."

We got to work, pressing every inch of the fanciful, swirling designs carved into the top and sides in search of a hidden button or catch, tilting it this way and that, peering at it intently. Nothing happened. The box seemed to be a solid piece of wood. Shaking it produced no sound of anything inside, and if there were seams that might indicate a lid or drawer, they were cunningly concealed by the exterior carvings. Jack finally resorted to thumping his fist against it a few times, more out of frustration than any hope that it would work.

Dusk began to settle over the cottage, and eventually I paused to turn on some lights and make us each a peanut butter sandwich. Jack checked in with Cassie at the detachment office and reported back that Samuel's body was in Campbell River awaiting a full autopsy tomorrow morning. Tracing the mysterious car seen around the time of his death was proceeding slowly, as neither of the two witnesses had been able to read the license plates. I pointed out that, on the bright side, at least no one else had turned up dead, but Jack didn't seem to find that very funny.

After my ill-advised attempt at humor, we sat opposite each other and quietly chewed our sandwiches. "Not much of a cook, huh?" Jack finally observed, one side of his mouth quirked upward in a sardonic little smirk. He'd removed his tactical vest and draped it across the back of another chair, and now he leaned back, seeming entirely at ease, and dusted a few crumbs from the front of his uniform shirt.

"I cook," I responded, a trifle defensively. "I just didn't feel like making anything fancy."

"Uh-huh." The corners of his eyes crinkled a little as he smiled. "Sure."

I threw a piece of crust at him. "Let me guess—you can cook like a dream because you're perfect at everything."

"Hardly. Though I *can* make a mean pot roast."

I studied him for a moment. It was good to see his habitual seriousness fade a little. "And what about your boyfriend?" I asked casually. "Does he cook?"

Jack's dark eyebrows rose in surprise. "My boyfriend?" he repeated.

"Yeah. I assume you're spoken for. How could anyone resist falling for this?" I gestured meaningfully at him. "I mean, the uniform alone . . ."

He snorted and folded his brawny arms across his chest. "I don't have a boyfriend, Luke."

"Really? That's surprising." I kept my tone light, but somewhere deep inside I felt a warmth begin to suffuse my body.

He shrugged and said, "It's a small place. There aren't a lot of . . . possibilities here."

"Apart from Kieran Collingwood, you mean," I murmured, and his expression darkened.

"Let's not bring that up again."

"Well, I think you're pretty amazing," I said. "Even if you did accuse me of murder."

His lips twitched. "I never accused you of murder."

"You basically did. Admit it: for a while there, you were just itching to throw me in jail."

He shot me an amused glance. "Only because you deserve to be locked up. You're a menace to society."

I assumed an expression of wounded outrage. "How dare you!"

Jack laughed quietly and shook his head. "This is nice," he said, after a pause. "Kind of like old times. Even down to the terrible peanut butter sandwiches."

This time, my outrage was real. "*Terrible?*"

"You always use way too much peanut butter. It's like eating glue."

With an indignant harrumph, I got up and grabbed his empty plate. "Well then, see if I ever feed you again," I growled, before taking my own plate and stalking into the kitchen.

When I returned, Jack was still smiling. "It's strange, being back here after so long," he mused as he looked around.

"You're telling me."

"I loved going through your aunt's library when we were kids." His smile turned wistful. "She was pretty great, wasn't she?"

I tried to speak but couldn't get anything past the sudden lump in my throat, so I just nodded instead.

Another silence fell between us, and when I looked up from the table, I found Jack watching me. "Are you really going to walk away from this?" he asked quietly when our eyes met. "Again?"

I swallowed convulsively. "This?" I repeated huskily.

He gestured with one big hand. "This house. This town." He touched the center of his chest, then pointed at me. "This."

I stared at him for a long time. "I'm not sure there's anything here for me," I finally said, my voice barely above a whisper. "Not anymore."

Jack's gaze was direct, almost challenging, as he leaned forward and said, "You'll never know if you don't stick around."

There were so many things I wanted to say in response to that, but I never got the chance. From the kitchen came the sudden sound of breaking glass. Jack's head whipped around and he bolted to his feet, reaching for the gun still holstered at his side. I stood as well, my heart pounding now for a different reason, as a familiar voice said clearly, "Don't move, Sergeant Munro."

A figure moved into view, a gloved hand coming up to push back the dark hood covering their head. But I didn't need to see their face to know who had broken into the cottage.

It was Evelyn Collingwood, and she was holding a gun.

Chapter Twenty-Six

"Place your gun on the floor," Evelyn instructed Jack, her low voice tight with tension. She was wearing a black hoodie and dark jeans, her silver hair pulled back into a ponytail and her turquoise eyes cold. Those same eyes flicked to me just for a second as she waited for Jack to comply, and in them I saw nothing but steely determination.

Moving very slowly, Jack unholstered his gun and then crouched to place it on the woven rag rug positioned beneath the dining table. "Kick it to me," Evelyn said as he straightened, and he did so, sending the gun skittering across the floor until it came up against one of her muddy hiking boots. "Thank you for being reasonable, Sergeant."

"You're not leaving me much of a choice, Evelyn." His deep voice was calm, almost preternaturally steady, as he raised his hands to show that they were empty.

"No. I'm sorry about this, but you've come much too close to my little secret." She glanced at the table—no, I realized, at the box resting in its center. "You really should have left things alone, Luke dear," she went on, turning her gaze on me.

I tried to swallow and found my throat dry as sandpaper. "I couldn't do that," I told her hoarsely.

Unexpectedly, she smiled. "I suppose you couldn't. The dogged investigative journalist. Marguerite would be so proud of you."

"Except she's dead," I observed, my voice shaking. Her smile vanished. "Did you kill her?"

A long silence descended on the three of us. It was raining, I realized belatedly as I heard the drops tapping against the window behind me. Evelyn didn't move from where she stood, eight or nine feet away from Jack and me. I couldn't stop staring at the gun in her gloved hand, its dark metal seeming to absorb the cheerful light surrounding us.

"I don't know how Marguerite ended up with that box," she finally said. "I don't know who removed it from the estate. A servant, perhaps. My father had hidden it away, you see."

"Your father?" I asked incredulously, and she nodded once.

"Yes. But it was my grandmother, Leticia Collingwood, who met Joel in Toronto. She was over a hundred years old by that point, and probably senile." Her voice, normally so melodious, roughened as she went on. "He laughed when he told me how confused she was, how she sometimes thought he was my father, her dear son. I never met her. She left Crescent Cove before I was born and moved to Toronto. But at the very end of her life, she had the misfortune to meet Joel Mackenzie, and talked to him about the shameful past that haunts my family."

My mind spun as I tried to understand. "And the box . . ."

"Marguerite dug it out from the junk piling up in her store. She recognized the Collingwood crest immediately, of course. It used to be everywhere at the estate, and she spent a lot of time there when we were younger." Her smile this time was faintly supercilious. "We Collingwoods made our fortune first in timber, and then in shipbuilding. My great-great-grandfather commissioned a family crest that reflected that fact."

I closed my eyes for a moment. Of course. Trees and anchors.

"So Marguerite had the box," Jack said calmly. "What happened then?"

Evelyn let out a long sigh. "She told me about it, but not before that young man who worked for her photographed it and displayed it online. She didn't see the Collingwood crest until after it went up for sale. And that was the problem." She turned to look at me, and her expression was earnest as she said, "Had she noticed it and told me *before* she put in on her website, I could have gotten it back from her and none of this would have happened. But she didn't. She thought I wouldn't care. The estate is overflowing with knickknacks, after all. What did it matter if a small box went up for sale?" Her voice tightened. "And meanwhile, Joel Mackenzie had cajoled and weaseled his way into my grandmother's confidence. He knew that she was a Collingwood, and that her son—my father—was at the center of a terrible secret. She must have mentioned the box before she died, and so he did his research, the odious little vermin. When he found the photos of the box online, he knew what it was. What it contained. And he came to Crescent Cove." I was startled to see unshed tears shining in her eyes. "It was all just a terrible, terrible series of coincidences."

My fists clenched at my sides as I listened. "Coincidences didn't kill my aunt," I told her, my voice raw. "You did. Didn't you?"

She flinched, and for a moment the gun wavered in her grasp. But then she steeled herself with obvious effort. "Marguerite tried to help me, once she knew that Joel was up to no good. She hid the box away, even closed up the shop so that she could avoid him. But then she started asking me why he wanted this box so badly, and I knew . . . I knew she wouldn't stop wondering. Wouldn't stop asking questions." She gazed at me sadly. "You're just like her in that regard."

Across the table from me, Jack shifted slightly. "You're admitting to Marguerite's death?" he asked.

"Yes." She was as calm as him now. "I begged her to give me the box. Joel had already contacted me, demanding money in return for his silence. Not much, at least at first, but I knew he would keep asking for more. If I had the box, I could send him packing. But Marguerite told me it would be safest where it was while Joel was snooping around. She refused to give it to me. Even though it was mine, even though I *had* to have it! I drove out here one night to . . . to talk to her, or confront her, I don't know. I was out of my mind. And there she was, walking along the side of the road. I didn't even think about it. I stomped on the accelerator and drove her down. I thought I could run to the cottage, take what belonged to me, and leave. But . . ." Evelyn trailed off and closed her eyes for a moment. "But then I realized what I'd done. I was horrified.

Heartbroken. So I drove back to the estate and hid the car in one of the old stables."

Icy tendrils crept through me as I listened. Involuntarily, I wrapped my arms around myself as I stared at the woman who had murdered my aunt. I couldn't stop picturing her final moments, dying on the edge of the road just a few hundred feet from the house she'd loved. It had been a cruel and senseless end to a good life.

"How could you?" I demanded, my words choked with rage. Without thinking, I took a step closer to her. In response, she leveled the gun straight at my face.

"I'm sorry," she said as I halted. "I truly am. But she should have listened to me."

Jack said, very quietly, "Luke. Don't."

I turned to look at him. Something fierce burned in his eyes, and his jaw was set with a steely determination. In that moment, I knew he would do everything he could to end this and keep me safe. A tiny spark of warmth flared deep inside my chest, beating back the cold that threatened to engulf me. I met his gaze and then slowly eased back a step.

Jack gave me an infinitesimal nod in return before turning his attention back to Evelyn. "What about Joel Mackenzie?"

She scowled, the expression curiously out of place on her patrician features. "I think Marguerite's death spooked him. He'd been bothering her, stopping by the store and the cottage, trying to get the box from her." I remembered Barnabus saying that my aunt had been acting strangely before she died. Presumably, this was why. "After she died, I hoped he would give up and leave Crescent Cove. This place was locked up and so was her shop, when they weren't filled with lawyers and police and all kinds of people coming and going, settling her affairs. It was too risky to search for the box. And then I heard from Daisy Simpson that you were expected in town." She looked at me as she said that. "She told me that you intended to sell both the cottage and the shop, and I knew I was running out of time. After you encountered Joel here, I assume he realized the same thing."

"But how did you know he would be here that night?" I asked.

"Because he told me." She laughed in disbelief. "Can you imagine? He was drunk, of course. He was always drunk. He called me to boast that my secret was going to be his, and then he would bleed me dry for all the trouble I'd caused him. So I came out here and settled myself in the woods to wait. I was there for hours. I nearly froze to death. But finally he showed up, stumbling through the trees. I'd already found the perfect rock while I was waiting." She lifted her other hand, fingers curled as if still holding it. "I could smell the whiskey on him at twenty paces, so it wasn't difficult to sneak up behind him in the back garden and hit him on the head as hard as I could. Then I shoved him into the pond." She smiled, an expression of quiet satisfaction. It made my skin crawl.

"And then you entered the cottage, didn't you?" I guessed, and she shot me a shrewd glance.

"I did, yes. I came in through the back, just like I did tonight, though I didn't have to break any windows. I still had a key. I intended to search the cottage, but then I heard you moving around and panicked. I left and hid in the woods again, in

245

case you decided to investigate, but when nothing happened, I made my way back to my car, which was parked on the other side of the woods. Before I got there, though, I found Joel's truck on that same little road. I decided to search it in case he'd left anything incriminating, but all I found was this." She waved the gun almost playfully.

Jack and I exchanged a glance. "What about his phone?" he asked.

"Oh, that. Yes, I was afraid you'd find my number in there, so I took it from his pocket before I left and threw it into the woods. I should have just taken it with me, but I wasn't thinking clearly. My blood was up." She gave us both an apologetic smile, as if we were grading her on her performance.

"Then you went to the Seahorse Motel the next morning," I said.

She nodded. "You're quick. Yes. I needed to know if Joel had kept anything that might tie him to me. I couldn't ask Silas for the key, but he was blaring that awful music of his, so I knew he wouldn't hear the gun. It made such a racket! Terribly exciting, though. I was in the middle of searching Joel's room when I heard a car pull up outside." She gave me a faint frown. "It was you, Luke. That's when I started to suspect that you might become a problem."

I gave her a cold smile but said nothing.

"Fortunately, I was able to leave while you were in the motel office. And then I watched from the trees across the road while your constable arrived, Sergeant Munro, and Luke escaped just as I had." She tilted her head to one side as she considered me. "Did you find anything in there?"

"Proof that he was blackmailing someone," I replied shortly.

Evelyn let out a quiet, "Ah." Her eyes were cool as she paused. "I'd already contrived to run into you the day before, after you found Joel's body," she finally said. "I needed an excuse to get back into this house."

"So you came calling with a casserole," I finished, shaking my head. "I remember thinking you were gone an awfully long time before you showed me that album. You were searching, I presume."

She shrugged. "Not well enough, apparently." Her gaze lingered once more on the box sitting innocuously on the table. "Where was it, out of curiosity?" she asked as her attention returned to me.

"Go to hell."

She *tsk*ed softly. "That's not very polite, Luke."

"Yeah, well, I'm not feeling too sociable at the moment." I glanced at Jack and saw him shift again, bringing him closer to his tactical vest where it hung across the back of the chair. In an effort to distract Evelyn, I moved forward as well and watched her eyes narrow. "I know why you killed Samuel Beckinridge," I prodded her. "He recognized the crest."

"Yes," she agreed. "He called me as soon as you left the library. I mean, he was the town historian. Of course he recognized it. More importantly, though, his call confirmed that you'd found the box somehow. Unfortunately, like Marguerite, he started asking inconvenient questions, and I knew I couldn't trust him to stay quiet. He was a nice man but a terrible liar."

"And so you tried to kill me."

She offered me another apologetic look. "It was an act of desperation."

Out of the corner of my eye, I saw Jack ease forward another couple of inches. Evelyn's attention wavered from me—she'd seen it too—so I blurted out, "What is this all about? What's this terrible secret that's already cost three lives?"

She watched me for a long moment, her features impassive. "I might as well tell you," she decided at last, "since neither of you will survive, I'm afraid." Keeping her gun trained on me, she started to shuffle backward, into the kitchen. "There's going to be a terrible fire. It will devastate the town, losing both of you like that. But we'll recover." She felt her way around the small island and moved toward the gas range, turning her head just for a few seconds as she twisted the knobs to start the gas flowing. One by one, the burners sputtered to life and began to burn with a fierce blue light.

With Evelyn distracted, Jack managed to reach the walkie handset attached to the shoulder of his tactical vest. He rapidly pressed the button on its side, keeping an eye on her as he did so. I felt my armpits prickle with sweat as I waited for her to turn and see him. The tension was unbearable. But as the final burner flared into flame, Jack let go of the walkie and retreated half a step, sparing me the briefest of glances as he did so. I tried to feel reassured, but his expression was inscrutable.

With the burners going, Evelyn turned back to us. "I've never seen what's inside the box myself," she said as she slowly approached once more. "I only know what my papa told me when I was a girl. He died young, from cancer, but he couldn't leave me until he'd confessed the truth." She drifted out of the kitchen, past Jack's gun still lying on the floor, and neared the dining table, her gaze fixed on the box. With a sharp movement of her own weapon, she made Jack step back several paces so that she could take the box and then retreat back to the kitchen island with it cradled against her chest. "I must admit, however, that I'm curious to see its contents before they're destroyed along with everything else here." Moving with something approaching reverence, she placed the box on the polished granite countertop and stood looking down at it for several long moments. When she spoke again, her voice was soft, and I had to strain to hear her over the quiet hiss of the gas burners.

"His father, my grandfather, was Adolphus Van Alstyne, a descendent of one of the oldest families in New York. He married into the Collingwoods when his fortunes fell into decline and took my grandmother's surname, as is the tradition in our family. My husband did the same when we married." Her mouth twisted. "Adolphus was a man of enormous appetites, by all accounts, and his wife—my grandmother Leticia—turned a blind eye to his depredations until he got one of the servants pregnant. Then, rather than endure the scandal and humiliation, my grandmother concocted a simple ruse. She and the unfortunate parlor maid left Crescent Cove for several months, and when my grandmother returned—alone—she presented my grandfather with his heir: my dear papa. She raised him as her own son and never once hinted that he was a lowborn bastard. But we can assume she made her husband's life hell for what he'd done, and in time Adolphus grew to despise the boy as a living reminder of his own weakness and depravity.

"It wasn't until Papa was nearly sixteen years old that his father told him the truth. Adolphus was drunk, and in a rage, he told Papa everything. It was horrifying, he said to me on his deathbed, the contempt that his own father had for him. Then my grandfather showed him the letters he'd written to Papa's real mother, the maid abandoned to fend for herself as soon as she gave birth. All of the letters had been returned, Adolphus sneered, because Papa's whore of a mother didn't love her son."

I listened in silence, drawn into the story despite myself. Across the table from me, Jack studied Evelyn with a grim intensity. "Letters," I repeated, and she nodded. "That's what's in the box?"

"Proof of my papa's illegitimacy," Evelyn corrected me. "Signed confessions from Adolphus of his infidelity, yes, but also of the fact that my father was not a Collingwood by blood."

I let this sink in for a moment. "That's it?" I finally said. "That's what all this is about? The fact that your dad was illegitimate?"

Her eyes narrowed. "These letters"—she tapped the box with a gloved finger—"would cost me everything. Worse, they would cost my son everything. Our wealth comes to us through the Collingwood Trust, and it's administered by a pack of bloodless lawyers. If they ever learned that Kieran and I aren't descended from the Collingwoods . . ." She trailed off as if her voice had failed her.

"So maybe you have to sell your fancy penthouses in New York and Paris, the Caribbean mansion, the expensive cars," Jack growled. "Maybe you have to live like an ordinary person. So what? How is that worth people's *lives*, Evelyn?"

"Being a Collingwood is who I am!" she screamed in response, and I jumped at her sudden fury. She stared at us like a wild thing, her features distorted into something unrecognizable as tendons stood out sharply on either side of her neck. "I won't allow that to be taken away!"

The gun shook crazily in her hand as she pointed it at him, and I knew she was about to shoot. "Wait!" I shouted, taking two quick steps until I'd positioned myself between them. "Wait. Help me understand." Behind me, I heard Jack's ragged indrawn breath as I moved in front of him. I could practically feel him preparing to spring past me, and I reached back blindly to place a hand against his chest. I had no idea how long I could stall Evelyn, no idea how we were going to get out of this alive, but I knew I would never forgive myself if I watched her gun Jack down without trying to stop her. His heart hammered against the palm of my hand as we stood there, both of us bracing for the end.

Slowly, so slowly, she lowered the gun. I felt my chest loosen as the demented rage in her eyes began to dwindle and fade. Carefully, she placed the gun on the kitchen island with a soft *click* of metal on stone. Then she took up the box, turned it over, and began twisting its stubby legs. "Papa told me how to open it," she said, as calmly as if she were commenting on the weather. "Though he died before telling me where he'd hidden it." She frowned in concentration as she rotated one leg ninety degrees, then another. "The very last thing he ever spoke to me was a confession. He killed Adolphus, his own father. Bashed his head in with a fireplace poker." The matter-of-factness in her tone sent a shiver through me, but she wasn't looking at us. "It was the story of the century here in our little town: philanthropist murdered in his home, that sort of thing. The local paper reported on it for weeks. My grandmother left Papa in the care of the servants and moved to Toronto shortly thereafter. I think she knew what my father had done, and I suspect, in her senile confusion, she talked about it to Joel. That's why Joel knew he could blackmail me. Even without the box, he had something to hold over me. Something to keep me at bay while he tried to get the box from Marguerite."

We watched as, with one final twist of a leg, the bottom of the box slid open. Evelyn let out a low cry as she reached inside and retrieved a small bundle wrapped in thin, gauzy fabric. When she stripped it away, there they were: folded pieces of paper covered in dense handwriting, the letters that Adolphus Van Alstyne had written to the long-abandoned object of his brutish affections. Evelyn's hands trembled visibly as she gazed down at them, and I saw tears glisten on her cheeks.

"My poor papa," she said softly. "He couldn't bring himself to destroy these letters, no matter how dangerous they were. This was the only link he had left to his real mother. So he hid them away and counted on me to do it for him."

With one smooth motion, she turned and cast the letters onto the burning stove, where they flared into flame and ash.

For a moment, everything was very still. Evelyn stared at the burnt remnants of her family's terrible secret, and I could see her lips move as she whispered something to herself. Then I saw her shoulders lift, her back straighten, as she turned to pick up the gun from where it rested next to her. With an eerie, icy calm, she leveled the weapon at me once more.

"Well, that's done," she remarked. "Just two more loose ends to tie up here. I'll get rid of my car in case anyone thinks to search the stables, and everything will return to the way it was. When they find your bodies in the burnt-out wreckage of this cottage, I doubt they'll bother checking for bullet wounds. But if they do, this gun will be long gone at the bottom of the ocean." She offered me a wistful little smile. "I'm sorry, Luke dear. Say hello to your aunt for me."

Time slowed to a crawl as I watched her finger tighten on the trigger. Then, behind Evelyn, the French doors burst open from a powerful kick, and a small figure barreled inside. Evelyn wheeled around, her gun going off with an ear-shattering roar. A piece of the kitchen wall exploded into dust as Jack placed both hands on my shoulders and shoved me to the ground. Stunned, I watched him leap past me and perform a truly impressive flying tackle over the kitchen island, slamming into Evelyn and bringing her down with a loud grunt. The gun went off again and I heard a choked-off cry.

Scrambling back to my feet, I ran into the kitchen and almost collided with Cassie Perkins, whose eyes looked to be as wide as they could go as she brandished her sidearm with both hands. She was out of uniform, wearing jeans and a baggy sweatshirt instead—apparently, she'd been off duty. Together we came to a halt at the sight of Evelyn's willowy form huddled on the floor, arms wrenched behind her and held in place by Jack, who knelt with one knee planted firmly in the middle of her back. He looked around at us and barked, "Restraints, Constable!" Cassie reached down to the tactical belt she'd fastened rather bizarrely over her sweatshirt and swiftly tossed a zip tie to Jack, keeping her sidearm trained steadily on Evelyn all the while.

For my part, I sagged against the island as I struggled to bring my breathing under control. My heart was pounding so fast that I thought I might pass out. "Are you all right?" I asked Jack, who nodded once.

"I'm okay. The second shot just grazed me." I stared down at him with increasing panic, noticing for the first time the dark blood staining the upper arm of his short-sleeved shirt.

"Oh my God." I turned helplessly in place, looking for some way to help, finally grabbing a tea towel from the counter and stooping to press it firmly against his arm. He hissed quietly at the pressure but kept his attention fixed on Evelyn as he wrangled her into the restraints. Only once she was secured did he move the knee that was pinning her in place and then slowly rise to his feet.

Putting one big hand on top of mine where I was holding the towel, he said quietly, "Would you mind turning off those burners?"

Nodding hurriedly, I left him to keep applying pressure to his injury and circled the island to the other side of the kitchen. Snapping off the burners, I leaned down to examine what was left of the letters Evelyn had risked everything to destroy. Apart from a few small pieces of yellowed paper, there was little more than flakes of soot and ash. I couldn't help feeling a pang of disappointment at that. I would have liked to read them, if only to understand a little better the secrets that had cost my aunt her life.

I turned and stared down at Evelyn Collingwood. She lay there, face pressed against the floor as a soft keening moan escaped her lips. I wanted to hate her, to revel in this ignominious end to her terrible crimes. But I couldn't. Her father had made her privy to a shameful secret, one that she'd carried with her for most of her life. It was tragic, and unbearably sad, and its poison had touched us all in the end.

Looking up, I found Jack watching me and once again felt my heart give that dizzying little jump I now associated with him. Cassie had withdrawn into the dining room and was speaking into her phone. It was just the two of us, for the moment.

"I'm sorry you got hurt," I murmured.

He lifted his broad shoulders in a shrug. "It's nothing. I'll have the doc stitch me up."

I tilted my head to one side as I studied him. "She'd better make sure you're still pretty."

"*Pretty?*"

"Sure. It'd be a shame to have such a perfect specimen ruined by a lousy little scar."

He cocked an eyebrow at me. "Perfect, huh?"

I smiled and looked away. "Must be the adrenaline talking."

There was an entirely unsubtle throat clearing from the direction of the dining room. We both turned to see Cassie standing there, looking at us with an expression of faint bemusement. Flirting, apparently, was a no-no under the circumstances. "I gave Doc Kestenbaum a call, and she's on her way, Sarge. Ranjit too. You want anyone else here?"

Jack shook his head and then glanced down at Evelyn where she lay at his feet. "The situation's under control, Cassie. Excellent work, by the way. I'm sure glad you had your walkie switched on."

She offered him a grin and headed for the back door, sneakers crunching over broken glass. Outside, I could see red and blue lights strobing against the darkened trees as another RCMP vehicle arrived. Doors slammed and voices called out as Jack and I stood in my aunt's kitchen and looked at each other in silence.

Chapter
Twenty-Seven

A s it happens, it takes a while to wrap up a case like this. Even before Evelyn could be carted away, Juliana Kestenbaum appeared and took charge in her usual inimitable style. Ignoring Jack's protests, she stripped his shirt off him and bundled him into a chair at the dining table. It took her no more than ten minutes to stitch up the long, shallow wound on his upper arm while I watched with considerable interest. My prurience was entirely medical in nature, of course, and had nothing to do with the impressive sight of Jack's lightly furred bare chest. He glowered at both of us until she told him to stop pouting, after which he gritted his teeth and stared forbiddingly into the middle distance.

Later that night, Evelyn Collingwood was charged formally with the murders of Joel Mackenzie, Samuel Beckinridge, and Marguerite Tremblay. She refused to say a word to anyone, though an extremely well-dressed lawyer from Vancouver appeared the next day at the RCMP detachment office to represent her, accompanied by a hollow-eyed Kieran. Her dark-blue

Mercedes was found under a dusty tarp in a derelict set of stables on the Collingwood estate, its front bumper battered and scuffed. Preliminary analysis revealed traces of blood as well. Combined with the confession she'd unwisely made while holding us at gunpoint and the ballistics report that linked Joel Mackenzie's stolen weapon to Samuel's death and to the bullet casings recovered from the attack on yours truly, there was more than enough evidence to convict Evelyn even without her grandfather's letters.

The damage sustained to the cottage was relatively minor. One bullet had pulverized a small section of drywall, while the other had lodged itself in the ceiling. I called Eve, who had done such a good job fixing Forget-Me-Not's door, and she made short work of the repairs, also replacing the French doors that first Evelyn and then Cassie had wrecked. In remarkably short order, things returned to something approaching normal . . . whatever that meant now.

Two days after almost being shot, I found myself pottering around the front garden, pulling what I hoped were weeds as the warm sunlight beat down on the back of my neck and shoulders. Apart from the constant lapping of waves from the beach below and the occasional cry of a solitary gull, it was very quiet. That made it easy to hear the crunch of tires on gravel from behind the cottage, followed by the sound of a car door opening and closing. I straightened from my weeding and absently rubbed my dirt-covered hands together as Jack came strolling into view from the side of the house. He was dressed in a plain green T-shirt and jeans, and I could see the edge of the bandage still wrapped around his left bicep.

"Hey," I greeted him as he wandered across the lush grass. "Hey yourself."

"Finally taking some time off?" I asked with a meaningful glance at his casual attire.

He grinned for a moment. "I think I've earned it."

I nodded as he drew closer. "More than earned it. You saved my life, you know. I don't believe I've thanked you for that yet."

He came to stand next to me, his perfect side part ruffled a little by the breeze coming off the ocean as he tilted his head. "Just doing my job."

"Well, thanks all the same." I looked up into his hazel eyes and felt my heart start to beat just a little faster. "I've, uh, still got some coffee inside. Want some?"

"Sure, thanks." He watched me with an inscrutable expression, though one corner of his mouth quirked upward just slightly.

"Wanna sit outside?" At his nod, I gestured to the pair of Adirondack chairs at the edge of the bluff. "I'll be right back. Milk, no sugar, right?"

He looked faintly surprised but nodded again. When I returned a few minutes later, coffees in hand, he was leaning back comfortably in one of the chairs, gazing out at the water. "Thanks," he murmured as I handed him a mug and then settled into the other chair with a faint sigh.

We sat there in companionable silence for a few minutes, enjoying our coffee and the view. "I meant to ask," I finally said. "How did Cassie know we were in trouble?"

"Morse code," he responded. "Part of a protocol I set up a while ago now. If an officer requires urgent assistance but can't communicate directly, they tap out an SOS on their walkie. At least one of us has their radio on at all times, even at night. Cassie knew I'd be here, keeping an eye on you."

"That's smart," I said admiringly, to which he shrugged in a self-deprecating sort of way.

"Just a basic precaution."

I studied his profile as he gazed out at the water. "I'm really glad you were here."

His mouth turned up at the corners. "Likewise," he said quietly as he turned to look at me. "You saved my life too, you know, when you stepped in front of me."

It was my turn to shrug, a little embarrassed. "I'd never hear the end of it if the valiant Sergeant Munro was gunned down while I just stood there."

Jack's eyes were warm as he watched me. "Well, thanks all the same."

I had to look away. Clearing my throat, I asked, "What will happen to Evelyn now?"

After a momentary pause, Jack said briskly, "I'm confident she won't go to trial. The public scrutiny would be intense, and she wants to spare Kieran that. She'll start cooperating sooner or later, and then she'll go to prison for the rest of her life."

I hadn't really thought much about Kieran, though now I took a moment to consider what his life would be like as a result of his mother's crimes. "And the Collingwood Trust?" I asked, glancing back at him.

"Who knows?" he said with a curt shake of his head. "I expect things will be tied up in litigation for years. Kieran's still a wealthy man, and probably will be for the foreseeable future."

His voice changed a little when he said that, and I eyed him curiously as he turned his attention back to the water. His hand clenched and unclenched where it rested on the arm of his chair.

Was Jack *jealous*?

"That's a relief," I said earnestly. "You know how I feel about rich men."

His head swiveled and he gave me a fierce glower that faded only when I started laughing. Then, rolling his shoulders irritably, he turned away once more.

"You know," I finally said, "I asked an old colleague of mine to track down this mysterious woman who told Joel her family's secret. He emailed me this morning with a list of names from the last nursing home where Joel worked, and one of them was Leticia Collingwood. That email would have solved this whole case if Evelyn hadn't grown desperate enough to come after me first."

"You're not half-bad at this whole investigating thing," Jack observed. "Now, if you could just do it in a way that didn't annoy me."

I rolled my eyes at the backhanded compliment. "Where's the fun in that?"

A long silence fell between us as we both stared out at the ocean. Then Jack said in a casual tone, "So when are you putting the cottage up for sale?"

"I'm not." He turned to look at me, and I smiled at the expression on his face. "I've been doing a lot of thinking since I almost died. Reflecting on what's important. And I realized that I don't really have anything waiting for me back in Toronto. Just an empty townhouse that I never liked and a bunch of people I met through my ex." I paused for a moment, then cleared my throat. "You asked me if I was really going to walk away from all this."

"This?" he repeated softly, his eyes searching mine.

"This town. This house." I reached out and placed a hand on his where it rested on the arm of his chair. "This."

His mouth curved upward. "And?"

"And I think I'm going to stick around, if that's okay with you."

His hand turned until our fingers interlaced. "It's okay with me," he assured me.

We sat like that for a long time as the sun rose overhead. I felt my heart expand as it drank in the beauty around me and Jack's solid, familiar presence at my side, the feel of his hand in mine. For the first time in a very long time, I felt at peace.

I think my aunt would have approved.

Acknowledgments

I had a lot of help getting here. First and foremost, I want to thank my amazing agent, Melissa Edwards. Without her support and guidance, this book simply wouldn't exist. I also want to thank my editor, Faith Black Ross, who fought for this project, and the rest of the fantastic team at Crooked Lane who worked to get this book out there: Rebecca Nelson, Madeline Rathle, Dulce Botello, and Hannah Pierdolla.

A special shout-out to copyeditor Rachel Keith, who made the manuscript so much better, and to illustrator Brandon Dorman for the wonderful cover: thank you!

Going from aspiring writer to published author has been a whirlwind, and it would have been impossible to manage without the incredible friendship and support of my #TeamMelissa siblings. You're all awesome and I'm lucky to have found you.

Finally, words can't describe how grateful I am to my amazing, beautiful husband, Matt. I love you, and our little family, more than I can say.